Jarod's Heart

A KING BROTHERS STORY

TROUBLE IN TIMBISHA TOWNSHIP
BOOK TWO

ELISE MANION

*For my husband,
and all the sacrifices he has made for me.*

Contents

Jarod's Heart

CHAPTER 1
The Boycott

S eptember…

"YOU'RE ARRESTING ME?" SHE SCREECHED.

"Not if I don't have to. Now get in the car, Lauren." Jarod didn't understand her attitude. A madman was on the loose and she was out parading herself around as a target.

What had she been thinking, walking to her car by herself with Billy on the loose? He'd already brutalized one woman, burned down Jason's house, and set his goons on Julie.

"Jarod, take your hands off me. I'm hungry and I'm getting lunch." She shook her arm out of his gentle hold and continued on toward her car.

"I'm not asking again, Lauren."

"You didn't ask the first time, Jarod," she threw over her shoulder.

"Billy's still out there and you want to play Miss Independent? I don't think so," he said, as he grabbed her upper arm again and spun her around. Their noses came within touching distance. He looked down into her baby blue eyes and got lost for a moment.

A car horn brought him back to reality. "You can't be alone right now," he pleaded. "He's already hurt one woman. Do you want to be the next?"

She was so close and breathing so fast, it was hard to keep his eyes from roaming all over her body, but maintain eye contact he would. He could see her mustering up another argument. Before she got a word out, he began to drag her to his cruiser.

She's hungry? Fine. He'd head out to The Estate. His mom would have lunch going, or, better yet, Julie might have whipped up something out of this world. Lauren would be much safer there than being alone in a random fast-food joint.

"Jarod, stop this! You're making a scene," she hissed.

"The only one causing a fuss is you. Now stop fighting me and watch your head."

He opened the back door of his cruiser and pushed her pretty blonde head down so she wouldn't bump it on the doorjamb. He closed the door comforted by the fact she was now safe inside—until she looked up into his face through the glass, her expression one of shock.

Uh oh. A chill of warning ran up his spine when her lovely face morphed into her infamous you-are-so-dead look.

He'd be damned if he was going to worry about it, though. Her safety was all that mattered.

Once in the driver's seat, he felt the heat of her anger sear the back of his neck. He started the engine and put the cruiser in reverse. When he turned his head to back out of his parking spot, he noticed her beet-red face, and swore smoke might've been coming out her ears. A twinge of panic tingled a warning down his spine, but he continued to ignore it.

This is Lauren, he reasoned. If she wasn't flirting with him, then she was mad at him. There was no middle ground, and it had been that way since the day they'd met. That was their relationship, and she always came around.

Besides, she was the best damn secretary a man could have, and he'd be damned if he'd lose her to a psychopath on a rampage because she failed to take proper safety precautions. *She's a professional*, he told himself. She'd never let her anger affect their working relationship.

They were all on edge because of Billy's shenanigans. Once Jarod had the creep behind bars, this would all be a funny memory the two of them could laugh about later, he assured himself.

"I hope you realize, Jarod, I am never speaking to you again."

Her voice sounded like a rough gravel road. He peeked in the rearview mirror and, yes, she had tears in her eyes, but they hadn't spilled over yet. It meant she was miffed. Nothing to worry about.

"Whatever, Lauren. Just simmer down. We'll be at The Estate soon."

"I was headed to The Estate, *Jarod*." This time she said his name between gritted teeth. "I could've driven myself!"

Well, hell. How was he supposed to know? She usually hit one of the drive-thrus for a salad. Not that he paid much attention to her daily itinerary.

"Think of it as me saving you some gas money," he assured her.

"I'm serious. I'm never speaking to you again. This is the last straw."

She turned her head to look out the window. From his side mirror, he studied her profile. Damn it, her glossy bottom lip quivered. Maybe this wasn't such a good plan after all. The tingle in his spine was back, and a little bit of bile now churned in his gut.

But he had always enjoyed their sparring, and certainly this was all they were doing. She liked the verbal debates as much as he did.

She'll speak to me again once her anger's calmed down, he thought with confidence.

Lauren was a fixture in his life—an annoying, efficient fixture—but something he could count on nonetheless. She'd get over it.

Just in case, though, he'd better lay things out for her one more time, so she'd know he was doing this for her own good.

"He's out there, Lauren, and he's about to snap. He knows we've got him cornered, and being cornered makes him more dangerous and unpredictable. He's proven time and again that brutalizing women isn't beneath him. I don't want you, or anyone else I know, to be one of his victims."

Don't you understand? You're smarter than this, honey.

"I know, Jarod. Do you think I don't take precautions? My firearm is in my purse, I've been utilizing a yellow-to-orange awareness like they teach in self-defense class, and I've got mace on my keychain. I'm not an idiot." Her low-volume voice carried an edge she'd never used on him before. He didn't like it.

"It's not enough."

He could have sworn he heard her growl. He ignored it and drove into his parents' driveway, parking in his normal spot by the side entrance. He got out and opened the back door. Before she had the chance to walk away from him, he took hold of her arm and spun her around again, this time caging her between his arms against the cruiser.

"Billy is off his rails. Being on 'yellow to orange'"—here he used air quotes before resting his hands back on the cruiser—"and keeping your weapon in your purse, for God's sake, is not going to be enough protection if he gets his hands on you." He inhaled a breath. "Can't you see that?"

He saw one of her famous smart-ass retorts coming, but before she could answer, his mouth landed on hers. He didn't know why he'd done it, but damn it, he couldn't think how else to keep her from arguing with him. He had to make her see reason without her sassy attitude getting in the way. He'd known her too long to let anything bad happen to her. He needed her compliance, not her defiance.

As he deepened the kiss, he felt her soften, causing an involuntary moan to issue from his chest. Right before he wrapped his arms around her, she stomped on his instep.

"How dare you!" She stormed off toward the house, her blonde locks whipping behind her like wheat in a cold autumn wind.

At least she's heading in the right direction this time. He had to jog a bit to catch up to her.

"Look, I'm sorry. I don't know why I did that."

They'd made it inside the entry by now. Lauren was full steam ahead as she sailed into the kitchen.

"You might be my boss at work, Jarod, but you are not my *anything* after hours! You have no right to dictate to me where I can go on my own time!"

"Calm down, Lauren."

"I will NOT calm down. I'm getting sick and tired of you ignoring me except when you feel like paying attention, which usually means you want to dictate how I should live my life! I'm sick of it!"

He almost ran into her back when she stopped dead in the kitchen, where everyone had congregated and were now listening intently to their argument. Perfect, now the whole family knew they were fighting.

He'd deal with Lauren later. Right now, he needed to explain to everyone what was going on with Billy and his cohorts, and try to make a plan to keep them all safe.

Monday morning, October...

He looked up at the dark sky, feeling a kinship with the clouds. The oncoming storm reminded him of those chaotic, black days when his ex-wife had broken his heart, scattering its pieces to the four corners of the universe.

He coughed a disgusted laugh at such melancholy nonsense before he unlocked the door and folded his six-foot-three-inch frame into the driver's seat. He turned the key in the ignition and the cruiser purred to life.

Sheriff Jarod King drove away from his parents' palatial family home in the High Sierra desert. He switched the heater on, and the sweet tang of wet sage billowed through the air vents in the dashboard. The aromatic flavor was much better than the crusty funk coming from the back seat, where drunks and petty criminals had all left a little something of themselves behind. He'd ask Lauren to call the detailer to schedule the cruiser for a good cleaning.

No, she still wasn't speaking to him, but it hadn't affected her job performance... much.

The forecast called for ice and possibly snow in this freak October storm, so the chances weren't good he'd have it freshened up any time soon. The wrecks would keep him busy most of the day.

Jarod was the oldest son of James and Camille King, a prominent family in this little corner of Nevada. His father built the family construction company from the ground up before Jarod was even born. King Construction was now one of the leading outfits in the state. But Jarod had eschewed his birthright, handing over his legacy to Jason, the eldest of his two younger brothers, whom Jarod loved dearly. He preferred law enforcement, working with and helping the people of his community.

This morning's dark mood had nothing to do with the job, but everything to do with it marking the fifth anniversary of his darkest hour: the day his high school sweetheart, Miranda, left him for her drug dealer. After their bitter divorce, he'd moved back home with his parents into his suite of rooms at the King Estate. Since then, every morning had been a carbon copy of the last: Wake up, get dressed, and go to work.

It'd be funny if it weren't so damn tragic, he thought with disgust.

A gust of wind blew sand and rocks into the windshield, startling him. He gripped the wheel to keep from drifting into oncoming traffic when the pickup in front of him blew a tire.

Sighing out loud, he pulled his cruiser over to the shoulder behind the disabled vehicle and called it in to dispatch. He needed a fortifying drink of coffee to warm him up before he left his vehicle, but as he reached for the much-needed elixir, he realized he'd left his travel mug on the counter at home. Disgusted with himself and his own sour mood, he watchfully opened his door and stepped out of his vehicle to approach the disabled pickup. Halfway to the driver the skies opened up in a downpour of icy rain.

Thank you, Monday, for wasting no time punching me in the trachea.

An hour later, he'd made it to the Timbisha County Sheriff's Office, drenched to the bone. He sloshed through the doors, hoping no one would make eye contact with him.

"Good morning, Sheriff!"

Today's just not my freaking day.

"G'morning, Marguerite," he intoned before shutting his office door without a backward glance at his receptionist. The last thing he needed at the moment was to get caught up in a gossip session with the town crier. Oh, she was pretty enough, and she had impeccable customer service skills, but something about the woman rubbed him the wrong way.

Not that Jarod was interested in conversing with any woman. He had *been there* and *done that*, before and after the divorce. The experience taught him women were only good for one thing: making sure his office ran with smooth efficiency.

Okay, he was a man, but currently his only interest in women was for impeccable office skills. If he got the itch for something more, he went out of town and gave a fictitious name...

And a fake number.

He closed his office blinds before grabbing the extra uniform he kept in the armoire his mother had insisted he have installed in his office. Sure, the station had a small locker room, but he seldom used it because it often smelled like the back of his cruiser.

Once he was dressed, he hit the intercom and buzzed

Lauren. She hadn't been at her desk when he had walked by, but he hoped to beg her for a cup of coffee to warm him up. Unfortunately, she wasn't back yet, so he began the report on the flat tire he had assisted with that morning. As it turned out, the driver had a bench warrant out for his arrest. He was being booked downstairs at this very moment.

Once Jarod finished the report, he shoved his chair back and stood. He needed coffee in a bad way, but the break room was located on the other side of the station. He'd have to trek through reception again, which was one big room partitioned off with padded cubicle walls separating his deputies from the main area. Marguerite worked the long counter which divided the room from the public. In order to reach the precious coffee pot, he'd have to cross paths with her again, something he really didn't want to do.

He peeked out his door and looked around. When he stepped out, he kept his head and eyes down and hurried to the break room. Lucky for him, Marguerite was helping someone at the counter and didn't see his reappearance. He sighed with relief when he managed to push his way through the break-room door unnoticed.

He reached into the dishwasher for his favorite mug, only to discover it hadn't been run. Frustrated, he grabbed a soap cube from the box under the sink and added it to the dispenser in the door of the washer, closed the door, and pushed the *Short Cycle* button. Then he reached into the cupboard and got lucky. There was one plain mug left. All the rest bore vulgar sayings, flowers, or holiday themes. He'd rather drink straight from the pot than use one of those.

He put his mug next to the coffee pot and grabbed the empty carafe.

Son of a...

Digging down deep for a calm he did not possess, he jerked on the faucet before angrily swishing water around inside the dirty carafe, then dumped it out to refill it. He poured the water into the reservoir, added a new filter and coffee grounds to the basket, and—out of sheer spite for his lazy coworkers—dumped in two extra scoops.

Finally feeling a bit of satisfaction, he pressed the *Brew* button.

As he leaned against the counter whistling a jaunty tune, Lauren crashed through the door soaked to the bone. Her clothes stuck to her perfect, curved body, and she looked as if she might commit a homicide if pushed in the right direction. Right now, Jarod felt like pushing.

"Nice outfit," he deadpanned.

Frosty beams of anger shot from her winter blue eyes, causing him to unintentionally place a hand over his heart. She still wasn't speaking to him. It'd been over a month since forcing her into the back of his cruiser in an effort to keep her safe from Julie's crazy ex-boyfriend. They'd all been in danger, as Billy tried to enact vengeance on Jason. Thankfully, Billy had been apprehended, but at the time of their fight, Jarod couldn't help but worry Billy might kidnap Lauren to play one of his sick games.

Jarod hadn't been willing to take the chance, and Lauren hadn't appreciated his efforts to keep her safe.

Women.

She shoved a soggy, brown paper sack into the refrigerator before moving to the cupboard to grab the mug with the words, "HAVE A NICE DAY," on the front. Slamming the mug on the counter, she reached over for the carafe before she realized it was still brewing. She narrowed her eyes at him again.

"It was empty when I got here," he said with innocence,

showing her his empty mug. "So I made a new pot." He grinned evilly.

She closed her eyes and took a deep breath before she went back to the refrigerator for the artificially over-sweetened creamer. She slammed it on the counter next to her mug. She tapped her manicured fingernails on the counter, staring daggers at the pot.

He knew how she felt. It appeared she was in the same mood he'd arrived in over an hour ago.

He frowned. Was she just now getting to work? Thinking about it now, she should've been here before him this morning.

Genuinely concerned by her soggy appearance, he asked, "Run into any trouble on the way in?"

She took another deep breath through her nose, probably working out how to answer his question without speaking to him aloud.

Before he had a chance to ask if she was all right, she closed her eyes and shook her head. "A stupid flat tire."

That explained the wet-cat fashion statement she sported.

Ticked she hadn't had the sense to ask him for help, he admonished, "Why didn't you call for road assistance? One of us would've come changed it for you."

She grabbed the now-full carafe from the burner and poured a small amount of the very strong, black coffee into her mug. He watched, mesmerized, as she measured in a healthy amount of creamer and four packets of stevia. She mixed her concoction with vigor, turned to face him, and very deliberately took a drink.

As she tipped up her mug, the image on the bottom was hard to ignore: a hand flipping him the bird.

He glared at her.

She smirked back with a raised eyebrow, turned back to the

counter to fill her mug with more of the bitter brew, and then stormed out of the break room. He couldn't take his eyes off the feminine sway of her rounded hips as she sashayed to her desk before the door closed in his face.

LAUREN SLAMMED HER *HAVE A NICE DAY*/BIRDIE MUG onto her desk, tossed her purse in the drawer, and headed for the ladies' room to try and dry off.

Call in for help, indeed. Like she'd use up precious manpower for a lousy flat she could change herself. She wasn't helpless, for heaven's sake.

She looked at herself in the mirror and wanted to cry. Her blonde hair hung in matted ropes with water dripping from the ends. Her makeup was smeared, giving her raccoon eyes.

But what embarrassed her most was that her white silk blouse was plastered to her body, wet and transparent, as if she'd entered herself into a wet t-shirt contest. Thank goodness she'd worn the white lacy camisole underneath her blouse, or she could have been cited for indecent exposure.

And, of course, it'd be her luck Jarod would be the first person to see her in all this miserable glory. She didn't know who was worse, him or Marguerite.

Okay, that's unfair. No one's as bad as Marguerite.

Her slim shoulders drooped in defeat. It didn't matter what they fought about, she would always love Jarod King. She'd fallen hard and fast the day she'd first laid eyes on him, and no matter what her heart would always belong to him.

Whether the jerk knew it or not.

At first, it'd been a school-girl crush on the older bad boy. Back then, he had worn his brown, wavy hair a bit longer than the crew cut he sported for his job now. But his eyes were the same sapphire blue that changed with his moods. Since his divorce, his eyes had ranged from sapphire gems to blue fire in an instant. He was harder than he used to be, but her feelings for him had never gone away and, in fact, had only grown over the years.

Lauren and her best friend, Julie, had been freshmen when they'd met and become best friends with Josh King, Jarod's youngest brother. All three were as close today as they had been back then. Now, Julie was marrying Jason, the middle King brother.

Lauren was about to embark on a new adventure with the Kings, as well. Jarod's mother, Camille, had offered her a partnership in a new business venture which also included Julie. They'd be coordinating and catering charitable events in their community. They hadn't finalized the business details yet, but Lauren was excited to start a new adventure and a new career.

She'd miss seeing Jarod every day, but leaving her position with the sheriff's office would be a relief. Seeing people at the lowest points in their lives, even some folks she'd known since she had been a child, drained her mentally and emotionally. It killed her soul little by little. When you added in the normal office backstabbing and workplace gossip—she was so over it. If she had to spend one more moment with Marguerite, she thought her head might pop.

And Marguerite... working with her was a living hell. The stereotypical bossy, ambitious Queen Bee had been captain of the cheer squad and homecoming queen in high school. She'd graduated in the same class as Lauren and Julie, who'd always skirted the fringes of the popular crowd. To Lauren's dismay, Marguerite came on at the department not long after Lauren had been promoted to her current position as administrative assistant to the sheriff.

Marguerite was also a notorious flirt, and Lauren suspected something was going on between Marguerite and Deputy Brad Anderson. In Lauren's opinion, Brad could do a whole lot better.

Even though he was the same age as Jarod, Brad had been with the department a few years longer and took Jarod under his wing, so to speak. And then Brad shocked everyone by passing up the opportunity to run for sheriff. He'd claimed it wouldn't suit him and thought the community would do better with someone like Jarod. Both Brad and the old sheriff endorsed Jarod for the position. With no other candidate on the ballot, Jarod became the youngest sheriff to be elected in Timbisha County.

Lauren thought it odd for Brad to pass up such an opportunity, but he remained a good deputy, backing up Jarod when needed while giving Jarod enough space to be a great leader. She'd have to check, but it was possible Brad held the record for most drug arrests in the department.

She looked in the mirror and took a moment to collect herself. There wasn't much she could do to tidy herself up. It was going to be snowing later anyway, so she brushed out her long blonde hair and pulled it into a neat ponytail. Her shirt was damp but no longer as transparent as it had been when she'd first walked through the door. She wiped the rest of her makeup off and reapplied her lip gloss.

It'll have to do.

She took a fortifying breath, straightened her shoulders, and walked out of the ladies' room to face what was left of the day.

As she took a seat at her desk she noticed Marguerite

smirking at her from the reception counter. Of course, Marguerite was perfectly put together from head to toe, not a hair out of place or a makeup smudge to be seen—the hag.

Ignoring her, Lauren logged onto her computer and began her work. People waited at the counter, so Marguerite turned on the professional mien and addressed their needs. That was the only compliment Lauren would offer the woman: professional to the point of sickening. Unfortunately, there was nothing in Marguerite's employment record that would lead Jarod to let her go, much to Lauren's dismay.

"Lauren! Are you okay?" Deputy Eli Wallace asked with genuine concern.

He was new to the department now that the county finally had the funds to hire an extra deputy to handle the rising crime in Timbisha County. Methamphetamine was the number-one culprit, which led to petty theft and property damage, along with the ruin of lives and families.

"Yeah, I'm good, Eli. I got caught with a flat tire this morning. How are you?"

He frowned at her. "Why didn't you report it? One of us coulda helped you. You shouldn't have had to deal with it by yourself."

"I didn't want to bother anyone. I'm sure I wasn't the only person having trouble this morning. Besides, I know how to change a flat," she said with a smile to erase her dismissive attitude. Ever the gentleman, but clearly about to argue with her, Lauren deflected Eli with, "How's Caroline doing? She's getting pretty close to her due date, isn't she?"

That was all it took to redirect the conversation. Eli and his wife were expecting their first child soon, and he was a very excited daddy-to-be.

At around one o'clock, Lauren grabbed her lunch from the break room fridge and took it back to her desk. Normally, she used her lunch hour to run errands, but because of the flat, she needed to catch up on her work.

The sack was still soggy from this morning's downpour. Being careful not to make a mess on her desk, she gently pulled the contents of a small sandwich and yogurt from the bag. She'd desperately needed water after swallowing Jarod's idea of coffee, so she'd rinsed out the sludge from her HAVE A NICE DAY/birdie mug and refilled it with water to hydrate herself. The bitter concoction had been so strong she was afraid she'd have to stop at the store on her way home to pick up a new razor—to shave off the hair that likely now grew on her chest.

Men.

As she settled in for her meal, she noticed Marguerite still staring daggers. Making eye contact with her, Lauren lifted her mug in salute before deliberately taking a swig.

Marguerite narrowed her eyes just as the phones began to ring.

CHAPTER 2
Talk To Me

"We received another call to the Decatur house. Brad's en route now. Something about an explosion."

Marguerite stood in Jarod's doorway, leaning on one hip, one arm outstretched above her head. She looked as if she were relieving pain from a bad case of scoliosis.

"Good grief, there's always something going on out there," Jarod said. "Tell Brad I'll meet him at the scene." He needed to get out of the office. "What's his ETA?"

Marguerite shrugged delicately and shook her over-styled, crispy blonde curls. "Not sure," she replied on a husky breath.

It was all he could do not to roll his eyes.

"I'll radio him from the cruiser," he muttered as he shouldered past her.

He approached Lauren's desk, shaking off the creepy crawlies from Marguerite's aggressive attempt at sex appeal.

Lauren, concentrating on her computer screen, still only spoke to him when absolutely necessary. So, without warning, he launched into his agenda. "I'm heading out to the Decatur house again," he announced, making her jump and causing her to frantically reach for her mug, which she had bumped and almost knocked over onto her keyboard.

Damn it. He hadn't meant to startle her, but it sure was hard to hide his automatic chuckle.

Recovering with grace, she acknowledged him without saying a word. He stared at her for a moment, wishing she'd get over her pout. It was easier talking to Lauren than Marguerite while at work. Lauren kept things professional and got the job done. He didn't have to put up with any female nonsense from her unless they were off the clock. Then it was a whole different story. Her smart mouth and sassy attitude drove him crazy, but this silent treatment was far worse.

"Have juvenile services on standby; might be minors involved... again," he added with disgust.

"Of course," she said, surprising him. She crinkled her forehead, as if she were going to say something else, but at the last minute she must have changed her mind. She nodded again and turned back to her computer, dismissing him entirely.

Normally, he'd shrug off her temper, but this conversation boycott had gone on for over a month—a record for her. He'd have to do something about it because it was beginning to piss him off. He needed their easy rapport at work. His job was hard enough without having to walk on eggshells around his secretary, and he certainly didn't need the added attentions of Marguerite, as Lauren buffered his receptionist's attentions.

Frustrated he would have to put their situation on hold, he slammed out of the building and into the parking lot. Right now, he had to head out to a possible child-endangerment situation, the type he hated most. He usually shared these cases with Lauren. They'd talk through a case together because she had a unique perspective on the subject.

Being in law enforcement fulfilled his natural instinct to

protect those who needed it. Cases involving the most innocent —children—were the hardest on him because he didn't understand that kind of criminal mindset or abuse.

The temperature was too warm for the snow level to drop, but the sky rained down upon him in sheets. He jogged to the cruiser and started the engine, turning the heater on full blast. While he waited for the vehicle to warm up, he picked up the radio and hailed Brad.

"What's your ETA to the Decaturs'?"

"Five minutes out."

"I'm on my way."

"Jarod, I've got this. There's no need for both of us to be out in this mess."

"See you in twenty."

Jarod set the handheld mic back in its cradle on the dash and backed out of his parking space.

The Decatur homestead was a dilapidated old farmhouse located in a rural part of Timbisha County, on the other side of the valley from Timbisha Township. Avery Decatur was the youngest son of the family, and the only one who'd stayed on the old family land. Jarod had put Avery in cuffs many times over the years, usually for drunk and disorderly conduct or disturbing the peace. Avery wasn't exactly the ambitious type, and neither was his girlfriend, Luanne. They often shared a holding cell together.

Over the past few months, Jarod and his deputies had been called out to the farmhouse, either by Luanne or their guests, when fights broke out and gotten out of control. As inept as Avery was, it wouldn't be surprising if he blew up his barbecue or some other nonsense.

Upon entering the property, Jarod estimated around twenty vehicles crowded the dirt driveway. Smoke billowed from an outbuilding behind the house, and a foul, chemical stench emanated from whatever had been inside it. The fire department had already put out the flames.

"What happened?" Jarod walked up to Brad and a battered and handcuffed Avery, who stood on the crumbling front porch steps.

"Cookin' meth is what happened," Brad seethed.

"You're kidding. Anyone hurt?" Jarod asked as the other emergency vehicles pulled into the driveway.

"They're all too out of it to be hurt, but I called for an ambulance anyway," Brad said, shaking his head in contempt.

"Avery is our meth dealer?" Jarod asked incredulously. *Avery the Imbecile, who failed at petty crime?* He wasn't smart enough to run an operation big enough to fuel the current meth epidemic in Timbisha County.

"Looks that way," Brad answered, anger roiling off of him like a volcano about to erupt.

No, Jarod didn't believe it and, apparently, neither did Brad, but they would investigate once they cleared the scene.

Jarod surveyed the property. "Where's Luanne?"

"Sitting in the back of my cruiser." Brad gestured with his chin in the direction of his parked vehicle. "I needed to separate them."

Jarod nodded once, then stepped into the house. Not surprisingly, it was a complete pigsty. It resembled one of those places you see on reality TV, the kind that's so filthy you can't believe it was ever habitable for humans.

His shoes shuffled through fast food wrappers and crumpled beer cans. Empty liquor bottles covered every surface. Broken and dirty red plastic cups country songs were sung about acted as a decorative burst of color. A thick layer of dust and cigarette smoke residue covered it all.

It appeared all the dishes Avery and Luanne owned lived in the sink, crusted over with dried food and mold. Drug paraphernalia was strewn all over the place, left for anyone to pick up and use.

And his nose told him somewhere in the house, a toilet was backed up.

As Jarod wandered through the filth, he began to notice juice boxes and prepackaged, child-sized deli trays on the ground and on the low tables among the detritus. The hair prickled on the back of his neck.

Searching in earnest, he went down the dim hallway and noticed a door locked with a padlock anchored high up on the frame. He leaned his head against the door and heard nothing at first, but then... sniffles.

From his utility belt he grabbed his knife and pried the cheap locking hinge from the doorjamb, effectively removing the padlock. He shoved the door open and stepped into what could have been a child's room, but instead of a bed he found a nest of dirty blankets and a flat pillow in the middle of the floor. A dirty stuffed animal lay in the center of the pallet.

When he heard more sniffles, he turned his head in the direction of a raised square, probably a small table, covered with a blanket. Jarod knelt down and pulled the blanket back, revealing a small boy in dirty footed pajamas. He was sucking an even dirtier thumb and clung to another filthy stuffed animal. It looked and smelled like he hadn't had a bath in weeks.

Jarod smiled at the pathetic waif and extended a hand. Speaking softly, he said, "Come on out of there now. It's okay."

The little boy gulped in some air on a hiccup before he crawled toward Jarod. He was small. Jarod estimated his age at between two or three years.

As he carried the boy out of the house, Jarod glared at Avery. Luanne, sitting in the back of Brad's cruiser, didn't even look up when Jarod walked past her carrying her child in his arms.

By then, the ambulance had arrived and chaos reigned everywhere. Most of the people were adults and were being treated for minor burns and other injuries. The little boy began to cry in earnest now, frightened by the flashing lights and periodic sirens. Instead of approaching the EMTs, Jarod decided to head to his cruiser, hoping to calm the kid down a bit before handing him over to Child Protective Services.

The rain diminished somewhat as the temperature began to drop with the heart of the storm front moving in. Though the car was still warm, Jarod started the engine to get the heater going again. He used the extra jacket he kept in his cruiser to cover the little boy's small, shivering frame.

He withdrew his cell phone from his pocket and dialed Lauren's number. Sure, he could've used proper police channels but, for reasons he didn't want to examine too closely, he needed to hear her voice, and he didn't want others listening to his conversation. As her cell began to ring, he prayed for her to answer his call.

"Jarod? Why are you calling my cell?"

Her irritated voice soothed him and made him smile. He glanced at the little guy next to him and said, "Sorry, Lauren. I need you to call in CPS. I found a little boy in the mess out here."

He described the squalor the poor child had been living in, holding nothing back. He had her attention now, and he heard her putting in the call on the landline while he continued to talk to her over their cell phones. *This is okay*, he thought. *At least I'm having a private conversation with her*, and he could hear her voice. Why that mattered he couldn't say, but he'd known her a long time and it just helped.

The little boy had been standing on the seat next to him, but now he climbed into Jarod's lap and rested his head on Jarod's chest. The boy's crying slowed down until it became sporadic hiccups. Jarod rubbed the toddler's back while Lauren listened to his story.

"CPS is on their way, Jarod. Is there anything else?"

She was back to being curt, probably realizing that, by calling her private cell number, he'd tricked her into actually conversing with him, breaking her vow of silence. Her sassy attitude usually brought a smile to his face, when she wasn't annoying the shit out of him. Right now, though, he didn't want this feud to go on any longer.

"Yeah, actually there is, Lauren." He cleared his throat. "I'm sorry."

He waited for a response.

And waited.

"Okay, you're forgiven."

He heard her own intake of breath before she asked, "Should I call your mom or something?" with genuine concern in her voice.

Relieved their fight was over, he said, "Nah, I'll be back to the office as soon as we clear the rest of the people out of the scene. Avery and Luanne will be heading to a holding cell after they're booked. Brad can't take them both back in his car, so I'll wait for CPS to pick up this little guy, and then I'll haul Avery's pathetic ass in."

"I'll get everything ready for processing."

"Thanks, Lauren." He wanted to stay on the line with her a little longer, but he'd run out of excuses to keep her, so he hung up.

Okay, that was awkward.

He sat for a moment longer in the quiet of the cruiser until his little friend fell asleep.

The condition of the house reminded Jarod of the last time he'd seen Miranda alive. His beautiful wife had been missing for three days, and he'd been out of his mind with worry. He'd just been hired on with the sheriff's department and assigned long hours, so spending a lot of time with his new bride had been impossible, and she had been lonely.

He couldn't remember what the awful fight had been about, but Miranda had gotten into her car and driven off. He thought for sure he'd hear from her within a few hours, but that hadn't been the case. One hour turned into twenty-four, making her an official missing person.

She'd been found three days later when deputies were called to an out-of-control party. She was so high she didn't even recognize him. The house had been as filthy as Avery's was today.

She hadn't been pleased to be back home with him. She'd told him she'd found someone else and would be leaving in the morning.

Later, he found out the "someone else" was her drug dealer. True to her word, she hadn't contacted him again until the divorce papers reached him by mail. The envelope had a Las Vegas postmark.

He hadn't seen her in five years and, in his broken heart, he knew he never would again.

LAUREN PLACED HER CELL PHONE BACK IN HER PURSE and stared at the computer. To her annoyance, talking to him had felt good. Trying to stay mad at Jarod King was like trying to change her DNA—impossible.

The past month had been harder on her than it should've been. Now that they'd broken the silence between them, tension eased from her shoulders, and her focus became clear.

The self-imposed boycott on Jarod sounded good a month ago, when her anger had been white hot, but now she realized she'd lost valuable time with him. Jarod was one of the best men she'd ever known, even if he was a little bit broken in the heart department.

Unfortunately, her anger usually led to foolish behavior, and she'd foolishly believed she could flick a switch to erase him from her own heart. Being at odds with him only caused her pain every time she'd been around him, which was daily. It made working with him nearly impossible.

She prided herself on her professionalism, but now she felt ashamed. One's administrative assistant must speak to one's boss, for crying out loud!

Her silent feud had even pushed the boundaries of her relationship with Camille. Lauren wasn't a chef, nor was she all that handy with a glue gun, but she knew how to talk to potential clients, and Camille wanted her to be a part of her team.

Lauren's feud with Jarod had stressed everyone out.

Her heart had gone out to him as she'd listened to the utter dismay in his voice. The little boy's condition obviously upset him. Jarod's career choice was a noble one, but it meant he dealt with people who were at their worst. His innate sense to defend and protect people often put strenuous demands on his emotional well-being, whether he wanted to admit it or not.

She understood what he was going through. Every time CPS came in to pick up a child, she had to fight back the tears.

She understood what it was like for those kids because she'd spent time with foster parents herself.

Shaking off the gloomy memories of her childhood, she got busy with her work. Unfortunately, Marguerite hovered nearby, trying to glean information through Lauren's one-sided conversation with the sheriff.

Lauren understood why he called her on her cell phone instead of going through proper department channels. Jarod wanted to protect the little boy, but the news about Avery and Luanne would be out soon enough. They didn't need Marguerite's talent for storytelling to move the gossip along. News got around fast enough in Timbisha Township, and it had taken Lauren years to wipe out the reputation her mother had built for her. She'd do everything possible to keep Jarod's trust regarding the little boy.

Maybe that's why no one knew what Miranda was really like? Jarod had protected her. She'd have to think about the situation when she got home. Right now, she needed to get busy.

Two hours later, Jarod and Brad returned to the station with their prisoners. Eli's shift had ended earlier, but he'd logged in overtime at the Decaturs' and would be back again this evening for the night shift. Rookies had the worst schedules. She worried Jarod was making Eli work too many hours, especially with his wife being pregnant.

She sat at her computer trying to focus, but she had too many unsettled thoughts spinning around in her head. Her distraction was exacerbated by Jarod, who sat at his desk, directly in her line of sight, filling out his part of the reports.

"I think he's gay."

"What?"

Lauren spun her office chair around to find Brad leaning against the wall with a teasing grin on his face. From his vantage point, he'd witnessed Lauren gazing into Jarod's office.

"I've never seen him with a woman. He doesn't even talk about women."

Lauren wanted to smack the fake puzzled expression off his face. "You're rotten. You know he's private, Brad." She turned back to her computer to try to ignore him.

"He lives with his parents," he began to tick off each item on a finger, listing reasons for believing Jarod played for the other team. "He doesn't date, and he doesn't even go out. I think the evidence is pretty clear," Brad stated, a dimple showing in his cheek.

He was being ornery, trying to get her goat, and it was working. Before she could defend Jarod again, Marguerite's heels clicked across the tile floor to stand next to Brad. She must have smelled blood.

"I agree with Brad. Not once has he ever complimented me. It's not normal." She was completely serious.

Brad stifled a laugh at Marguerite's arrogance behind a choking cough.

"Look, you guys, I've known him a long time. He's not gay, I promise," Lauren whined, sounding a little too frustrated with them.

What's with these two?

"Answer me this, Lauren: besides that skank he called 'wife,' have you ever seen him with a woman? Because I sure haven't," Brad smirked, stoking Marguerite's thirst for blood, who fiercely nodded her head in agreement.

"I knew Miranda in school," Marguerite informed them. "She probably left him because, well, you know...," and here she began to whisper loudly, "he's *gay*, and he probably didn't know what to do with a woman in bed."

Brad laughed out loud at Marguerite's ridiculous explanation, unable to control himself any longer.

"All right, knock it off you two. I don't want to hear another word on the subject." Lauren was standing now, shaking her head.

The invocation of Miranda's name always pushed Lauren's buttons. Jarod had become a different man after Miranda's shameful departure. He'd once been a confident and outgoing guy, but now he was merely going through the motions of life, competent in his job but quiet and withdrawn from the human race.

After speaking to Jarod today, she wasn't in the mood for Brad's teasing or Marguerite's stupidity. The only person allowed to mess with Jarod was her, and she always teased him to his face, not behind his back, like these two.

Of course, Brad was teasing *her* and not Jarod.

She was so confused.

Brad stood away from the wall, palms out in an "I give up" gesture. "Sounds like you care a little too much for your boss, Lauren."

Marguerite zeroed in on that possibility. "Oh, I get it. Lauren's got a crush on the sheriff. Well, surely by now you realize he has no interest in you or any other woman."

She winked at Brad in a satisfied way, and slithered back to her workstation on the other side of the room.

Lauren turned back to Brad and gave him a disbelieving look.

"Sorry," he said. "I took it too far."

"You're damn right you did. Why do you always get her going?" she asked.

"Because she is so full of herself and it entertains me."

He walked back to his desk, glancing at Marguerite as he went.

"You're really sick, you know that Brad?" Lauren yelled.

"So I've been told," he replied without turning around.

Puffing out an exasperated breath, she returned to her work.

On the way home that evening, she remembered the first time she'd learned Jarod would be committing himself to Miranda.

"Is he going off to college, Josh?" she asked despondently.

"He's staying local, Lauren. Don't worry," Josh answered with a sigh, putting his arm around her slumped shoulders. "You'll see him after he graduates, and he'll be around this summer, too."

"I don't understand why you're so upset, Lauren. He's with Miranda," Julie said as she popped some grapes into her mouth.

"I don't care. She's not the girl for Jarod."

"Lauren, honey, he told me and Jason last night he was saving up for an engagement ring. He really loves Miranda." Josh gave her shoulders a squeeze to soften his betraying words.

Lauren stared at the love of her teenage life, who stood across from their group in the cafeteria courtyard. His brilliant blue eyes were adoring as he looked at Miranda, the love of his teenage life.

Lauren refused to believe Miranda was anything but temporary. As she watched them, Jarod pressed his lips to Miranda's. Lauren turned away when Miranda's eyes connected with hers and her tongue jetted out to meet Jarod's.

Gross.

"*Why do you think she isn't right for him?*" Julie asked.

Lauren shook her head. She couldn't quite put her finger on the reason why she didn't like Miranda, other than the fact she had Jarod's affections and Lauren didn't. She'd never witnessed Miranda cheating or anything bad, but there was something wrong with the way she clung to Jarod. It didn't feel right.

She'd heard rumors about Miranda and what she did when Jarod wasn't around. But nothing could be proven. If the rumors were true, then Miranda didn't have any self-respect.

Shrugging, Lauren said, "All I know is that she's not good for Jarod."

"And you think you are, Sassy?" Josh teased her.

"Of course I am!" Lauren said with a laugh.

Two big guffaws sounded behind them before Josh was tackled to the ground by Jason. Billy slicked his arms around Julie, giving her a sloppy kiss on the neck and then on the mouth, which made Lauren want to gag.

Billy's cold eyes always creeped her out. She didn't understand what her best friend saw in the ugly toad. She also didn't understand why Jason was friends with him in the first place because Billy was not right in the head.

"Jarod doesn't even know you're alive, Lauren," Billy smirked.

Creep.

Julie elbowed him in the gut. "That's not nice, Billy." Lauren noted Julie gave him The Look. Lauren grinned. She appreciated Julie coming to her defense.

Jason and Josh stopped wrestling long enough for Jason to say, "Jarod's found his soul mate, Lauren. Sorry, but I don't think you're it. Ooof!" Jason bent in half when Josh slugged him in the stomach.

"Don't listen to Jason's crap, Lauren. Jarod thinks you're a good friend and he likes you." Josh gave her a reassuring smile.

"Dude, don't encourage her. Her moony-eyed expressions can get a little embarrassing," Billy laughed. "Come on, Julie. I'll walk you to class."

Lauren stuck her tongue out at Billy's retreating back as he walked away, his arms around Julie. Lauren noticed the narrow-eyed look Jason gave them as they disappeared inside the cafeteria.

Then, Jason turned his pretty green eyes on her and said, "I'm only teasing you, Sassy Pants, but I don't want you to get hurt. Jarod's going to marry Miranda."

Jason intimidated a lot of people, but he was her friend, too, and she understood his teasing came from a good place.

Josh batted the grass and dirt out of his shaggy hair. "Told ya."

"Marry her?" Lauren whined. "Oh, you guys have to talk him out of it," she pleaded.

"Talk who out of what?" Jarod asked from behind her. Miranda clung to his side like fungus on a tree trunk, and her haughty eyes laughed at Lauren.

She let out a surprised gasp, but Josh, seeing Lauren's distress, covered for her. "Billy wants to fight the assholes we met up with last night."

Jason eyed Josh, and for a moment Lauren thought he would give her away, but when Jason nodded his head in agreement, she relaxed.

"Yeah, we're gonna talk to him about it."

Lauren explained, "Julie would never forgive him." She smiled innocently at Jarod.

Miranda scowled.

"Well, I hope you do talk him out of it, cuz Miranda and I

have plans tonight, so I won't be available to watch your backs. What does Billy think he's doing, anyway?" Jarod asked with disgust.

"Just being Billy," Jason said with equal distaste for Julie's boyfriend.

Lauren felt Miranda's stare. Looking Lauren in the eye, she cuddled impossibly closer to Jarod. Never breaking eye contact, she said, "Well, kids, we gotta run." She tilted her head in a coquettish fashion and asked, "Jarod?"

He kissed Miranda on the lips before saying, "I'll catch up with you two dweebs later." But before he turned away, he looked back at Lauren and said sweetly, "Later, Lauren."

She watched them go, sucking in a large breath and quietly letting it out.

"Thanks for covering for me, guys."

"No problem, Sassy." Jason ruffled her gently on top of her head.

Josh helped her up and draped a negligent arm around her shoulders as they walked back into the school.

"Besides," he grinned, "Shit-for-brains really does want us to fight those creeps, so it wasn't like we were lying to Jarod."

Lauren shook her head. "Julie has no idea what a jackass Billy is. Want me to try and talk to her again?"

"Only if you think you can get through to her," Jason said, before storming off without another word.

By the time Lauren arrived at her townhouse, the snow floated down in thick, wet flakes. Once inside, she turned the lock on the deadbolt and headed straight for the small gas fireplace, flipping the switch on the wall to light the flames. She set her purse on the dining room table and headed up the stairs to her master bedroom.

It was the larger of the two bedrooms upstairs, with an en suite bathroom. A second full bathroom was located in the hallway to accommodate any overnight guests. Her townhouse wasn't huge, but it was hers and she loved it.

She stripped out of her work clothes, noting the white silk blouse would need to be dropped off at the cleaners. She put on some fleece yoga pants and a long-sleeved thermal top. Reaching into her drawer, she found the fluffiest pair of spa socks she owned. Once she had her feet properly ensconced, she padded back downstairs to the kitchen.

As was her normal routine, she opened the freezer and withdrew a low-calorie frozen dinner. She pealed back the plastic wrap on one corner to make a vent, placed the cardboard tray in the microwave, and hit the number six on the panel. Her dinner would be ready in six minutes.

She jumped when the phone rang.

"Hello?"

"Hey, it's me," Julie said on the other end. "Wanted to make sure you made it home safe. It's really nasty out there."

"I skated into the garage about ten minutes ago. Weren't you out at Jason's job site with Cafe Armstrong today?"

Lauren referred to her friend's restaurant on wheels. Julie was an amazing chef, but she'd purchased her small food truck in order to earn enough money to survive when her parents had died, and she'd been granted legal guardianship over Charlie, her little brother.

"Yes, but Jason made me drive it back to the estate right after lunch. He wouldn't even let me clean up first. He insisted on following me all the way home, too." Lauren heard the happy exasperation in Julie's voice before she asked, "Isn't that sweet?"

Lauren giggled, "Yes, it is, honey. Jason is the best thing that's ever happened to you."

"He really, really is." Julie paused in reverence. Her friend had had a tough five years on her own raising her amazing brother, but ever since Julie let Jason into her life, she was smiling and happy again. "How was everything today?"

Lauren launched into the day's events, beginning with the stupid flat tire that had made her late for work and soaked her to the bone.

"After Jarod found the little boy, he called me on my cell phone," she explained.

Julie gasped, "So the vow of silence is broken?"

"Yes! And quit laughing, you traitor!" Lauren exclaimed, but not unkindly.

She paused, thinking about how despondent Jarod had sounded. "I've never heard him so upset, at least not since Miranda skipped out on him."

"Why?"

"The home was in pretty bad shape and the little boy had been neglected for a long time."

"What happened to his parents?" Julie growled.

Since Julie had stepped up to take care of her brother at a young age, Lauren knew her friend found it incomprehensible that some people neglected their own children.

Lauren understood Julie's feelings all too well.

"The usual. Both Avery and Luanne are in jail, and the child is in foster care." Lauren shook her head at the stupidity of it. Some people didn't deserve children. "I'm so glad you were able to keep Charlie. I can't imagine how he would've turned out if he'd gone into the system."

"Or how I would've turned out if I'd lost my brother and my parents at the same time."

"Good point," Lauren agreed.

"The best thing to come out of my situation is how close Charlie is to Jason and Josh. Heck, even Jarod helped, even though it was about the same time Miranda walked out on him," Julie said.

"Gosh, you're right. Sometimes I forget everything happened in the same year—your parents' death, you dropping out of college to care for Charlie, and then Miranda, the cow, broke Jarod's heart." Lauren was angry all over again. "I never liked that woman."

"Me neither," Julie agreed.

After another twenty minutes of Miranda-bashing, Lauren finished her pow-wow with Julie and hung up the phone.

CHAPTER 3
Daddy

Visions of the little boy's room and the stench of its filth plagued Jarod all night. He kept imagining how the neglected Decatur boy had survived, and it reminded him of the pigsty where he'd found Miranda holed up, doing drugs. He couldn't fathom why anyone would want to live in such filth. Every drug bust he made left a painful reminder of that horrible time, a big punch in the gut, because it made him question what kind of husband he'd been.

How could a man—especially one trained in law enforcement—not notice his wife was a drug addict? Had he been so neglectful, so self-centered that he'd missed all the signs? They'd been high-school sweethearts, each other's first love, or so he believed, and she'd run away from him instead of working out their problems.

Thank God they'd never had any children. Finding the little boy in—he wouldn't call it a home, more like a prison cell —hiding in fear amid the filth and chaos, suffering from God only knew what horrors, was almost too much for Jarod.

The way Avery and Luanne ignored their child was incomprehensible. The boy could've been a stray dog, for all they cared. Jarod didn't understand how someone could forget their own flesh and blood like the refuse strewn about the scene.

Family meant everything to Jarod, and his father had made damn sure all three of his sons understood three things:

Family is the most important thing in the world. Next is honor, integrity, and standing up for those who can't defend themselves and it's your duty to protect them. But most importantly, there's nothing more precious than a child.

Jarod strongly believed a special place in hell existed for parents like Avery and Luanne. He sincerely hoped the boy would be placed in a good home and not be lost in bureaucratic red tape. Jarod would do everything in his power to see the Decaturs never got their little boy back, even if it meant going to every parole hearing until their sentences were up.

He contemplated all of this on his way to work the next morning. The small amount of snow which had stuck to the ground last night melted before the morning commute began. It should be a relatively calm day for traffic, thank God.

He wasn't looking forward to any drama when he entered his office. Alas, Marguerite waited for him when he walked through the door.

"How bad was it this time, Jarod?" she asked without preamble.

She must be starved for information this morning, he thought with disgust.

"'Bout what you'd expect from two lowlifes who care more about getting high than caring for their kid," he said without looking at her as he cruised through the break-room door, effectively cutting her off.

"Hey."

Lauren sat at the break table eating from a small yogurt, blue eyes soft with concern.

"Hey," he replied, a little chagrined. He hadn't meant to dump on her yesterday. It wasn't his way.

Seeing his regret, she immediately slipped into her professional persona, which he greatly appreciated.

"The Decatur reports are typed and ready for your signature. I've put them on your desk. A public defender was sent over to conference with the couple for their arraignment hearing." She stood and threw her empty yogurt container away.

He couldn't take his eyes off her.

She wore a pretty red dress this morning. It emphasized her amazing figure and his gaze drifted to bare legs, which gave him a shock. Wasn't she cold? The heating system in the building worked well, but she still had to walk from the parking lot to the building, and this morning's weather was brisk and damp from yesterday's storm. The sky was blue, and the weatherman promised the temperatures would rise back up to the low sixties this afternoon. Maybe she was banking on the warmer temps today.

"Is there a problem with my legs?" she asked with a raised eyebrow.

Startled by being caught ogling his secretary, he jerked his eyes back to hers. Humor clouded her baby blues, easing his embarrassment. He smirked and said, "Absolutely none, Ms. Lockwood."

A throaty giggle issued from her, hitting him square in the gut. "There is no way in hell I'm calling you *Mr. Grey.*"

He had no idea what *the hell* she was talking about. He felt his eyebrows lower at her when she laughed outright at his confusion.

"Never mind, Jarod. I'm flattered all the same." She turned

with her offensive smiley face mug and walked out of the break room.

Shaking his head, he grabbed his plain mug and poured himself a cup of coffee. The carafe was full, so she must have just made a fresh pot.

God bless her.

Brad stopped him on the way back to his office.

"Avery won't say who he's cooking for, and any evidence was destroyed in the explosion and subsequent fire."

Jarod laughed. "So you don't believe he's the ringleader any more than I do?"

Brad shook his head, "Avery is too stupid to lead anything, Jarod."

"I know. Whoever he is, the bastard's too crafty to leave behind any evidence. Hell, we don't even know if it's one man or a group of people. We've got nothing."

Jarod stalked into his office and closed the door. Crystal meth was a serious problem in Nevada, getting worse by the month, spreading into Timbisha Township and the surrounding county, and he had no leads. Nothing pissed him off more than chasing his tail while trying to figure out a puzzle. He needed to start looking at the problem from a different angle.

Until a few years ago, Timbisha had been a sleepy little community untouched by the problems of the big cities of Las Vegas and Reno. Now the problem had become his personal white whale. He'd made several busts in the past five years, swearing to clean up the problem which had forced his wife to leave him, but even though he had put some dealers behind bars, the bigger problem remained. He was missing something. He had to find the source, but none of his busts led him to any answers. They'd all been dead ends.

LAUREN CONCENTRATED ON HER WORK, IGNORING Jarod as much as possible. Any attention between them would only embarrass them both, especially after the teasing she'd received from Brad yesterday. She didn't want any rumors floating around for Marguerite to spread. But it was hard to keep her mind on anything else with Jarod only a few feet away in his office.

When Eli strode in, he answered her prayer for a distraction by plopping down in the chair next to her desk. She frowned at his bloodshot brown eyes and droopy eyelids. His uniform sagged in places indicating he'd lost a little weight, too. The late shifts and lack of sleep were obviously taking a toll on him. He'd arrested a teen last night for a Minor In Possession, or MIP. A high school kegger had gotten out of control, and neighbors called the cops.

"Hey, Lauren," Eli sighed.

"Hey, Eli. You okay?"

"Oh, sure. A little tired, though. I hate busting kids as a rule, but it's especially hard when they're so high on whatever they're using that they don't even understand why they're being taken into custody." He shook his head.

"Have you contacted his parents yet?"

"Yeah, they came down and got him last night." He swiped a hand down his face. "I don't think he'll have much of a social life for a while."

"Pretty upset, were they?"

"An understatement. I don't envy his morning when he sobers up," he chuckled.

"It means they're good parents."

"I don't think so. They appeared more upset over the

inconvenience of picking him up than the fact their son was using drugs."

Lauren thought for a moment. The family was part of Timbisha's upper echelon, so maybe the partying had been a cry for help.

Before she could expound upon her theory, Eli said, "God, I hope my child doesn't rebel too much as a teen." Eyes bleak, he admitted, "I don't know if I could handle it."

"Oh, Eli, you and Caroline are going to be wonderful parents, you'll see." She gave him a quick pat on the shoulder.

"I hope you're right." He sat in silence for a second before he asked, "What kind of monster intentionally hooks a child on a lethal narcotic? How do they live with themselves?"

"I don't know," she said, "but I'm sure you'll catch them."

Brad walked in the door and headed for them. "Who's a monster?"

"Drug dealers," they said in unison. She grinned at Eli. "Especially those who deal to children," she clarified.

"Ah," Brad said. "You busted Aiden Lawlor last night. Congratulations."

"Yeah, at a high school kegger." Eli explained what had transpired. "Sophomore. Too damn young."

"Agreed," Brad said, pausing for a moment before he continued. "I suppose the kid didn't volunteer who was supplying?"

"Not before his dad picked him up. I'm hoping he'll talk some sense into Aiden to help us apprehend the ringleaders. Maybe the DA could make a deal with them," Eli pondered.

"You're willing to cut a deal?"

"It's the kid's first offense. Why ruin his life when he can help us catch the bigger fish?"

Brad sighed. "Well, let me know how I can help, Eli. Maybe

one of us could reach out to the Lawlors. I know your wife is getting close to her due date. You should be home with her, right?" He put a hand on Eli's shoulder.

"Oh, I will, but this could make my career, too," he said, and then added, a bit hopefully, "Maybe I can get my shift changed, at the very least."

From Lauren's standpoint, she didn't care who busted the creeps responsible, so long as the ring leaders were off the streets.

JAROD LOOKED OVER ELI'S ARREST REPORT AND grimaced. The teen's family ran in the same social circles as Jarod's parents, but Derek Lawlor made his fortune in mining instead of construction. Most of the mines had closed down, but Derek still had a few producing.

Jarod didn't know the Lawlors very well, but he didn't believe them to be bad people.

Of course, Jarod didn't consider himself a bad person either, yet Miranda had still gotten herself involved in the drug world, exactly like Aiden Lawlor. The lingering question of why she'd done it sometimes kept Jarod awake at night.

The drug culture had rapidly spread in the five years since her departure from his life. All his investigations had led to nowhere. His informants either clammed up or disappeared altogether. Just when he thought he'd made some headway, the trail ran cold or led straight to a dead end. It was almost like they'd known his next move before he did.

A perfunctory knock on Jarod's open door grabbed his attention before Brad stepped into his office. "Heard about

Eli's bust. Can't believe any kid of Derek Lawlor's would be involved with selling meth. And where the hell is he getting it?"

Jarod leaned back in his chair and gestured to one of the two padded chairs in front of his desk. Brad acknowledged the invitation to sit with a nod.

"Yeah, Aiden is a rich, sixteen-year-old little snot, whose parents are parishioners of the same church as my family." Jarod rolled his eyes.

"Do you know the kid?"

"Not personally, no. But Dad worked with Derek to remodel his mining office, and I've heard rumblings about a hotel remodel. I'm not sure if their relationship extends beyond business."

Jarod tapped his pen on the desk in an agitated fashion before admitting, "I'm desperate enough to use my parents' connection to help persuade the Lawlors to allow Aiden to be interviewed, with their lawyer present, of course. Or at least to point out the benefits of him cooperating with us."

Brad nodded as if he agreed, but said nothing.

Jarod was disgusted with the circumstances, but he needed answers. He gave Brad an assessing look and asked, "What do you know about the kid?"

Brad shook his head. "Nothing, only the family name, pretty prominent, like you said, and I don't recall Aiden ever being in trouble before." He shrugged. "You sure you want to involve your parents in this case?"

"Hell, I'm not sure of anything anymore," Jarod sighed, tossing the pen in his hand onto his desk. "I'm hoping someone will get overconfident and sloppy so we can catch these bastards."

Brad stood up. "Agreed." He turned and said, "I'm heading

out on patrol. I'll make a few passes by the high school, see what's shakin'."

"Good idea. Keep me in the loop," Jarod said, unnecessarily. He trusted Brad to inform him of everything. From the beginning, Brad had been as frustrated as the rest of them, taking it as personally as Jarod did.

As Jarod's gaze followed Brad into the main office, his eyes landed on Lauren, who was busy at her desk. Her pretty red dress was modest and professional. Her blonde hair hung down her back in soft, shiny loops. He couldn't see her soft, clear blue eyes, which were surrounded by long, thick lashes that she darkened with mascara. Though she wore makeup at work, he knew their natural color was a shade or two darker than her hair. She'd spent many summers with his family at the lake, camping out, bare-faced and carefree. She enjoyed the outdoors as much as he did.

And then it dawned on him, not in an epiphany sort of way, but more like a punch to the gut: Lauren Lockwood is an extremely beautiful woman.

A rough breath soughed out of his lungs, as if he'd shot rotgut from a dirty glass in a cheap bar. Of course, he'd always known she was pretty, and there'd always been some subliminal attraction he'd known was mostly coming from her (not from him because he had loved his wife), but the realization of this new attraction felt as though a switch had been flipped in his head, and no matter how much he wanted to he couldn't switch it off again.

Unbidden and unwelcome, the memory of the kiss he'd forced upon her last month came to mind and tightened every muscle in his body.

Damn it. Maybe he needed to take a trip into the next county and take care of some personal business.

As the idea took hold, Lauren turned her head toward his office, and their eyes caught and held.

Screw it, he thought to himself. He let her see what was in his mind and smiled when she blushed.

Interesting. Lauren was not a shy woman. In fact, other than his mother, she was the most self-assured woman he knew. The fact he could draw a blush from her intrigued him in ways he didn't want to contemplate.

The intercom dinged, startling him before Marguerite's grating voice informed him of a phone call.

"Send it," he said. The phone on his desk rang and he hit the speaker, opening up the line. "Sheriff King."

"Sheriff, this is Detective Cane, Las Vegas PD. I have an urgent matter I need to speak with you about, in person and as soon as possible."

"In regard to?" Jarod let the question hang in the air. He didn't care much for his state's largest city, or its brand of law enforcement, but every now and then they had to work together on cases. If they'd done a better job, maybe their drug problem wouldn't have spread this far out into rural Nevada.

"We would prefer to do this in person. I'm already in town, staying at the Super 8. Will six this evening be all right?"

"I'll still be here." He hung up.

Uncertainty clawed at him. Detective Cane must be new on the job, otherwise they would've shared information over the phone.

He glanced back out at Lauren to see a frown marring her forehead. She'd overheard the conversation from her desk. He shook his head at her but smiled as he did so, putting her at ease.

At a quarter to six, the office had emptied out, except for Marguerite, who sometimes stayed later depending on how busy the office was. She rushed around, tidying up, when Jarod noticed a group of people coming in; the leader wore an ill-fitting brown suit jacket, stereotypical of a crusty detective—underpaid and overworked, along with a highway patrol officer and a woman whose appearance screamed Child Protective Services, with her overly friendly smile, cartoonish voice, and eyes that took in everything. She spoke softly but animatedly down toward her right hand, where she held the hand of a child whom Jarod couldn't see below the counter.

Jarod's neck hair prickled.

Why are they bringing a child here at this time of night?

Instinct propelled him out of his office to greet them before the detective could fully inform Marguerite who they were and whom they wished to see.

"Right this way, please," Jarod instructed, gesturing toward an interrogation room, out of Marguerite's line of sight. She wore her plastic smile, but she was annoyed at him for not allowing her to discern the identities of his mysterious guests.

"That'll be all for tonight, Marguerite. Make sure you lock the front doors when you leave," he commanded.

She studied him for only a second before giving him a nod, then turned to continue closing down her computer.

Assured now he wouldn't be interrupted, he turned down the hall and opened a door to a small room containing a table with four chairs. He again gestured for them to enter, but the woman stayed back and told the child—who, Jarod could now see, was a little girl—to sit on the bench outside the interrogation room and wait until the adults finished speaking.

For the second time today, Jarod's breath got stuck in his lungs when he caught the little girl's gaze. He stared into a pair of deep blue eyes which were as familiar to him as his own. His prickling neck hairs became a stinging chill down his spine.

The detective placed a hand on his shoulder, breaking the spell. "Sheriff," he said with something Jarod recognized as compassion, "come on in and we'll get this business taken care of."

Jarod didn't miss the sympathy in the man's voice.

"Uh," was all he could manage. He met the man's weathered eyes and followed him inside. The patrolman stood guard with the woman and child outside the room.

The detective sat down first with a file in his hands. The last thing Jarod wanted to do was sit and look through a rap sheet, so he didn't. Instead, he began to pace the small room in an attempt to control his boiling temper because, deep down in his gut, he knew what the detective was going to say about the little girl.

Detective Cane cleared his throat. He opened up his file and said, "I can see you're shaken up, so I'll make this brief. Miranda Becker King was killed in a car accident three days ago. She was with a man named Michael Trapp. She had no identification on her when she died. I'm sorry it's taken us this long to contact you."

"Miranda's dead?" He didn't know how to feel about the news—at least, not yet. He hadn't seen her since she'd walked out, and now she was... dead. He had trouble processing this information.

His heart began to beat faster because he suspected this wasn't the only news the good detective was about to impart.

"Yes, sir. We did some investigating, and the little girl sitting outside is Miranda's daughter." The detective cleared his throat again.

"Miranda's daughter," Jarod repeated. Inside his chest, he felt his heart beating.

k'thump-k'thump-k'thump.

Detective Cane flipped through the pages in the thick folder. Jarod spotted the edges of mugshot photos and other legal documents. "Yes, Mrs. King listed your name as the father on Jessica's birth certificate, Sheriff."

Jessica.

Stunned, Jarod finally sat down. He was working very hard to keep a cool head, but damn, his world had just been rocked off its axis.

Detective Cane sat patiently. Jarod looked at him and pointed to the file folder. "May I?"

"Of course," he said and passed over the documents.

Jarod flipped through the thick folder and found detailed arrest records. Miranda had been busted for selling meth several times; Jessica's birth certificate did, indeed, list him as the father. He noted by her birth date she was almost four and a half years old, but the little girl outside the door looked a lot younger.

BecauseMiranda used meth while she was pregnant.

Jarod fought hard to keep the red haze of his anger from obscuring the rest of the documents. He found reports indicating Child Protective Services had been called and Jessica had been taken from her mother on several occasions. He counted at least three periods when Jessica had been placed with foster families while Miranda was in jail—the first time at only six months of age.

Just a baby.

The red haze blazed across his vision.

"Why wasn't I informed when my... daughter," he swallowed, choking on the word, "was collected by CPS?" He jabbed his finger at the reports.

"We never found any record of shared custody filed with the State of Nevada. We didn't know you were her father until

Miranda's death. They're calling it a glitch." Here, the detective looked ashamed and looked down at the table, not meeting Jarod's eyes. "We didn't bring Jessica into our care until last night."

"What do you mean?" Jarod's voice was whisper calm.

"The wreck was reported three days ago on Highway 160, a few miles outside of Pahrump. We believe Mr. Trapp lost control of his vehicle and rolled it off the embankment. An autopsy will show whether any drugs or alcohol were in their systems at the time of the accident. But by the time Mrs. King had been identified, CPS was sent to her last known address, where they found Jessica, in good health," he assured Jarod. "She was then brought into the state's care, until it was determined that you're her only next of kin."

Jarod had a lot of questions to ask, but his poor befuddled mind still grappled with the fact he was a father and his child was outside needing him badly. His experience of late, and the Decatur boy in particular, weighed on his heart like an anchor. Reclaiming his control was almost impossible, but he did it as he stood up.

"Thank you for coming to me directly, Detective. I appreciate all you've done. I'd like to take my little girl home now to meet her family, if you don't mind."

"Of course," he said. Cane looked at the birth certificate Jarod still held in a death grip.

"I'd like to keep this, if possible?" Jarod motioned to the folder on the table. His voice only quavered a little. "I'd like to know what my daughter has gone through since her birth."

"Certainly, Sheriff. Let's get you introduced to your daughter."

They walked out to the hallway, where the woman sat with a protective arm around the back of the bench, surrounding

Jessica. Engrossed in a picture book, the woman read it softly to the little girl. They both looked up when the door opened, and Jarod stopped dead.

Jessica was small but beautiful. She didn't smile, but she wasn't crying, either. Did she know her mother was dead? Did she care?

Detective Cane bent down in front of her and said, "Jessica, this is your father. His name is Jarod King, the same last name as yours. He's a sheriff, and he wants to take you home now."

Jessica's blue eyes met Jarod's and studied his face while Jarod studied hers.

In a voice almost too quiet to hear, she whispered, "Ah-right."

She gave the book back to the woman, to whom Jarod had not been introduced, and hopped off the bench. She turned to the miniature backpack sitting next to her on the bench and put it on like a pro. Then she picked up the dirtiest blue blanket Jarod had ever seen and clung to it for dear life. She turned and looked up at Jarod expectantly.

It was clear his little girl had been passed around from person to person since her birth, and that this was not her first rodeo when it came to being dumped with someone new. He wondered if she even knew what it meant that he was her father.

He wanted to break things.

He wanted to howl at the moon and then kill his ex-wife all over again.

CHAPTER 4

Jessica

Jessica was quiet on the ride home. In fact, she hadn't said much at all since they'd left the station.

She was safely ensconced in a state-appointed car seat in the back of the cruiser, the well-worn blue blanket clutched tightly in her small fists. He could see her in the review mirror as she gazed out the window at the passing landscape.

Her temporary caregivers had dressed her in skinny jeans with pink sparkles on the pockets and were too big for her small body; the legs were rolled up at the ankles, showing off her pink sneakers. A white collar peeked out under the pink zip-up hoodie, which was also too big for her, and the cuffs were rolled up, thick and bulky, at her wrists. Her dark hair had been divided into two long braids with neon-colored hair ties on the ends. The child-sized backpack lay next to her on the back seat. The dirty blanket and the backpack were her only possessions.

Her shiny, dark hair, the same color as Miranda's, set off her deep-blue eyes, which were the same eyes he saw every morning staring back at him in the bathroom mirror, or when he looked at his own father.

He focused again on the road, trying not to let the anger set in, when a small sniffle issued from behind him. He met her gaze in the rearview mirror. She stared back at him with a tear trailing down her rosy cheek and a quiver in her bottom lip.

"Am I 'rested?" she whispered.

Jarod swallowed the lump in his throat. "Of course not, Darlin'. Why would you think that?"

She wiped her nose on the dirty blanket and whispered back, "Mommy and Big Mike hadda ride in the back seat of the policeman's car when they got 'rested."

Jarod ground his teeth together in an effort to keep his anger in check. He didn't want to frighten her. He could only guess at all the horrible things this sweet little girl, *his child*, had seen in her short life.

He took a deep, calming breath through his nose. "Who's Big Mike?" he asked, to distract them both from the circumstances. Of course, she was referring to Michael Trapp, the bastard who had dealt meth to Miranda and killed her in his car.

"He's mommy's slumber party friend," she explained.

Jarod closed his eyes for a moment. This kept getting better and better. He was afraid to ask her more, but he had to know. "Did your mom have a lot," he hesitated a moment by clearing his throat, "...of slumber parties?"

She nodded the affirmative, her eyes round as saucers and very serious. "Uh huh."

"Where were you when mommy had her parties?" He tried his damnedest to keep the wretched anger from seeping into his voice. Unfortunately, the last word came out as a growl, and her tiny shoulders hunched up to her ears.

"In my secret house with Teddy." Another tear rolled down her pretty face. "Teddy couldn't come with me." She squeezed her blanket even tighter.

Jarod's heart ached at the thought of his daughter being taken away from the only home she knew, even if it was most likely a living hell. It made him even madder that she mourned the loss of her "teddy" and the clothes on her back weren't even hers. All she had was the blue blanket she clung to for dear life. She'd come to him with nothing, and it was killing him.

At a loss for words, he concentrated on the road and getting them safely home to his family. When he pulled into the driveway, he squirmed a bit at seeing Lauren's car parked in what was slowly becoming her normal parking space. She'd been spending quite a bit of time at The Estate lately, working with his mother and Julie on the wedding.

His mother, Camille, had set Lauren up with her own room, so she didn't have to drive home late when they got carried away in the craft room (better known to him and his brothers as the Room of Doom), where his mother ran her business. It was Camille's way of appeasing her own guilt at monopolizing so much of Lauren's time. To be honest, he was glad she wasn't driving home alone on those nights as well.

He parked in his normal spot between the barn and the main house and shut off the engine. He heard an intake of breath from the back seat, a small, excited gasp before Jessica's small voice exclaimed, "Horsies!"

He grinned when he opened the door to unbuckle her from her car seat and helped her out of the cruiser.

"Do you like horses?" he asked as he set her tiny feet on the ground. This first smile took his breath away, as it changed her entire sweet face.

"Yes," she said seriously.

"Well, after we get you settled in, maybe we can go out to the barn and visit them. What do you say?"

She looked up at him with those big blue eyes and the sweet smile still gracing her delicate face. "Yes please!" she said and did a little hop.

He laughed and took her hand in his. His heart swelled in his chest when her tiny fingers tried to grip onto his large hand as they walked to the mud room. He had to keep his stride small in order for her short legs to keep up with his pace.

Though he'd grown up here, he still referred to The Estate as his parents' home. The main house was massive. The mud/utility room had more square footage than some living rooms he'd seen and contained more than a washer and dryer. There were a variety of items, including a vacuum, a broom, an iron, and an ironing board. Lots of cubbies for shoes, and hooks for coats hung on the walls and benches to sit on to remove dirty footwear, either from chores or play. He'd used the a large washbasin many times after mucking horse stalls.

This room led into the "small" family dining room and kitchen. The house had two, the other being commercial sized. Jarod's father constructed it so his mom could entertain properly for business and social events.

Laughter came from the next room as they approached the doorway. Jessica stopped in her tracks and clutched her blanket to her chest. Gone was her happy smile, replaced with the same wary expression she'd worn since she'd arrived at the station.

He knelt down on one knee in front of her. "It's okay, Darlin'."

"I don't like slumber parties." She shook her head at him, her eyes huge and luminous.

"This isn't a slumber party, Jessica. This is my family. And guess what? This is your family, too," he said softly.

"Mommy said family don't like me."

He saw red and growled, "Mommy was wrong."

"How d'ya know?" she whispered.

He touched her chin, rubbing his thumb across her baby-soft skin. He waited for her to meet his eyes. "Because I'm your family now, and I like you very much."

She smiled and he scooped her up in his arms. She was feather-light and was almost swallowed up by his big body. She held her blanket in a tight grip as he strode through the doorway and into the dining room.

Everyone stopped and stared when they saw what he held in his arms. His mother recovered first.

"Who do you have there, Jarod?" she asked as she approached them with a big smile on her face.

Jessica tensed up in his arms. He rubbed her back in a circular motion to offer comfort. She was so small that his big hand spanned her entire body.

His mother still wore a smile, but now a puzzled crinkle formed on her brow.

He cleared his throat, feeling nervous all of a sudden.

"This is Jessica Rose King. She's my daughter."

Jarod watched their different reactions to the stunning news. Josh's jaw hung open on its hinges, Lauren gasped, his father's eyebrows were stuck in his hairline, and his poor mother covered her mouth with her hand. Slowly, their shocked expressions morphed into watery smiles.

Jessica sniffled again and her lip began to quiver once more. That's when his mother remembered herself and slowly approached them, with tears in her emerald green eyes and a tender smile on her face.

"Hello, Jessica. I am your grandmother," she said, her voice cracking on the last word.

Jessica, still wary, whispered, "'Lo."

"Would you like something to eat?" As always, his mom's go-to plan in times of great emotion, whether it be happiness, stress, or shock, was food.

Jessica shook her head and leaned closer to Jarod's shoulder.

"We've had a lot of surprises today, but Jessica said she'd like to see the horses after she gets settled in, isn't that right, Darlin'?"

"Uh huh," she answered in her sweet little girl voice.

"Well, Jarod, why don't you take a seat at the table, and I'll bring your plate and a little something for this angel you've brought home to me." His mother smiled and went to the kitchen. She had her back to them, but her irregular breathing was a dead giveaway she was crying.

He understood how she felt.

Lauren pulled out the chair next to her for them to sit down. She grinned from ear to ear, her surprised blue eyes shining in welcome invitation.

"Hello, Jessie. My name is Lauren, and I work with your daddy." She held out her hand to the little girl, as if she were an adult. He kind of liked her easy way with his daughter.

To Jarod's surprise, Jessica slowly let go of her blanket with one small hand and let Lauren shake it. He took in a relieved breath, meeting Lauren's gaze with gratefulness. Something unnamed passed between them, but it was a good sort of something which made him want to hug her for all she was worth.

His father sat in stunned silence, watching Jessica's every move as if she were some kind of mythical creature. Used to boys, James didn't know what to do with a little girl, Jarod was sure. God knew he didn't have a clue himself.

Josh kept looking from one face to another with a big,

stupid grin on his face. All of a sudden he chuckled which startled Jessica. Jarod frowned at his baby brother, but Josh ignored him as usual and took one of Jessica's tiny hands into his own. "I guess that makes me your Uncle Josh."

Josh, ever the ladies' man, had an infectious smile to which even frightened little girls weren't immune.

Jessica smiled back. "'Lo, Hunkle Josh."

"After dinner, I'll show you the horses with your daddy, okay?"

"'Kay," she whispered, revealing one small dimple in her rosy cheek, which eased Jarod's tension a bit.

His mother placed a warmed plate of food in front of him, along with a small matching plate containing macaroni and cheese and apple slices. She smoothed her hand down one of Jessica's long, dark braids, unable to stop herself from touching the little girl. Jarod understood his mother's need to touch. Now that Jessica was allowing him to hold her, he was having trouble letting go; he wasn't sure whether she was real or not. He was perfectly happy with her sitting in his lap while they ate and she seemed perfectly happy being there.

James finally spoke up. "Well, young lady, I guess that makes me your grandpa, but you can call me Papa if you'd like. That's what I called my grandfather when I was your age." He smiled, and everyone at the table ignored the tears clinging to his lashes.

Jessica smiled back at her papa, but her attention focused mainly on the small plate in front of her. She wouldn't let go of her blanket, though, and Jarod was concerned she was still afraid.

Before he could come up with a solution, Lauren picked up an apple slice and handed it to Jessica. She took it with a smile. "Thank you," she whispered.

Jarod leaned into her ear and asked, "Have you eaten today, Darlin'?"

She shook her head in the negative.

Again, he saw red.

Lauren, God bless her, drew the small plate up in front of Jessica and handed her a fork. "Then you better gobble up this mac 'n'cheese before your nana gets her feelings hurt."

"Nana?" she asked.

"That's what I used to call my grandmother," Camille said, wiping tears from her eyes but smiling nonetheless.

Jessica took the fork from Lauren and dug into her dish. She kept a death grip on the blanket, and when asked if she wanted to sit in her own chair, she refused to leave Jarod's lap.

For now, he was okay with both.

While Jessica's attention remained on her food, James asked the question that was on everyone's mind. "Where's Miranda?"

"Died in a car wreck three days ago outside of Vegas. It took them this long to determine next of kin, which is me." Jarod cleared his throat as his voice cracked. He would not break down in front of his family or his little girl.

Lauren continued to help Jessica with her meal, but he felt her eyes on him. Then, ever so gently, she raised her hand and rubbed his back between his shoulder blades, offering comfort.

Under normal circumstances, her affection would've irritated him, but tonight, it felt like a balm. Just knowing she was here and the way she carefully treated his frightened child reinforced the tender feelings he was beginning to have for her.

Camille sat next to James across the table from Jarod, watching Jessica with fascination. All of a sudden, she whispered, "I assume Jessica wasn't in the car when it wrecked. Where has she been for the past three days?"

Jessica answered around a mouthful of pasta, "In my secret house."

James looked at Jarod. "Secret house?"

But Jessica answered matter-of-factly, "Uh huh." She took a drink of milk from her cup, with Lauren's help.

Jarod explained, "Not all the details are in yet, but I've requested a copy of the full report from NHP and Vegas PD."

Jessica whispered something to Lauren. Lauren smiled before they stood up. "I'll take you, sweet pea."

His little girl squirmed off his lap and took Lauren's hand like they were best friends. Her departure left him feeling a little empty.

His mother watched them go in silence before she turned back to Jarod. "She has your eyes." A tear slipped down her cheek.

Josh piped up proudly, "And mine and dad's. There's no denying that she's a King." He laughed at the double meaning.

The door to the mud room suddenly opened as Jason, Julie, and Charlie came through. Charlie made a beeline for Camille and hugged her tight.

"It smells like your macaroni and cheese in here. I'm starvin'!" He gave her a smacking kiss on the cheek and headed to the stove.

"What's going on?" Jason asked with a considering frown.

Josh stood up and hugged Jason. "You and I are *hunkles*!"

Jarod rolled his eyes but didn't miss seeing the pride in Josh's face.

"What are you talking about?" Jason asked, shoving Josh, who was now attempting to kiss Jason's cheek.

Right on cue, Lauren and Jessica made their way back from the bathroom. Lauren had the pink hoodie draped over her arm, but Jessica still had her blanket clutched tightly against her chest. Her eyes widened, and she stopped dead in her tracks at the sight of new people in the room.

"Holy shit," Jason breathed.

Julie gasped and leaned into Jason. Neither of them took their surprised eyes off of Jessica.

Charlie stared while he continued to chew the enormous amount of macaroni and cheese he'd shoveled into his mouth.

Ever the diplomat in these situations, Lauren said, "It's all right, Jessie. More of your family's arrived." She smiled reassuringly at Jessica. "You're a very lucky girl to have such a large family."

Lauren's statement tugged a bit at Jarod's heart, but his attention was on Jessica as she wrapped her tiny arms around Lauren's legs. Lauren picked her up and began the introductions.

"This is your Uncle Jason. He's your daddy's brother, just like Uncle Josh," she explained.

Jarod caught Jessica's eye and could feel her fear. Admittedly, they were all big men, but Jason was the biggest, covered in tattoos, and he could mean mug the most dangerous of men. Jarod shoved his chair back and took Jessica into his arms.

Wanting her to feel comfortable again, he asked, "Are you ready to see some horses?"

Keeping the blanket close, she wrapped one of her tiny arms around his shoulder and nodded her head.

Lauren said, "Then let's get your jacket back on," and proceeded to do so without taking her out of Jarod's arms, or relieving her of the blue blanket, something Jarod couldn't have done without some major maneuvering.

Again, Lauren had come to his rescue. She asked Jarod directly, "Does she have a hat or gloves in her backpack?"

She didn't. He'd have to take her shopping soon, which

brought on a little bit of panic. *What do I know about little girls?*

Letting Lauren see the answer in his expression, he hugged Jessica close and carried her out to the barn.

JAROD HAS A DAUGHTER!

Jarod was going to need a lot of help, and Lauren would be there for him, or else he'd completely mess things up. Heck, he hardly knew anything about women, let alone a female under the age of eighteen.

Jessica was so sweet Lauren was already in love with the waif. Her blue eyes mirrored Jarod's as if they'd been grown in a petri dish by a mad scientist. Her only resemblance to Miranda was in her hair and skin color, but Lauren didn't doubt Jessica was a little King.

How could she not love her already?

As Jarod and Jessica led the King family to the barn, Lauren decided to stay the night at The Estate. It was cold, the temperature dropping to freeze any leftover puddles from the day before. If anyone asked, she'd explain how she didn't want to take a chance of hitting black ice, but she was sure no one would bat an eye, since Camille had already given her a room of her own. Besides, she wasn't about to miss a thing now that Jessica was here. She seriously doubted anyone else would leave tonight, for the same reason. Knowing this family, everyone would want to learn all about Jessica's life before coming here, the good and the bad.

That sweet pea was going to need a strong female influence to undo whatever damage Miranda had inflicted upon her. Lauren held no fantasies Miranda had protected her daughter from her dangerous lifestyle, and she was extremely curious to know what a "secret house" was to a four-and-a-half-year-old child.

Jarod spoke quietly to Jessica, who was getting excited about the old mare standing in the stall in front of them.

"Do you want to give her some of your apple?" he asked.

"Yes, please!"

He gently put her on the ground and handed her an apple slice. He rolled up the sleeve of her oversized hoodie, so the mare wouldn't accidentally catch hold of it. Lauren studied his concentration and knew he was afraid he might break Jessica's delicate wrists.

"Hold your hand out like this, Darlin'," he instructed, unfurling her fingers and placed an apple slice on top.

With absolutely no fear, Jessica held her hand out to the mare, palm up, with the apple slice resting on the flat of her hand like Jarod had shown her. The old horse snuffled the fruit with a gentleness that surprised Lauren, and then took it out of the tiny hand holding it out for her to eat.

Jessica squealed with delight when the horse's lips tickled her palm. She even dropped the old blanket she'd been clinging to. She clasped her hands together under her chin and did a little tap dance while the mare chewed up the apple.

Josh reached around Lauren to hand Jessica another piece of the fruit. Jessica took it with a big grin and held it out for the mare once again.

Jason had taken up position on the other side of Jarod, no doubt to be caught up on the situation. Josh took advantage of their conversation and knelt down beside Jessica with a giant grin on his face.

Julie put her arm around Lauren's shoulders. She was still shaking her head slowly from side to side in amazement. She gave Lauren a little squeeze and said, "I can't believe it, Lauren. I just can't believe it! Where did this little angel come from?"

"Jarod walked into the kitchen with her in his arms." She met her best friend's eyes. "You should've seen the look on his face when he announced to everyone she was his daughter. He was so proud, Julie, and really pissed."

"I bet. This little girl certainly is a mixed blessing. What happened to Miranda?"

Lauren quickly explained the circumstances. "He hasn't said anything, but I have a feeling they'll open a criminal investigation." Lauren had worked with the sheriff's department long enough to know something didn't add up with the car accident. She'd bet money Miranda had been entangled in something terrible, and poor Jessica was probably going to be caught up in the middle.

"I thank God for bringing Jessica to us and getting her out of that life." Lauren hadn't meant to say it out loud.

Julie hugged her again and whispered, "Amen."

"I second that," Camille said, as she and Charlie approached.

With joy, the women continued to watch Jessica feed the old mare the rest of the apple her "hunkle" Josh had handed to her. He spoke easily with her, and eventually picked her up in his arms so she could pet the horse's mane above the stall rail.

Lauren shared a smile with Julie, who rolled her eyes. "The man definitely has a way with the ladies. And that's the God's honest truth."

In his typical fashion, Josh won over the newest female in the room, and Lauren adored him for it. When he finally settled down with his own family, he would be an excellent husband and, by the looks of it, a natural at fatherhood. Lauren grinned wickedly to herself, wishing lots of little girls on Josh, payback for all the womanizing he'd done in his young life.

It was funny how all of the adults, even Charlie, gathered around this one small child, watching her every move and smiling at everything she did and said. Lauren wondered how it would be with a baby.

Blocking that picture out of her mind, she turned to retrieve the forgotten blanket on the ground. She didn't want Jessica to miss it later if she needed it. It seemed to be the only item of comfort she'd been allowed to bring with her.

———

JAROD ALLOWED HIMSELF TO SMILE AS JOSH established his "hunkle" relationship with Jessica. Under normal circumstances, it would have annoyed him that his little brother so easily attracted the prettiest girl in the room, but there was nothing normal about this situation.

He'd feared a possible rejection from his family, but should've known better. He came from people who valued family, helped the helpless, and believed children were a treasure, a blessing from God. The only proof Jessica was really his came from a birth certificate belonging to a dead meth addict, and the color of her eyes. But his family had accepted her anyway.

Do I need a DNA test? Do I want to put her through that? Jarod wondered. Jason asked him if he was sure Jessica was his biological daughter. Initially, he'd had his own doubts.

His family interacted with Jessica with protectiveness and caring. He knew she'd been through hell in her short life. Why confuse her any more than she already was right now? Did it matter whose DNA was in her body? Instinctively he felt drawn to her, and he wanted her safe and happy. The thought of Jessica ending up in a situation like the Decatur boy turned his stomach. And, legally, she was his. Again, he looked around at his family and was confident she'd find love here. His family had a way with taking in strays. Julie and Charlie were proof. Hell, as far as his parents were concerned, even Lauren was part of their family. She'd been accepted almost immediately after Josh had introduced her to their mom when they were freshmen, only as a friend, of course.

Motherly arms wrapped around his waist, pulling him from pictures of the past. "She's beautiful, Jarod." Camille wore a watery smile as she focused her eyes on her new granddaughter.

"I know, Mom." He put his arm around her shoulders in return.

Sensing she was getting down to business, he pulled his eyes away from Jessica and paid close attention to his mother.

"I went through her backpack, and she doesn't have much," Camille said. "Only a large t-shirt which I suppose will suffice for a nightgown tonight, but I'll have to do some major shopping tomorrow. I'll set her up in your room for now. I doubt she'll want to sleep alone in a strange house for a while, and I'll be damned if I'm going to scare my granddaughter on her first night home." She swallowed back her tears.

"I'd planned on putting her on my sofa, so I'm glad we're in agreement on the issue," he agreed.

"Good," she said, having gained her control again. "We can make other arrangements for her later. As far as her clothes, I'll wash her things tonight so she'll have something clean to wear tomorrow morning because what she has on is it, Jarod."

"I hadn't looked in the backpack. There's nothing else?"

"Nope. Not even an extra pair of undies." She paused, then whispered, "My grandbaby has nothing."

"She's got us, Mom," Jason interrupted before Jarod could answer. Jason's protective instinct had ruled his life for a long time. Jarod was proud it extended beyond his brother's fiancée to Jessica.

"Of course, you're right." Camille visibly straightened and wiped the moisture from her eyes. Leaving his side, she marched right over to Josh and put her hands out to Jessica in a "can I hold you, too?" gesture.

Jessica smiled and went to her grandmother willingly. The smile that spread across his mother's face was all the answer Jarod needed.

He didn't need any testing. Jessica Rose King was home.

CHAPTER 5

Girls

Something's not right. Jarod blinked his sleepy eyes open and looked around his bedroom. Everything seemed normal except he'd left the bathroom light on by accident and now the glow of the fluorescent bulb spilled into the room. How he hated those things. Most times he took a leak in the dark instead of waiting for the damn bulb to heat up. In the time it took to cast any light, he was already back in bed.

Then he heard the noise that must have jarred him from sleep.

He laid perfectly still until he heard it again. Someone was in his bedroom breathing hard, as if in a panic.

What the hell?

He clicked on the bedside light and looked around. Through the bedroom door he could just make out the crumpled blankets on the couch in his sitting room, but no one was there.

Revelation hitting him, he sat up and looked around.

Where's Jessica?

The noise came again and he looked toward his armoire to find his little girl trying to open the tall doors.

"What are you doing, Darlin'?" Jarod asked.

Jessica startled and turned around slowly; her sapphire eyes were huge and frightened. Jarod went down to one knee and put his hands on her delicate shoulders. Her raven black hair fell like a cloak to the middle of her small back, wavy from the braids she'd worn earlier. The t-shirt from her backpack was about seven times too big for her, the neck hole hanging off to one side, almost to her elbow. Huge tears ran down her face, but she barely made a sound.

"Tell me what's wrong, Jessica."

"Blue is gone," she hiccupped.

"Blue?"

"Uh huh." Her lower lip quivered and another fat tear rolled down her face. "I hafta find Blue. I can't sleep without Blue."

Thinking "Blue" must be a toy he'd somehow missed seeing, he asked, "Tell me what Blue looks like and I'll help you find it."

"Blue is blue," she explained, as if he were mentally deficient.

Jarod scrubbed at his sleepy, beard-stubbled face and looked at the clock.

2:00 am

He turned back to his little girl and thought for a moment before the lightbulb turned on in his head and he grinned.

"Are you looking for that dirty ol' blanket?"

Lip trembling and eyes closing to squeeze out another fat tear, she nodded, still not making any kind of sound.

Aren't children supposed to be noisy when they cry?

Hell if he knew, but her silence did bother him. However,

he wasn't going to question her about it at the moment because he had an urgent matter to attend to.

He had to find Blue. His daughter needed her blanket.

Scooping her up, he hugged her to him and said, "Nana put Blue, and the rest of your things, in the washing machine when you fell asleep." He brushed a tear away from her rosy cheek with the tip of his large finger.

"But Blue is 'fraid of the washin' sheens. They live on the dark street and Blue needs ta be with me," she explained.

"Jessica, Nana has her own washing machine. Blue's here in the house. Actually, it's probably in the dryer." He studied her tearful face for another moment. "Do you want to see if Blue is clean and dry yet?"

She was clasping and unclasping her hands under her chin, but she nodded her head. Those fat tears still rolled down her face. He hugged her again and kissed her wet cheek, unable to stop himself from offering her comfort.

So, with her in a giant t-shirt and him wearing only his boxers, they padded downstairs to the washer and dryer to look for his daughter's beloved blanket.

When they entered the small dining room which led to the utility room, they found Lauren sitting at the table sipping from a teacup. Lauren's eyes bugged out of her head, obviously surprised to see them at this unholy hour in such a state of undress.

With a wicked grin on her face, she asked sweetly, "What's goin' on, guys?"

Jessica said, "We're lookin' for Blue."

Lauren raised her eyebrows.

"She needs her blanket," he explained.

Lauren immediately got up to open the utility room door.

"Of course you do, sweet pea. Let's see if it's in the dryer."

Good God, she wasn't wearing much more than either of them. Jarod watched her firm behind sway in soft gray yoga pants that hugged her heart-shaped tush. Her white camisole left nothing to the imagination, especially with it being a little chilly. The central heating system was set to automatically dip down at night so everyone could sleep comfortably.

He did not want to see her like this, right now, while he held his very afraid, and very new, daughter in his arms.

He closed his eyes and prayed for self-control.

Jessica squeezed his neck. "We need ta rescue Blue, Jar'd."

Hearing her mangle his name in her sweet voice distracted him from Lauren's rear end. And he was beginning to think his daughter might have some speech problems.

"Sorry, Darlin'," he said distractedly and followed Lauren-of-the-awesome-behind into the utility room, where she was bending over to dig through the dryer.

Damn. He squeezed his eyes shut again. *Get it together, Man!*

All of a sudden, she turned around excitedly to present the now-clean blanket, which did very interesting things to the front of her camisole. Lauren's eyes were bright with excitement when Jessica squealed at the sight of her blanket. Jessica squirmed to be let down, so Jarod gently put her feet to the floor.

She ran to Lauren, who bent down to hand the blanket over—*Lord have mercy*—giving him a perfect view of her fantastic cleavage.

He was never getting back to sleep tonight. No way. No how.

Crossing his arms over his chest, he watched the two females squeal with delight over the clean, ratty blue blanket.

Lauren picked up Jessica and asked, "Are you ready for bed now?"

Jessica hugged her blue blanket tight, nodding her pretty head.

"Do you want your daddy to take you back upstairs?"

He looked at both girls, one ebony-haired and one blonde, two pairs of blue eyes of different variation, looking back at him in contemplation.

"Yes," Jessica said definitively. Lauren put Jessica down, and Jessica hurried back to him.

"All better now, Darlin'?" He scooped her up as he asked her the question. Once she was securely in his arms again, he felt better. The blanket was warm, like Jessica, and she seemed content, her eyes drooping sleepily. She wrapped one arm around his neck this time and stared at Lauren.

"Is she comin' ta bed with us, Jar'd?"

Jarod jerked his eyes to Lauren, who laughed behind her hands, which didn't help his problem. All the giggling ran through her lush body and jiggled feminine things he shouldn't be noticing right now.

Lauren dropped her hands from her mouth to cross her arms under her chest which—God help him—pushed her assets up even more.

She collected herself enough to say, "No, sweet pea. Your nana gave me my own bedroom to sleep in." She continued to snicker. "You better take your daddy back to bed, though. He's gotta get up early for work."

Solemnly, Jessica said, "Ah-right." She turned her sweet face to him and said, "C'mon, Jar'd. Let's go back to our room."

Jarod couldn't hold back the chuckle at his daughter's command. "As you wish, Darlin'. Say goodnight to Lauren."

"'Night, Lorn," she said on a tiny yawn. Jessica laid her

head on his shoulder, cuddling her blanket close to her face, while her other arm stayed around his neck.

"Goodnight, sweet pea. I'll see you at breakfast."

Jarod gave her a thankful nod of appreciation. He turned with his sleepy burden and headed back upstairs.

Once in his room, he made his way to the couch where she'd been sleeping before her nightmare. He bent to put her down, but she clung to him like a baby monkey.

"What's the matter, Jessica?"

"Blue wants ta sleep with you."

"Blue does, huh?" He raised a disbelieving eyebrow at her, then looked at the clock. He only had time for a cat nap before he had to be up to shower anyway. "Come on, you two. Let's get some shut eye."

He didn't bother tucking her into the other side of his California king-sized bed, but carried her to his side and laid down under the covers. She didn't bat an eye. As Jarod settled down on his back, she cuddled closer to him with her blanket, let out a gusty, satisfied sigh, and fell asleep.

HER CELL PHONE WAS RINGING.

Maybe they'll hang up, Lauren thought as she rolled over and pulled the covers over her head.

Again, the loud techno beat of her ringtone sounded through the bedroom. She unwound herself from her warm cocoon and reached for her phone on the bedside table.

"Mmm... 'lo?" she mumbled. Her eyes weren't quite open as she ran her free hand through the chaotic mass of blonde curls covering her face and head.

"Howsh my gurl?" slurred a drunken female voice on the other end.

Lauren sighed as she looked at the clock. Three forty-five in the morning; she'd only just fallen back to sleep.

"Fine, Mom. I'm sleeping. You should be asleep, too."

"I mish you, baby."

Yeah, right. But Lauren could hear the pathetic sadness in her mother's inebriated voice. The reasons for her mother's late-night drunken calls always came down to her feeling sorry for herself.

"I know, Mom."

"I'm a terrible muther. You disherved musch better 'an me."

Lauren listened to her mother's pathetic ramblings for another five minutes before she convinced the woman to hang up the phone and go to bed.

Now awake, she wondered how Jarod was doing with Jessica, and whether he realized the importance of Jessica's blanket.

She automatically reached for Ribbit, a velvet beanbag frog her dad gave her when she was a little girl. Ribbit had accompanied her to every slumber party, every camping trip, and even to college. He'd especially been with her on every trip to social services. And now he was with her while she stayed in the Kings' luxurious home. She understood Jessica's need for something familiar, which was why she'd helped the little girl retrieve the ragged blanket out of the dryer as fast as she could.

Leaning back on the soft pillows, she thought of her childhood. There'd always been fighting and yelling, then the divorce, and finally her father's funeral. She had no good memories of living with her parents, but she smiled at the happy memories she shared with her two best friends, Julie and

Josh. Their unwavering loyalty had gotten her through the worst times in her life. Although the Armstrongs and the Kings couldn't do much to save her from her parents' behavior, they had always been supportive, especially when the town tried to paint Lauren with the same brush as her parents'.

Not wanting to remember any more, she turned her focus back to the here and now. She wondered if Jarod slept in those boxers normally, or if he'd worn them in deference to the presence of his little girl.

Holy cow, the only thing that had kept her from wrapping herself around him was the tiny child he'd been carrying at the time. With a smile on her face, she imagined what could've happened if he'd come downstairs alone.

———

THE NEXT TIME LAUREN OPENED HER EYES, THE digital clock on the nightstand read six-thirty. She scrambled out of bed and into the shower. Breakfast on a weekday with the Kings was normally hectic, but it would be doubly so this morning. The whole family had stayed the night, including Josh, who owned the townhouse next door to hers in the same development, using bad weather as an excuse. But with a new little girl added to the family ranks, it was obvious to Lauren everyone wanted to get to know Jessica better.

Upon entering the dining room, the first thing to catch Lauren's attention was the radiant smile on Camille's sophisticated face. The older woman loved her family so much, it made Lauren's heart swell. Many times while growing up, she had wished Camille was her mother instead of the drunk who called her in the middle of the night from time to time. As she'd grown up, Jarod's whole family had been something she'd desperately wanted to emulate.

Jessica was hanging on Camille's hip. She had her blanket and was dressed in the same clothes she'd been wearing the day before. Her hair had been combed but hung loose in long waves down her back. She was quiet as she absorbed everyone around her while she clung to her brand-new grandmother. And Camille, God bless her, bustled around one-armed, getting breakfast for everyone, happier than Lauren had ever seen her before, which was saying something.

"Let me help you with that platter, Camille," Lauren said, smiling at Jessica. "Good morning, sweet pea!"

"G'mornin', Lorn," she said with a quiet smile. "Me an' Nana are fixin' brefkist."

"I see that," she said as she pushed a strand of silky black hair behind a tiny ear.

The three of them set the platter of eggs and bacon on the table, where the men were gathered with their coffee, juice, and toast.

Lauren's mouth began to water when Julie brought over a platter of homemade cinnamon pancakes. Their delicious aroma wafted up to Lauren's nose and made her stomach growl.

Camille had taken seat cushions from furniture in the family room and stacked them on the chair next to Jarod. She sat Jessica down on the cushions, and Jarod put a plate in front of his daughter. Lauren took the open seat between Jessica and Josh. As soon as everyone was seated, Camille got down to business.

"I thought, after breakfast, I would take Jessica shopping. Do you have anything specific you want me to pick up for her, Jarod?"

"She needs everything, Mom." Then he asked Jessica, "Do you have a favorite color?"

"Blue," she said matter-of-factly.

"Well, that clears things up," Jarod chuckled, lifting his shoulders in a negligent shrug.

He wasn't fooling anyone. There were smiles around the table, but no one contradicted him because Jessica did need everything.

"Good. Then after everyone is off to work and school," she hugged Charlie, who always sat next to Camille, "Miss Jessica and I will head to town to fill her wardrobe. What do you say, sweetheart?"

Jessica smiled around a mouthful of pancakes and nodded her head.

Camille addressed Lauren and Julie, saying, "Later this evening, I'd like to start on the Halloween decorations for our haunted castle and the centerpieces for St. Anthony's harvest dinner. Are you girls planning on coming back tonight?"

"I'm free, Camille," Lauren agreed.

"I found someone to rent out Julie's house, so we thought we'd pack this weekend," Jason announced. "We're gonna stay here from now on."

"I'm kinda tired of going back and forth. Most of my stuff is already here, anyway," Charlie explained before he crammed another helping of pancakes into his mouth.

"Really?" Lauren said, astonished. "I didn't know you had decided to rent it out?"

"It's really too small for all three of us. But I don't want to sell it, either. It's all I have left of my parents," Julie said. "Besides, renting it out is extra income—"

"Jujyfruit," Jason warned.

"Well, it is," Julie countered, one eyebrow raised in challenge.

James cleared his throat, "I'd rather have you here than in town. I'm glad you guys are moving in."

Jason put his arm around Julie and smiled. "Glad to hear it, Dad, but we'll only be underfoot until the new house is finished. I want to get the foundation poured before it gets too cold."

The next few minutes were filled with construction talk which was over Lauren's head. She shared a smile with Julie, who'd never looked happier. Part of Jason's inheritance was a parcel of land subdivided off of James and Camille's property. It overlooked Timbisha Township and the mountains to the west. It would be a lovely place for them to start a family.

Feeling a little like an outsider, Lauren asked, "What time do you want us back tonight?"

"As soon as you get off work would be great. Don't keep her late, Jarod. I need Lauren's help with these projects."

Lauren noted Camille's no-nonsense look.

"She'll be here, Mom," he smirked and then, to Lauren's astonishment, he winked at her!

Shaking her head and hiding her smile, she helped Jessica finish with her plate and wiped the pancake syrup from the little girl's chin.

Melancholy, unwanted and unbidden, crept into Lauren's head. Her mother's late-night call lingered in the recesses of her mind, reminding her, as those calls always did, that these wonderful people were not her own flesh and blood. They were a family she admired, but would never belong to. She needed to back off before she embarrassed herself.

"All right, I gotta run," she said, and stood to take her plate to the dishwasher.

"Wanna lift? I'm heading out now as well," Jarod offered. "If your plan is to come back right after work, we might as well carpool."

She was so taken aback she stared at him for a good five seconds before he grinned, helping her recover herself.

"No, I have errands of my own to run, so I'll need my car today. But thanks, Sheriff."

She turned her back on him while she loaded a few lingering dishes from the sink into the dishwasher. When she returned to the table to collect more dishes, he had his arms around his daughter, talking softly to her.

Apprehensive, Jessica listened to him intently. Lauren could see her pretty face concentrating on his every word and then a ghost of a smile on her sweet face.

Lauren turned her head away from the private moment father and daughter shared, especially when her eyes burned with tears threatening to spill over.

Once she was in her car, she was able to breathe easier.

She couldn't remember a time when she wasn't in love with Jarod. He'd been all she'd ever wanted from a very young age and now, once again, he was involved with another woman —albeit a very small, younger woman who was sweeter than any creature she'd ever met, but involved nonetheless.

All of a sudden, Lauren's heart leapt with the idea of being Jessica's mommy. She wiped the single tear which had fallen down her cheek, admitting to herself there was nothing she wanted more, except to be Jarod's wife.

What did she know about being a mother? Her own was a complete mess. The only woman worth emulating was Camille, but since she was Jessica's grandmother, wouldn't Lauren be a redundancy?

Not to mention Jarod hadn't asked her to be Jessica's mommy.

I'm an idiot.

She pulled into a space in the parking lot and put on her administrative assistant façade. She needed routine, and hers was waiting for her in the boring county office. She hit the key fob, locking her car, and headed inside to deal with the dregs of the earth.

———

MARGUERITE WAS ALL OVER HIM LIKE A POISONOUS rash. She made her irritation known because she hadn't been able to discover whom he'd met with last night, and Jarod wasn't going to clue her in, either.

So far, the only person in the department who knew about Jessica was Lauren, and he wanted to keep it that way for now. The detective hadn't told Jarod the whole story about Miranda's death. Being a cop himself, Jarod could tell when someone withheld information. He'd be patient and wait for the other shoe to drop.

He grabbed some coffee from the break room and headed to his office, planning to stop by Lauren's desk on the way. She was talking on the phone when he approached, so he signaled for her to head into his office when she was done. She gave him a nod of acknowledgement as he passed by.

He set his plain coffee mug on the desk and flopped into his desk chair. Taking a fortifying breath, he pulled Miranda's file out of a drawer and opened it. He searched through her arrest records. Something was nagging at him, but he couldn't put his finger on it. This was how his mind worked. He'd get a gut feeling about something, and it plagued him persistently until he took it seriously.

His mother used to call him a stubborn child. He didn't agree with her; rather, he thought of himself as logical. So when he got these feelings, he ignored them until he had something tangible to work with, which was usually why it took him longer than it should to solve his cases.

Finally done with her call, Lauren took a seat in one of the chairs in front of his desk.

"What's up?"

Before he could filter his mouth, he asked, "Do you think I'm stubborn?"

She laughed out loud before she smoothed her expression. Clearing her throat to stifle another giggle, she answered him with another question. "Do you want me to tell you what you want to hear, or do you want the truth?"

Damn it, the minx was grinning.

"Never mind." He focused his attention on the file, then glanced up at her, still not speaking.

"What is it, Jarod?" she asked with concern.

"Don't tell anyone here about Jessica yet."

She raised her eyebrow. "May I ask why?"

He detected an angry edge in her voice. Based on his experiences with Lauren over the years, this could go either way. If he didn't answer her correctly, he could be facing another month-long radio silence. Since that scenario didn't work for him, he went with honesty.

"I don't want to give Marguerite a reason to spread rumors." He waited a moment for his reasoning to sink in, and before he could change his mind he admitted, "Something is telling me to keep it quiet here. I can't tell you why because I can't explain it myself. Will you help me?"

"Are you ashamed of Jessica?" she asked point blank. One of Lauren's best qualities was her straightforward nature.

"Hell no, I'm not ashamed of *my daughter*," he emphasized, making sure she understood his feelings for his child. "I want to protect her and, judging by what little history I have," he indicated the folder in front of him, "this will be the first time anyone has looked out for her best interests since her birth."

The tension visibly leached from her body as her full lips eased into a gentle smile. Seeing it did things to his gut again, but this time in a completely different way. He cleared his throat and sat up straighter.

"Of course I'll keep it to myself. Let me know how I can help, when you figure out why you want to protect her from your staff." She winked at him.

He chuckled at her. "It's not the staff. I don't know how to explain it, but I don't want to share it with anyone until I know exactly what it is. Do you think I'm crazy?"

She eyed him for a second, then shook her head and got to her feet. "No. Clue me in when you know which direction we're going to look, okay?" she replied, emphasizing the word *we*.

He relaxed. She understood him, and the relief was surprising as hell. "I will," he said, liking the idea of teaming up with her.

She walked out of his office to her desk. She sent him another wink before she went back to her work. Again, his eyes lingered on her a little too long to be proper before he returned his attention to the file in front of him.

He searched every arrest record looking for anything out of place. It made him edgy and frustrated. When he looked at the clock, it was almost lunchtime. He picked up the phone and called his mom.

"Hey, how's she doing?"

"She is a perfect angel. We're having a lunch break right now, then we are going to have a pedicure." The smile in her voice was hard to miss, making him laugh himself.

"A pedicure? Isn't she a little too young for those?"

"Jarod, a woman is never too young for a pedicure," she assured him. "Afterward, we're shopping for more clothes and other things she might need."

"More clothes?" he asked, shaking his head even though she couldn't see him. "How much does she need?"

"Well, obviously, she needs everything, so we stopped at Walmart for some play clothes and her under things. But she needs clothes for church and school. She needs something for the wedding, although I suppose we'll have time to have her fitted for a flower girl dress, but I really need to talk to Julie to make sure it's okay with her. I think she'll make the perfect flower girl. Do you think I'm overstepping? She also needs some toys, coloring books, crayons, and I'd like to buy her some prekindergarten learning books—"

"Mom! Okay, I get it," he said and laughed again. She was on a roll, and it made him proud to have Camille King as his mother. "You two have fun and don't break the bank on one little girl. A sheriff's salary only goes so far," he chuckled. "Give her a kiss for me, will you?"

"Done and done, Jarod. Love you."

"Love you too, Mom."

CHAPTER 6
Not Mine

Lauren stopped by her place to pick up a few more things after work for another night's stay with the Kings. The townhouse was dark when she arrived, and Lauren noted the staleness in the air from being closed up and unoccupied. She'd been spending more and more time at The Estate lately, working hard with Camille on various business, social, and charitable events, but the biggest event was The Wedding—Jason and Julie's upcoming nuptials.

Tonight, though, they'd be working on Halloween decorations for the two big functions on Camille's October calendar. Camille loved her church, and the Harvest dinner was a big deal for her.

Lauren wasn't much of a churchgoer, but she wouldn't let Camille down for anything. Camille King was her mentor, and Lauren really looked up to her. James and Camille were pillars in their small community, and Lauren had tried to emulate Camille's behavior from the first moment they'd met. Camille seemed to understand Lauren, even though Lauren didn't talk much about how she'd been raised, too ashamed to scandalize these good people with her life's story of parental drunkenness and divorce. Julie was the only person who knew the full extent of what Lauren's childhood had been like.

The Kings also did an impressive event on Halloween night with a big haunted castle for the teenagers, a mini corn maze for the younger kids, and homemade treats for everyone. It was mostly a neighborly get-together for the townsfolk, but Camille usually went all out. Even with The Wedding to plan, this year's Halloween party would be a big event.

Lauren wondered how Jessica had faired today and realized she could hardly wait to see the little girl again, so she gathered clothes appropriate for the office the next morning. She did a quick check to make sure all her doors and windows were locked, making a mental note that she needed to spend at least one day here this weekend to dust, vacuum, and air the place out. Shaking her head as she turned the key on her front door, she headed for her car.

Once at The Estate, she parked next to Julie's food truck, Cafe Armstrong, and grabbed her bag from the back seat. She entered through the side door into the mud room, then into the family kitchen, where she heard loud voices. Someone was screeching about "moving on."

There, she found Charlie attempting to serenade Jessica with the latest *Asking Alexandria* hit while Camille laughed her head off. They'd put the little girl on a barstool at the counter, where Julie had set up an assembly line of plates which—Lauren could now see—were filled with beaten egg, flour, and breadcrumbs. The girls were breading chicken fillets, while Charlie entertained them with his rocker's voice, complete with air guitar.

Lauren laughed.

"Hi Lorn!" An excited Jessica waved with fingers caked in flour.

"Hey, sweet pea. Are you cooking dinner tonight?" She put her stuff down to join them in the kitchen, giving Jessica a quick kiss on her forehead.

"Joojee let me dip," she answered with a sweet smile.

"Joojee?" she asked her friend.

Julie smirked before explaining, "Jessica overheard Jason say goodbye to me this morning."

Lauren laughed. "That explains it."

As if conjured from a dream, Julie's tattooed Prince Charming entered the kitchen, making a beeline for the chef. He kissed her soundly before softly saying, "Hey, Jujyfruit."

Lauren turned and picked up her things, not wanting to watch the newly engaged couple's intimate display. Everyone else scattered as well, Camille taking a smiling, gooey-handed Jessica to the sink to wash her fingers, and Charlie muttering something along the line of "get a room," began to set the table.

Lauren ran upstairs to change out of her work clothes and put the rest of her things away. She found Jarod on the stairs as she headed down, hoping dinner's progress had resumed.

Jarod stopped midway up and smiled.

She smiled back.

An awkward silence ensued, until, "Have you seen Jessica?" he asked a bit more loudly than necessary.

"Yeah, downstairs in the kitchen," she said, puzzled.

"Oh. Well, I'm gonna change out of this uniform and hunt her down," he stated before moving past her on his way to his room.

That was odd.

Sighing, she continued down the stairs and into the hallway toward the craft room. She wasn't in the mood to watch Jason and Julie making out in the kitchen, and if Jarod hadn't spotted Jessica there, then odds were they were still playing kissy-face. Sometimes their public displays of affection ruined her appetite—and she loved Julie's chicken fingers.

She found she wasn't the only person who had escaped the love scene. Camille was talking softly to Jessica in the craft room.

"It will be fun. There will be lots of children your age, and at the end of the dinner, Father O'Keefe will have a piñata set up full of candy," she explained.

"What's a yah-da?" Jessica asked, which nearly broke Lauren's heart. She wondered, not for the first time, how Jessica's life had been under Miranda's care. Did she even know who Santa was? The thought was depressing.

"Hey, you two," Lauren breezed in wearing her patented, no-worries-all-is-well-with-the-world smile.

"Lorn, what's a yah-da?" Jessie asked, still wanting to know. The poor child was starving for information.

"A *piñata*," Lauren emphasized the correct pronunciation, "is a cardboard container shaped like an animal or cartoon character and is filled with candy. It's hung up on a rope, and kids take turns trying to break it open with a stick or a baseball bat," she explained. At Jessica's confused look, she shrugged her shoulders and said, "It's fun."

Jessica didn't look convinced.

Jarod stuck his head in the room; Lauren noted he was careful not to cross the threshold. "How're my girls?"

"Jar'd!" Jessica squealed, running over to him, arms raised

up. Like a pro, he scooped her into his arms and gave her a resounding kiss on the cheek. Lauren was momentarily jealous but squelched the invidious feeling as it came, too thrilled at being included as one of "his girls."

"Hello, Darlin'! Did you have fun today? I see you have on a new blue shirt. It's very pretty."

"Yup, an' Nana found shoes with lights!" she squirmed out of his arms. When he set her on her feet, she jumped up and down, then pointed at the red flashers on the soles of her new sneakers, a big radiant smile on her face.

Jarod laughed and picked her up again. "Those are great, honey." He kissed her cheek again, and Lauren noted how Jessica wrapped her little arms around his neck.

Jarod caught Lauren's eye. She felt something pass between them that, to her disgrace, made her blush. Then the devil grinned wickedly before he turned his eyes to his mother.

"Did you have fun, too, Nana?" he asked with a smile.

"My granddaughter and I had a great deal of fun."

Camille had been gathering supplies from the plethora of inventory she kept, in what she humbly referred to as her "craft room." It was a vast room made specifically for Camille's passion for crafting and event planning. James had built it with plenty of space and storage to rival a Hobby Lobby. Camille had dragged her delinquent sons inside, kicking and screaming, to help her whenever they had gotten into trouble, which explained why Jarod still hadn't set foot over the threshold. It was why the King boys referred to it as "the Room of Doom."

"Dinner's ready," Charlie announced, walking right into the room. As he was not an actual King, he had never suffered one of Camille's punishments.

Jarod gave him a cockeyed look that made Lauren chuckle.

THEIR NOSES LED THEM BACK TO THE DINING ROOM, where scents of homemade chicken fingers and french fries permeated the air. Lauren loved family meals like this. It was so much better than her microwaved dinners alone.

She took her spot next to Jessica, who now possessed a new blue booster seat in the chair next to Jarod. A large, tattooed arm stretched between them, placing a new child's plate with a cute blue dog pictured on it, full of chicken fingers and fries.

"Here you go, Princess."

"Thank you, Hunkle Jase," Jessica said as she concentrated on her plate of food, picking up a chicken finger and dipping it into some ranch sauce before taking a huge bite.

"I think my granddaughter has some catching up to do," James observed from across the table. Jessica grinned with ranch in the corners of her mouth.

"Yes she does, Dad," Jarod said, handing her a napkin.

Lauren thought of her blanket and noticed Camille had strategically laid it across her chair underneath the booster seat. *Clever.*

As usual, a lively discussion took place around the dinner table about everyone's day and familial camaraderie. Brotherly jibes between the men were the most common. Since the big engagement, Charlie and Julie had been welcomed to this awesome family.

Lauren sometimes let the demons in her head rule, and tonight they made an unwelcome appearance. They told her she wasn't good enough for these people and that she didn't belong. It was her own childish insecurity playing with her self-esteem. If she wasn't careful, it would sink her into a black hole of depression.

She must have let her melancholy show because Jarod placed his hand on her shoulder, his thumb moving in a small circle. He had to stretch an arm across the back of Jessica's chair to reach her. She looked over Jessica's head into a pair of deep-blue eyes.

"Hey," he said quietly. "You okay?"

"I'm great." She smiled to cover her mood. "Julie's chicken strips are one of my favorites."

"Julie's everything is one of my favorites," James said, making everyone laugh in agreement.

Camille slugged him in the arm. "Geez, you'd think I starved you all your life."

He kissed her cheek. "I didn't say you were a lousy cook, my love. I'm only saying Julie is better." He flashed a big Cheshire cat grin. "Isn't that why you teamed up with her?"

"Well, let's just say it's not the only reason I teamed up with her."

Camille winked across the table at Lauren, who smiled back. There was no denying Lauren's best friend could cook.

AFTER DESSERT, THE WOMEN HEADED OFF TO THE Room of Doom to work on their decorations, Jessica tagging along with them. Jarod missed her already. He'd missed her infancy and most of her toddler years, and he didn't want to miss anything else.

But no self-respecting man with the last name of King would ever set foot in that room of his own free will. So he joined the men of his family, who'd congregated in the family room.

James had the gas fireplace going, and the Giants' playoff

game was on the television with the sound muted. Charlie and Josh sat on the floor at the coffee table in a grudge match of Chinese checkers. Jason and their father were conversing about the family business, King Construction, and going over plans for Jason's new house. Jarod's brother had decided to begin building it after Julie's good-for-nothing ex-boyfriend burned his house down.

Jarod zoned out on the game while his family went about their evening. He was thinking about his daughter and how lucky he was to have her when his cell phone rang. Checking the number, he answered the call rather than sending it to voicemail.

"What do you have for me, Detective Cane?"

"I need to bring you up to speed on the deaths of your ex-wife and Michael Trapp."

"I'm listening," Jarod said.

"I told you they were killed in a car wreck, but what I didn't tell you was there had also been a fire. The bodies were badly burned, which was the main reason it took so long to identify your ex-wife. However, the coroner sent the autopsy reports back, and they found bullet wounds to the skulls of both victims. They were shot at close range, execution style. No bullets were recovered. This case is now a murder investigation."

Jarod wasn't surprised. Miranda had been living a hard, dangerous lifestyle.

With my daughter.

Keeping his voice as quiet and unemotional as possible, he said, "Understood. Any leads?"

"No, none yet. But we'll need an accounting of your whereabouts on the night they were killed."

"Of course, you have my full cooperation. I'll have my on-duty log sent to you. Let me know what else you need and it's yours," Jarod said without hesitation as he ended the call; he was a man of few words, and he'd expected to be the first person on the list of suspects. He had records proving his whereabouts. But that damn nagging feeling was back, causing tension to coil up his neck and into his shoulders. He was missing something, and the good lord knew he was tenacious when it came to solving a puzzle.

"What's happened?"

Jarod mentally rolled his eyes. His father had always known when something was wrong with one of his sons.

"Miranda's death has been ruled a homicide," he said.

"Care to explain why?" Jason asked.

Jarod swore he came from a family of genetic mutants with superhuman hearing.

He gave Jason a blank face while he worked out in his head what he wanted to say, and he needed to say it before the girls returned. He'd fill Lauren in on things later when he asked for the attendance logs.

He repeated what the detective had told them, finishing with, "I've asked Lauren not to say anything about Jessica to my staff."

Josh frowned, "Dude. Mom's had her all over town today. People are going to find out about her, and if they don't already know by now, the horse will be out of the barn at the Halloween dinner at St. Anthony's."

"You're right. Of course you're right." He sighed, closing his eyes as he pinched the bridge of his nose. It was the curse of living in a small community; everyone knew everything about everybody.

Unless you're a drug-dealing murderer. But he couldn't connect the two crimes yet; it was just a gut feeling. He rubbed his temples to ease the ache that had set up house in his head.

From down the hall he heard small feet running for all they were worth and Lauren's laughing voice saying, "Slow down before you fall and hurt yourself, silly!"

Jessica took the corner into the family room at full speed, sneakers blinking like a red strobe light. "Look!" She laughed as she climbed onto the couch next to Jarod and held up an orange and green cloth pumpkin in front of his face.

"Did you make that by yourself, Darlin'?" He took it from her and it felt soft and cushiony.

"Guess what's inside?" Giggling and clutching her fingers together under her chin, she waited for his answer.

He smiled at her as he turned the item around in his hands. Her amusement was infectious. "I give up. What's in it?"

"TOILET PAPER!"

She was so worked up she didn't realize she was standing on the couch. She laughed so hard she held his shoulder with one hand to keep herself steady while bending over holding her tummy with the other.

Jarod started laughing. "Who gave you that idea?"

"I read it in a magazine," Lauren answered as she sat down next to him on the couch right as Jessica jumped down.

They laughed as she presented her toilet paper pumpkin to everyone in the room, each person pretending they hadn't just heard her squeal what was inside. Pretty soon the room filled with warm smiles and laughter.

"Where's Mom and Julie?" Jason asked in between chuckles.

"They're cleaning up our mess. Jessie was too excited to show you all her project to stay and help, so we left them to do the dirty work," Lauren explained in a conspiratorial whisper.

"How many of those are you making?" Charlie asked.

Camille strolled in and answered, "Since my granddaughter enjoyed putting it together so much, I think we'll take the supplies to the dinner and make this a craft activity for the kids. So my guess is we'll need enough supplies for fifty children."

"What do you mean?" James chuckled.

"I'll show ya," Jessica said proudly. She wriggled out of her grandfather's arms. Once on the ground, she put the pumpkin on the coffee table. Green felt strips stuck out of the top end of the roll. She plucked out the strips and set them aside. Next, she carefully pulled out the four corners of the orange cloth, which had also been pulled up from around the bottom of the roll and tucked into the hole in the top, where the stems had been removed. The whole roll of toilet paper now sat in the middle of a square of orange cloth.

She looked up and smiled. Then she pushed all four corners back into the top hole of the roll, followed by the green felt strips Jarod could now see were shaped like vine leaves.

"Ta-dah!" She threw her hands in the air and grinned from ear to ear.

Camille explained, "Our volunteer committee is ready to go at a moment's notice. We can have them cut the orange cloth squares and the green felt leaves and then load them into individual brown paper sacks. When the kids are gathered, we'll hand each child a sack, explaining there's a surprise Halloween craft inside that we're all putting together at the same time. Each child will open up the sack to find the orange and green material, plus a roll of toilet paper. When they are instructed to put it all together, it will be a hoot. And because there's no glue involved, it won't be messy. We'll also add a felt marker so they can draw a jack o'lantern face on their pumpkins if they wish. Kids of all ages can participate."

"It's good, wholesome family fun," Julie said as she wrapped her arms around Jason's middle.

Josh said, "You're going to have to soothe them with some candy inside those bags, Mom. If I opened a bag that was supposed to contain a surprise but got nothing but a roll of toilet paper, I'd feel like I got gypped."

"Or tricked instead of treated," Charlie said. "Gotta fill those bags with candy, Camille. It's Halloween, after all."

THE EVENING WOUND DOWN AS THE BASEBALL GAME ended in extra innings, and Charlie had creamed Josh at Chinese checkers. Their taunting had quieted down somewhat with another challenge issued for the following evening, if Charlie didn't have too much homework.

Jessica crawled onto the couch between Jarod and Lauren, taking apart her toilet paper pumpkin and reassembling it over and over again until finally her head dropped into Lauren's lap. It was then Jarod realized he'd put his arm on the back of the couch and his hand idly twirled a curl of Lauren's pretty blonde hair.

Her face was turned down toward Jessica, her own hand petting Jessica's long black locks.

Suddenly, she looked up and met his eyes. Heat flared in his blood. With his child in her lap, she was the most beautiful woman he had ever seen. His desirous thoughts must have shown because her lips parted as she took an involuntary gasp of air. The pulse of her heart beating in her neck inflamed him further, before she soughed out the air from her lungs and gave him a shy smile.

Shy?

Lauren was anything but shy and they both knew it. What-ever it was happening between them was getting stronger by the day, and God help him, he liked it.

He liked *her*.

LAUREN GOT HER BREATHING UNDER CONTROL AND smiled at Jarod. He was so handsome it hurt to look at him, especially when he looked at her like she was a delicious piece of candy he wanted to suck on and lick to his heart's content.

Maybe I should let him unwrap me.

She didn't like feeling unsure of herself, so to cover her insecurity, she winked at him, thereby breaking the spell. If she didn't do something fast, they'd spontaneously combust right in front of everyone and embarrass themselves.

"You better put that princess to bed. I think I wore her out today," Camille said from across the room.

"You're right, Mom," Jarod said. "Where's her blanket?"

"I'll get it. She ran out of the craft room so fast she forgot all about it," Lauren explained. She gingerly moved the sleeping child off her lap, but before she was out from under her, Lauren felt Jarod's strong hands lifting Jessica. As he did so, his fingers grazed her thigh and sent a shockwave of awareness zipping through her body.

"I've got her. You get the blanket and I'll meet you upstairs."

What he said was completely innocent, but the heat in his eyes and the soft, sexy tone of his voice said he intended to do more than put Jessica down for the night.

While she'd dreamed for years about Jarod having those kinds of ideas about her, tonight was not the right time to fulfill her lifelong fantasy. She loved him, no doubt about it, but there was no way she would engage in a random affair with Jarod King. She respected him—*and myself*—too much to let that happen. If he wanted her, he would have to want her for the rest of their lives.

Having decided not to give in to temptation, she smiled at him and said, "Sure, be right there."

She followed behind him as he carried Jessica, admiring the man who loved his child. She found him even more attractive now that he was a doting father.

She expected him to head straight for the stairs, but instead he led her to the craft room, standing just outside the entrance.

"Aren't you coming inside?" she asked as innocently as she could.

"Not if I can help it," he deadpanned.

Chuckling, she hurried in and grabbed the blanket. Her smile broadened when she draped the blanket over Jessica's small shoulders, noticing the pumpkin tucked up in her arms.

"Follow me up to my room. I need to tell you something," Jarod whispered.

"Okay," she agreed, knowing full well he had a lot more on his mind than talking.

She admired his delectable derrière as he climbed the stairs ahead of her. His tush was right at eye level, and it took everything she had not to slip a hand into one of his back pockets.

She snickered at the thought.

When he reached his room, he pushed the door open, gesturing with one hand for Lauren to enter ahead of him while he kept hold of Jessica with the other. She'd never been inside his suite, only viewed it from the hallway when she'd accidentally-on-purpose strayed to the wrong side of the massive house. It was exactly how she pictured his living space to be: neat and tidy, and very utilitarian. The sitting room consisted of a small entertainment center, a contemporary couch and recliner, a coffee table, and a small end table with a lamp. Bookshelves lined one wall, with pictures of him and his family sporadically strewn about.

She followed him into his bedroom, which was decidedly *not* what she had expected. A huge, king-sized, four-post bed sat in the center of the room with a matching armoire to the left, and two night stands on either side. A highboy dresser sat on the opposite wall at the foot of the bed. The door to his large walk-in closet stood open. All his clothes were hung up and evenly spaced apart, his uniform the first to be seen. His shoe rack contained a variety of shoes, including cowboy boots. What really surprised her were the many fluffy throw pillows strewn about the large bed and plush duvet in soft, earthy colors. Where the sitting room was almost sterile and blah, his bedroom was warm and masculine, looking like something out of an eighteenth-century castle.

And, of course, the whole place smelled like the man who slept here, putting her in a trance.

She was staring at the bed when he asked, "Can you pull her sneakers off, please?"

"Oh! Of course."

She carefully untied Jessica's shoes and pulled them off. Unsure of where he wanted them, she placed them near the armoire.

He sat down on the bed and cradled his daughter, who didn't stir, in his arms. "Do you think we should try to wrangle her into her pajamas or what?"

She offered a smile to this capable alpha male who'd been taken down by a four-year-old little girl. "I think we can get her jeans off, but let's leave her in her t-shirt for now. She needs sleep more than she needs jammies, and she's catching some good Zs now. Better not interrupt them, don't you think?" she asked.

"Yeah, I think you're right," he whispered, then looked up into her eyes. "They grow in their sleep, did you know that?"

"Been doing research, huh?"

"A little," he said on a chuckle.

Together, they undressed Jessica as much as possible without waking her. When Lauren pulled back the covers, Jarod slipped his little girl underneath. He made sure her blue blanket was nestled in her arms, and he placed her toilet paper pumpkin on the nightstand next to her.

"If she wakes up, she'll be sure to see it," he whispered.

Lauren smiled, warmed by his need to explain his endearing thoughtfulness.

However, as soon as Jessica left his arms and he stood to face her, she noted the seriousness of his expression.

Cop mode. She immediately went on alert.

"What's happened, Jarod?"

"Let's go into the sitting room."

She followed him into the next room, noticing he'd left his bedroom door ajar.

"I received a call from Detective Cane while you were in the Room of Doom."

She shook her head at him. "I can't take you seriously when you call it that, Jarod. You sound like you're twelve."

He sucked in a big breath through his nose and stared at her. He rolled his eyes heavenward before his dimple surfaced in his left cheek. "Fine. The craft room. Can I finish?"

"Please do, sir," she said, barely containing her mirth.

He sat down on the couch, signaling for her to sit next to him.

Scrunching up her brows, she waved a hand at him, indicating for him to continue.

"Miranda was murdered."

"I thought you said she died in a car crash."

"That was the initial story. The truth is she and her lover were burned beyond recognition. The autopsy just came back, and both victims had been shot first. Detective Cane will need my attendance logs for the day they were killed, to rule me out as a suspect. For good measure, I'd like you to give him a full month's worth, three weeks before the murders and up to today. I don't want to leave any doubt I haven't left the area. Understood?"

"Absolutely. I'll do it first thing." She stared at him, trying to process everything he'd told her. "What do you think they were doing in the middle of the desert?"

He shook his head and leaned back into the cushions of the couch. "I have nothing to go on, but I'm thinking it was a drug deal gone bad. Her file is full of arrest records and CPS reports, which is proof enough my little girl grew up around crystal meth, or at least in a house where the owners used it every night. I'm praying she wasn't around while they cooked that crap. The chemicals in the air," he trailed off and rubbed his eyes with the heels of his hands. "She's so tiny, Lauren," he whispered.

"I know, but she seems healthy enough. She's definitely smart. Camille said she was an angel while they were out. It's probably why she's so tired, too. I've been shopping with your mother. It's almost like waging a military campaign."

He slowly reached over and twirled one of his fingers around a curl in her hair, like he'd been doing downstairs. "You are so beautiful. You know that, don't you?" he asked softly.

Before she could say anything, he sat up and took her face

in his palms. He kissed her lips sweetly, softly. Her heart rate began to race and warmth shot through her limbs from his gentle touch. Before she could tell him to stop, he brushed his warm lips over hers one last time and rested his forehead to hers.

They were both breathing hard when he whispered, "Thank you for being with her tonight." He paused and swallowed whatever else he might've said.

She leaned away from him, holding both of his hands in hers. She whispered back, "You are most welcome."

Then, she stood from the couch and walked to the door before anything more could happen.

"Goodnight, Jarod."

He seemed surprised by her retreat but schooled his features, like the good cop he was.

"G'night, Lauren."

She walked through the door into the hallway and made her way across the huge house to her room. Fighting the tears, she gathered up her things and decided to go home instead of staying. She was getting too comfortable at The Estate.

As much as she wanted it to be so, Jarod and his family were not her own. Jessica was not her daughter. And Jarod needed time to bond with his child. Distancing herself felt like the logical thing to do right now, before she got too attached.

I'm not walking away forever, she told herself. Plenty of things needed to be completed at work before she went into business with Camille, like actually giving Jarod her resignation.

She had the parish dinner to work on, as well as the Kings' trick-or-treat event. She'd be back here often enough, working on the wedding, too.

She needed her own space to think and clear her mind

before the inevitable panic crept in. She hated that horrible voice which told her so often she wasn't worth being loved. Shoving her unpleasant thoughts as far back as she could, she put her car into gear.

As she drove out of the driveway, she ignored the tears falling down her cheeks, concentrating on the road instead, and the possible suspects in Miranda's murder.

CHAPTER 7

Avery

Avery Decatur was pure pond scum. He'd like to put ol' Avery in a hole for being so sloppy, but he still needed information from the imbecile.

Keeping his hat pulled low over his face and avoiding the security cameras, the man signed the visitors' log with an alias while showing his fake ID to the guard, who didn't bat an eye.

Idiot.

Shaking his head, the man was allowed access to the visiting area.

Avery had already been ushered to a stall and was waiting for him. He bared his teeth in a semblance of a smile, and the man was somewhat mollified by the look of fear on Avery's face as he approached the cubical that separated them by a thin layer of bulletproof glass.

He picked up the phone receiver at the same time as Avery, who now looked a little pale.

"'Lo, Avery," he ground out.

"Wha'choo doin' here? You crazy or somethin'?" Avery asked in a panicked whisper, eyes wide with disbelief.

"Watch your mouth, Avery. Or I'll have someone remove your teeth without anesthetic," he threatened.

Avery blanched, then scanned the area as if someone might be behind him with rusted dental instruments.

"What happened when you met with Trapp?"

Avery sighed. "I told you. They didn't have the money."

"What else?" he commanded, letting Avery know his life was on the line if he wasn't forthcoming. Avery began to fidget.

"Mike said he was keepin' a fee for all the years he'd been helpin' you out. Said he wasn't gonna keep launderin' the money if you didn't give 'em a bigger percentage."

He knew this part. Trapp, that jackass, had been on this rant for a while. It was the main reason the man had run them off the road. He'd shot them before he'd discovered they'd fooled him. And he didn't like to be made a fool. He'd doused the wreck in gasoline once he'd realized the money wasn't in the car. There was half a million in cash missing—cash they'd stolen from him. He was going to find his money, even if he had to kill everyone he was associated with, including the dickhole in front of him. Once he found the stash, he'd be set for life and could start over somewhere else.

But he couldn't do that if he couldn't find the money. It was obvious this puke knew more than what he was telling. He'd get it out of Avery before he had him shanked. The fewer people who knew his identity, the better.

"Do you know what happens to assholes who hold out on their employers, Avery? Especially bosses in this business? It's no skin off my nose if you don't exist anymore. Do you read me?"

"Loud and clear," he whispered, but then said more forcefully, "but I ain't holdin' out on ya, you know that!" he whined.

"We'll see."

He pulled his hat down, hung up the receiver and walked out on ol' Avery.

CHAPTER 8

Missing Lauren

The next two weeks were a blur of arrests, pediatric appointments, and preschool registrations.

None of the recent arrests had been meth related, and Jarod heard from Las Vegas that the homicide investigation was at a dead end. He couldn't remember the last time he'd been so frustrated with a case.

He and his deputies tightened up their watches at the high school and community center, apprehending petty thieves and vandals. Some of the suspects did have drugs on them but nothing connected to the current murder or the elusive meth supplier. He absolutely hated it when a trail ran dry.

Not to mention the house was in chaos with all of the Halloween prep and parish dinner crafts. The yearly Haunted-Castle-Trick-or-Treat-Extravaganza his family held on their property was right around the corner.

Jarod was exhausted, but what bothered him the most was how much he missed Lauren. She hadn't stayed overnight at The Estate since he'd told her about the homicide investigation.

She hasn't stayed since I kissed her.

She'd sent the proper documents to Detective Cane in Las Vegas, and he'd been cleared as a suspect, but other than seeing Lauren at work and brief glimpses before she headed to the Room of Doom, he spent little personal time with her.

His daughter, on the other hand, spent more time with Lauren than she did with him. Of course, then all he heard from her was "Lorn this" and "Lorn that," making him a little jealous. He wanted to know where she was and what she was thinking. He liked a good mystery, and Lauren Lockwood was definitely mysterious, with her sad eyes and enigmatic smiles. He wanted to solve her riddle so he could be close to her again.

I want my friend back.

He hoped to remedy the problem tonight at the church dinner.

Jarod hurried into the house to change out of his uniform and freshen up. The dinner started in forty-five minutes, which gave him enough time for a quick shower and to stuff the bins containing all the paper sack pumpkin crap—er—craft material into his Ford Raptor.

His mother had gone a little overboard; there were more than a hundred paper sacks filled with Jessica's toilet paper pumpkin supplies. Her reasoning behind this ridiculous amount was because not all of the children in the parish would be attending the dinner, and she didn't want those who were absent to feel left out.

Jarod rolled his eyes heavenward and prayed for patience. He'd have to reign in his mother's generosity so she wouldn't spoil her granddaughter. She'd already requested Josh draw up some plans for the guest suite across the hall from his, to remodel it "for the perfect little princess."

Josh had only smiled and said, "I'm already on it. I just needed to know which set of rooms were hers."

Jessica had been in his care for less than a month and already she showed signs of being spoiled.

He couldn't imagine it being any other way.

HE PULLED INTO THE CROWDED CHURCH PARKING lot in search of a spot close to the doors so he could unload the bins as quickly as possible. He'd decided to pull up alongside the main entrance doors when he spotted Charlie on his way out.

Jarod rolled his window down. "Are you leaving already?"

Charlie walked up to the passenger side window and put his elbows on the rim. "Nah. The craft team needed some more stuff from their van. I guess they couldn't carry it all in by themselves. I just got here about three minutes ago when they sent me back outside to get it." He rolled his eyes but the grin on his face said he was fine with being bossed around by Camille's friends.

"Listen, I've got all the bins with the pumpkin sacks in the back. I'll start unloading while you grab their stuff, and then you can help me with my stuff when you're done."

"No problem, Jarod. I'll let Lauren know you're here once I'm inside." Charlie jogged off to the parking lot before Jarod could tell him not to bother her.

He put his truck in park, stepped out and around to the tailgate. A cool breeze blew some fallen leaves past his pickup, typical for Nevada in late October. He hoped the hard frost wouldn't hit until after the kids trick-or-treated. The days and nights had been pleasant since the last freak storm, but now it felt like fall was really here and winter beckoned at their doorstep.

As he put the tailgate down, Charlie sprinted into the crowded doorway, arms loaded down with more decorations. The boy's voice echoed through the parish hall, searching out Lauren.

Jarod stacked a couple of bins on top of each other and picked them up as Lauren came out the door with Jessica securely on her hip. It didn't look like Jessica was going anywhere by the way her knuckles clenched tight to Lauren's collar... and that damned blue blanket.

Uh oh.

Lauren covered both of their obvious distress with her patented sunny smile, which he loved more than he wanted to admit.

"Hey, you made it! Need help with the bins?" she asked sunnily, then directed her next question to Jessica. "Want to help Daddy carry in the bins?"

It was then Jarod noticed the terror in his daughter's eyes. Jessica looked at him and quietly asked, "Jar'd?" She reached her arms out to him, but his arms were already full with the bins.

He immediately set them back on the tailgate and scooped up his little girl, hugging her tightly to his chest. He gave Lauren a questioning look before saying, "Hey, Darlin'. What's all this about? Daddy's here." She clung tightly to him, and he could feel her shaking. She was scared to death, which kicked in his natural instinct to protect.

"What happened?" he demanded in a low voice that only Lauren could hear.

"We're not sure," she answered, wringing her hands. "She was fine all afternoon while we were setting up, and she fit in with the few kids who were here helping with their parents. But as soon as all the adults started showing up, she started clinging to either Camille's legs or mine. Once the DJ started playing music, she wouldn't let go of me. I've been holding her and reassuring her for the better part of thirty minutes."

Lauren shook her head, her concerned blue eyes focusing on his daughter. "I think she's seen one too many parties," she said, using her fingers as quotation marks around the P word.

Jessica squeezed him tighter. Rage boiled inside him at the return of his daughter's fear.

Lauren quelled his anger when he met her gaze. He relaxed his body, as he did right before a fight. He didn't want his enemies to read his body language and, right now, he certainly didn't want his daughter or Lauren to see him lose control. It dawned on him that it had been years since he had let loose on someone other than his brothers.

He managed a half smile for Lauren, who seemed to be able to read him better than anyone else.

She raised an eyebrow and asked, "Shall I grab a bin or send out the cavalry to help?" She cocked her hip to the side and rested a feminine hand on her curvaceous waistline, in her typical sassy-pants fashion.

"You grab a bin while Jessica and I find Nana to see where she wants this stuff."

Jessica clung more tightly to him as he began to walk toward the entrance, afraid to go back inside. However, now that she was in his arms, he wanted her to know he would never let anything bad happen to her. He needed her to trust him.

"Sure thing, Sheriff."

He stopped and turned toward Lauren, who wore that damned sassy grin of hers.

Lauren winked and grabbed a bin. He followed her inside,

loving the way the sparkles on her jeans pockets danced in the light.

"There you are!"

His mother took the bin from Lauren and opened it up. Lauren began setting the craft sacks onto the bales of hay which sat in one corner of the event space. It looked like his mom had designated this area as a mock pumpkin patch. Several children kept themselves occupied with the crayons and butcher paper someone had laid out for them to use in the center of the bales.

He really had to hand it to her. His mom was a great event planner.

"Don't you just love what Lauren's done with the hay bales?" she asked him.

Lauren did this?

"It's really great," he said to Lauren, who blushed.

"Jessica, honey, are you feeling better? Can you help Nana put the sacks on the hay?" She rubbed her back, trying to get her attention. "The other children will be so excited when they get to make their very own pumpkins, don't you think?"

Jessica lifted her head from Jarod's shoulders and nodded her head. She went to her grandmother, who stood her on the ground next to her, but Jarod noted the happy little girl he'd been getting to know the past few weeks was nowhere in sight. He eyed his mother questioningly.

"We'll be fine, honey," she assured him. "You go get the rest of the bins, and we'll be right here waiting for you, won't we, Jessica?"

His little girl clung to his mother's legs and her blanket. She looked up at him with those giant blue eyes and whispered, "Uh huh."

"I'll be right back, Darlin'."

He kissed the top of her head before heading out the front doors. He looked for Charlie for some help, but he'd been commandeered by Julie to work in the kitchen after delivering the rest of the party favors.

Thankfully, the people at his church were honest folks because his truck was still running when he got outside. He removed the keys from the ignition before grabbing two more bins. Once he was back inside, he dropped them off with Lauren while his mom kept Jessica distracted, and turned to head back out for more when he saw Josh and Jason walking through the doors with the rest of the bins.

"We saw your truck and decided to help," Josh said with a smile.

THE BROTHERS HAD DUMPED OUT THE BINS, AND now the paper sacks were in a large, unorganized pile in the middle of the floor. They were heading back out with the empty bins when Jarod caught Lauren's eye.

"I need to move my truck. Will you keep an eye on Jessica? Mom looks a little overwhelmed," he pointed out.

Lauren had done well at keeping Jarod at arm's length over the past two weeks, while she sorted out her feelings. However, keeping Jessica at a distance had been impossible.

How do you distance yourself from a child whom you already cared deeply for, but who also has lost so much in her short life?

The answer: You don't.

If Lauren had been at The Estate and Jessica knew she was there, she was on Lauren's lap, in her arms, or holding her hand, and Lauren happily complied with the little girl's every demand. Not that she demanded much—she only needed love and attention. Lauren had oodles of love to give her.

It also pleased Lauren greatly that Jarod was impressed with the design of the kids' play area. She supposed she should've been insulted by his surprise, but any time Jarod found something she did pleasing, it only increased her desire to please him more, which was just sad and pathetic.

She glanced over at Camille, surrounded by volunteers needing more direction. Dinner was about to begin, but Camille was running late with the sacks. Then Lauren noticed Jessica keeping a death grip on Camille's legs. She gave Jarod a reassuring pat on the shoulder and made a beeline to help.

After excusing herself to the people congregated around Camille, Lauren knelt down to Jessica's level and asked, "Your uncles brought in more sacks. Can you help me sort them out before dinner starts?" She smiled, trying not to baby Jessica but not wanting to scare her, either. The girl's earlier fright had been disconcerting. Not knowing what Jessica had gone through before she'd come to live with Jarod meant everyone had to exercise a little discretion when dealing with her behavior.

Lauren held out her hand, but Jessica reached up with both hands to be picked up, fear still in her eyes. What on earth had frightened her so?

Snatching her up again, Lauren met Camille's eyes; the older woman nodded gratefully. She walked back to the pile of sacks just as she heard a familiar, sweet giggle.

"Need an extra pair of hands?" Julie asked.

"Oh, thank God," Lauren answered with a relieved sigh. She felt Jessica relax a bit at the sight of Julie, who kissed the little girl on the forehead.

"All done in the kitchen?"

"They've got it handled, but you look a little behind. They're setting up the buffet now."

"Hi, Joojee." Jessica finally gave up her fear for a small smile.

Relieved Jessica was willing to be on her own two feet, the three women began to scatter the sacks on the bales of hay, while the guests began to form a line at the buffet tables.

Soon, Jason was back, not wanting to be away from Julie too long and, with everyone's help, it took no time at all to finish the mock pumpkin patch.

Father O'Keefe tapped on the microphone. "If everah one will stop whatcher doin' and bow yer heads, I'll give the blessin'," he announced in his soft Irish lilt.

As they bowed their heads to pray, Lauren watched Julie reach for Jason with a love in her eyes that made Lauren's heart ache, mostly because Jason returned the look. Jason and Julie only had eyes for each other, and Lauren longed for a relationship like theirs.

"Lauren, dear, why don't you get in line for dinner," Camille suggested when the prayer was over. James now held her hand.

"Oh no. I'm not sitting down until I know you're eating, too," she replied.

"I am, Lauren. I want us all to go together as one big family," Camille smiled as she ushered Lauren into the line behind Jarod and Jessica. The little girl turned her big blue eyes up to Lauren's face and reached for her hand. Jarod had her blue blanket hanging over his shoulder.

Josh squeezed Lauren's shoulder playfully, saying, "I'm cutting, so step aside."

"Rule breaker," she teased, giving him a playful shove with the hand not holding Jessica's.

Charlie swooped in next to Josh, saying, "Me too!" while making a silly face at Jessica.

"You're funny, Char-lee," she giggled, emphasizing the last syllable of his name.

"Oh yeah? Well you're pretty, Jess-ee," he mimicked back, rubbing the top of her head, making her giggle again.

Charlie knuckle-bumped Jarod as he passed him by, something Lauren hadn't seen them do in years.

Jason and Julie, oblivious to everyone around them, released each other long enough to grab plates and head through the buffet line. Josh and Charlie followed suit, simultaneously goofing off and placing food on their plates. Honestly, Lauren wondered how they kept their food from falling all over the floor.

When it was the trio's turn to take their plates, Jarod handed two, stacked one on top of the other, to Jessica, saying, "Hold these with both hands, Darlin'." Then he bent down and scooped her up in his arms. "Now you can see what's for dinner," he explained with a smile and pointed to the first dish on the buffet table.

Lauren took a plate of her own and followed them, knowing he was going to need a little help. She glanced at Camille, who merely shrugged.

As they moved down the line, Jessica would choose a dish, Jarod would put a helping on the plate, and they'd move on. When Jessica's plate was too full to hold any more items, Jarod began placing their choices on Lauren's plate.

Jessica wasn't usually picky, and tonight was no exception. Lauren also suspected Jessica was trying to please her father because every time she picked something out, Jarod would praise her with phrases like "You bet!" or "Ooh, that's a good choice."

Two overflowing plates later, they made their way to the table reserved for the Kings. Camille had rented round tables which seated ten each for this event, so the family had a table to themselves, plus one chair. Lauren sat down next to Julie, whose chair was touching Jason's. They were so close Julie was almost in his lap.

Jarod sat Jessica in the chair between himself and Lauren. Before Jessica could put her giant plate of food down, he lifted it up and retrieved the spare plate from the bottom.

"Good thinkin', Daddy," Lauren smirked.

"I have my moments," he deadpanned.

Jarod left the full plate of food in front of his daughter, transferring what he'd picked for himself onto his own plate. Then he scooted his plate near Lauren's and winked. She laughed as she added the few things they'd needed space for onto his plate from her own.

Jessica wriggled around to get comfortable, settling on her knees. Jarod gave her back a rub but said nothing more as his daughter dug into her plate with gusto.

"Are you feeling better, Jessie?" Charlie asked with a wink.

She gave him her serious eyes while chewing up her noodles. "Uh huh." Then her attention went straight back to the food in front of her, which only reinforced Lauren's guess that she had eaten sparingly when Miranda had been alive.

Jarod got his mom's attention and asked, "Do you know what set her off?"

"I'm sorry, honey. I wish I did. I can only tell you one minute she was playing well with the other children, and then, suddenly, she was glued to Lauren's legs." Camille shrugged her shoulders and looked to Lauren.

Jarod turned his questioning glare to Lauren. "Did someone scare her?"

"Honestly, I didn't see anything untoward happen to her. Brad stopped by to let us know he couldn't stay for the dinner because something had come up and he needed to go out of town. One minute Jessie was fine, and the next she was upset. I'm sorry, Jarod, but I really don't know what happened. We were all busy putting things together for tonight," she explained, clearly feeling like she was in trouble.

He continued to stare her down until he released his breath and looked at Jessica.

"Looks to me like she was just hungry," Jason said.

Jessica polished off all of her "Spook-etti." Most of the food items were Halloween themed. She'd chosen two "Frankendogs" for herself and Jarod and some Casper salad, which was an ambrosia. Lauren thought it was all very cute.

"All done, Jessie?" she asked.

"Yup!" Jessica grinned ear to ear and had more color in her cheeks. "Can I have a cookie, Jar'd?" she asked, putting her little hand on his massive shoulder, looking him directly in the eye.

Lauren laughed at the sweet, sing-song voice she used on her dad.

"As soon as we're all done, we'll go get a dessert plate," he said softly to her.

She clapped her hands and smiled, then turned to face Lauren in the same way she'd just done with Jarod. "Hurry, Lorn, so we can getta d'sert plate," she said with excitement.

Glad to be included, Lauren laughed, "I'm doing the best I can, sweet pea."

After dessert, Father O'Keefe introduced the youth ministry, who put on a short performance of choral music and a couple of skits on the small stage. Jessica crawled into Lauren's lap for a better view. Jarod mingled with some of the other parishioners, including Derek Lawlor and his wife, Debbie.

Eli walked in at the same time and approached the Lawlors as well, before heading back to their table with Jarod.

Lauren felt the little girl tense up in her arms. Jarod, unaware of his daughter's distress, reached for her, saying, "Darlin', come meet Eli."

Jessica shook her head, hiding her face in Lauren's neck and wrapping her tiny body around her like a vine. Trying to reassure her of the stranger, she offered, "He works with your daddy, sweet pea."

"Still not feeling good, Jessica?" Eli asked.

Jarod turned to his deputy. "Still? You were here earlier?"

Eli went on alert. "Yes, sir. I came in with Brad before he took off for parts unknown. Why?"

Jarod said nothing.

"I think she's overwhelmed with all the new faces," Lauren said, reassuring Eli. He was nervous enough about being a new dad. She didn't want him thinking kids didn't like him. "Let's go get ready to do your pumpkins," she said, smoothly standing up with her burden.

Camille and Julie followed her to the bales of hay.

"That was rude, Jessica. I think you hurt Eli's feelings," she scolded.

Jessica lifted her head to look at Lauren with her big, scared eyes and whispered, "Sorry."

Not wanting to prolong her discomfort, Lauren patted her back and said, "Are you ready for this?"

Jessica looked at all three women and then the bales of hay with the sacks of pumpkin material in them. When she turned back to them, she grinned and kicked her feet, the universal signal used by children everywhere indicating they want to be let back down to the ground.

Father O'Keefe, seeing Camille and Lauren were ready to begin, introduced them to the parishioners. Dozens of children gathered around the hay bales to listen to Lauren, with Jessica's help, explain the project.

Camille and Julie offered help where it was needed. In the end, the kids were happy with their project, laughing at the toilet paper, and enjoying the candy corns and gummy worms from the plastic baggy at the bottom of each sack.

Jessica interacted well with the other kids with no further signs of stress or shyness, and she had no other panic attacks before they left for the evening.

Lauren didn't know what to make of her behavior, but she knew real fear when she saw it, and Jessica had definitely been afraid of something. Whatever it was, it wasn't there anymore. She hoped the episode was random and due to the stress of meeting new faces, but something in her gut told her not all of those faces were new to Jessica.

JAROD LOOKED IN HIS REARVIEW MIRROR TO CHECK on Jessica, whose cheek was smooshed up against her car seat. To his right, Lauren's head lay sweetly relaxed on the headrest, her eyes closed in sleep. A warm feeling he hadn't experienced in years filled his body, making him pensive. He had two beautiful girls in his care, and his natural instinct to keep and protect them pulsed through his veins.

His girls.

Yes, Jessica and Lauren were his girls, no matter that one of them wouldn't call him *Daddy,* and the other one had no clue he'd claimed her. He wasn't sure exactly when he'd decided to keep Lauren, but it didn't matter. Now he had to convince her to stay.

Determination took hold as he glanced from the road to Lauren's face and back again. He needed to plan out his next conversation with her. She was a stubborn, sassy, wonderful woman. She was the best damn secretary he'd ever had, but the way she'd cared for Jessica proved to him how much he needed her in his personal life as well.

But did he love her?

Does it matter?

He'd loved a woman once, and look what happened. No, the only thing that mattered was how *Jessica* felt about Lauren. From the very beginning, the two of them had been drawn to each other. If Lauren wasn't around, Jessica asked repeatedly for Lauren. When she did find her, Jessica clung to the woman as if her life depended on it—and maybe it did.

Obviously the feelings between them were mutual because Lauren never turned Jessica away, and always gave in to his daughter's demands.

They were kindred spirits. Lauren's past was no secret; she'd grown up in and out of the system until she'd grown enough to take care of herself. She was capable and strong willed. He'd known her for as long as he could remember and her reputation was impeccable, even though her mother was the town drunk. Lauren had pulled herself up by the boot-straps and made something of herself. She'd be a wonderful mother.

He'd married Miranda because he had thought he'd loved her, only to have his heart removed with a spoon. If he were going to marry again (*Am I really thinking of getting married?*), then Jessica would be a major factor in his choice of spouse. The woman he married would have to have certain qualities.

He began a mental checklist and compared it to Lauren. His future wife had to be:

1. a good mother to Jessica, who was the most important thing in his life right now. *Check.*

2. strong and not clingy. *Check.*

3. accepted by their small community and fit in well as the wife of the sheriff. *Check.*

4. accepted by his family and his mother had to like her. *Check.*

He looked at Lauren again.

5. beautiful inside and out. *Check.*

He concentrated on the road, pressing the accelerator while he mentally prepared himself for battle. He would have to convince Lauren to marry him. The past few weeks without her had been hell. He shuddered remembering the month when she'd not spoken to him, before Jessica arrived. The more he thought about making her his wife, the more he liked the idea.

And when Jarod made a decision, there was no turning back. He was going to marry Lauren Lockwood, whether she liked it or not.

RELIEVED TO BE HOME, HE PULLED INTO HIS NORMAL parking spot in the driveway. The rest of the family followed suit. He shut off the engine and sat looking at his future wife.

He reached over and rubbed the back of his fingers along her cheek. Softly, he said, "Hey, beautiful, we're home."

He watched her eyebrows squish together before her lids fluttered open, revealing her confused baby blues.

"Oh, I'm sorry. I must've dozed off." She gave him a sheepish smile before turning her head to check on Jessica.

Just like a good mother would, he thought with satisfaction.

"She's out," he said, stating the obvious.

"She had a very busy day." She reached over the seat to gently undo the car seat straps.

"Careful, Lauren. You might hurt yourself by twisting over the seat like that."

He stepped out of the truck, hustled himself around to the passenger side, and opened the back door.

Ignoring her look of confusion, he wrangled his comatose daughter out of her car seat and slung her limp body halfway over his shoulder, rubbing her back. Jessica hung like a rag doll.

Lauren grabbed the blue blanket and her purse, then followed him inside without question.

They said nothing to each other as they walked through the house, hearing the rest of his family as they made their weary way to their own rooms. It had been an exhausting day for him, but now he was wide awake, anticipation fueling him like caffeine for what was to come next in his life.

Lauren followed him into his suite and then his bedroom without protest. Jessica still slept in his bed because her rooms were not complete, and she flat out refused to sleep on his couch. She'd probably slept on more couches than he could count. His little girl deserved a real bed, with real pillows and blankets.

Lauren moved ahead of him to draw back the covers. He laid Jessica down on her side of the bed, and together they managed to get her undressed as far as they could without waking her, leaving her in her t-shirt and undies, which seemed to be the routine lately.

A warm, homey feeling flooded through him when Lauren brushed Jessica's dark hair away from her forehead before bending down to kiss her.

"Goodnight, sweet pea," she whispered.

Jarod followed Lauren's lead, kissing his daughter good-night. He caught Lauren's smile as she left his bedroom. He pulled his door closed far enough to leave a crack in case Jessica woke up and was frightened, then caught up with Lauren before she could leave his suite.

"I'll walk you to your room," he whispered.

Lauren stopped in her tracks and turned to give him a quizzical smile. "I'm heading home tonight, Jarod."

"It's really late. I'd feel better if you stayed at The Estate tonight," he said, reaching out to her shoulder. At the last second she backed away, his fingers finding only air. He covered the near miss by rubbing his hand over his head.

"I'll be fine, Jarod. I've made the drive so many times I could find my way home in my sleep. Speaking of which, I'm really tired and need to get going."

She turned to head down the stairs.

Determined not to let her leave, he implored, "Wait. What are your plans for tomorrow?"

She stopped before she hit the first step.

"I haven't got any plans," she shrugged. "At least not in the morning. Why do you ask? You've never asked about my plans before, Jarod," she said accusingly.

Clearing his throat, he stated, "Halloween is next weekend."

"So?"

"Well," he stalled, trying to come up with a good enough

excuse for her to stay. "Jessica will want to go trick-or-treating. I'm not sure if she's ever done it before, and she'll need a costume."

Lauren studied him for a second, cocking her hip out. "Do you need help finding her a costume, Jarod?"

He studied her, gauging her mood. Would she help, or would she tell him to figure it out himself?

"Yes, I need help with finding her a costume. Plus, Mom wants us to start getting ready for the haunted castle tomorrow," he said, raising his eyebrow.

"Camille's starting set-up tomorrow?" she asked in a state of panic.

"Yep."

"Why didn't she say anything to me?"

"I don't know. Maybe she thought you already knew." He was such a liar, but he was desperate. They were moving the large items first and beginning construction for the fun house. His mother wouldn't start the smaller things until later in the week, but he wasn't about to tell Lauren that. Besides, he could feel her caving in.

"I really want you to stay here tonight."

Her blue eyes locked with his. "Why?"

"Because I hate the thought of sleeping in this house without you in it," he said honestly.

His eyes fixated on the rise of her chest as she sucked air into her lungs and was fascinated as her body began to shake, and a slight blush tinted her cheeks. It could go either way... she could slap him or stay.

He prayed for the latter.

"All right," was all she said before she turned around and headed away from his room toward the guest wing.

She didn't look back.

CHAPTER 9

Deal With A
Blue-Eyed Devil

Lauren closed the bedroom door and stared at the space which was irritatingly becoming more of a home to her than her own townhouse. She'd purposely distanced herself from Jarod and his home two weeks ago, with the intention of ridding herself of these misplaced feelings of belonging. Other than committing herself professionally to Camille and the events business, she'd tried to stay away from The Estate as much as possible.

But being in love with Jarod made staying away difficult, even though he could never return her feelings. Now she'd gone and done something really stupid. She'd fallen head over heels in love with Jessica.

She was on a collision course with heartbreak and didn't know how to change her flight plan. It had to be her damned biological clock clouding her ability for self-preservation.

She opened the second drawer of the highboy dresser sitting in the corner of her pristine room. The gentle fragrance of roses caressed her senses and filled her with welcoming warmth. Camille had added a scented sachet to her personal items. She ignored the tears pricking her eyes as she picked out her favorite pair of jammies and headed to the en-suite bathroom to shower and prepare for bed.

Unlike the master bath at her townhouse, this one was lavish. Camille had stocked it with all of Lauren's favorite personal hygiene products. It had taken her a while to figure out Camille had been subtly gleaning information from her for several weeks.

"My dentist said I need to use a good mouthwash, but I don't like any he's recommended. What do you suggest, Lauren?"

Or...

"I can't keep my skin from looking like alligator hide. How do you keep your's so smooth, dear?"

And her personal favorite: *"Just tell me what kind of body wash you use, Lauren. I'm heading to the store and don't have time for games."*

After a quick shower, she brushed her teeth with her favorite toothpaste and combed her hair with an exact replica of her own comb Camille had "picked up somewhere." Lauren slipped on the camisole top and yoga pants she used as her jammies and headed for the bedroom.

She slipped between fine linen sheets and relaxed against a pile of feather pillows. She thought of her own bed, which was comfortable but not nearly as luxurious as this one, and sighed with contentment.

As she relaxed, her mind began to wander. The past two weeks had been harder than when she'd refused to speak to Jarod for a month—because this time she wasn't angry with him. She'd tried her best to limit herself from being around him, except for work, where he'd been more respectful than usual. Their playful banter had disappeared and she missed it. She supposed his behavioral changes had everything to do with the fact he was a father now, but it didn't explain his request for her to stay at The Estate tonight.

Then there was Jessica, who'd been a force to be reckoned with because she had the same determination and stubborn streak as her father. If Lauren was on the grounds somewhere and Jessica found out, the little darling would call out, "Lorn! Lorn!" As soon as she found her, Jessica would climb into her lap or hold tightly to her hand, unless she could finagle Lauren into carrying her on her hip.

Lauren loved every minute of it, though. She hadn't had much of a childhood herself. Empathizing with the little girl, she didn't want to disappoint her, even at the cost of Lauren's heart. It was impossible to say no to her.

Lauren's eyes grew heavy, the last image in Lauren's mind was Jessica's sweet face, and then she succumbed to sleep.

"Lorn." An exaggerated whisper tickled her ear and tiny fingers tapped her cheeks. "Wake up. Joojee is makin' pang-cakes."

Tap, tap, tap.

Lauren opened one eye to see familiar blue ones blazing at her from a tiny hummingbird face surrounded by a halo of black tresses.

"What time is it, Jessie?" She struggled to see the alarm clock through her own tangled mass of blonde hair.

7:30 a.m.

On a Saturday.

After a late night.

"Bref-kist time," Jessica chirped.

Lauren's heart melted. Yes, she'd do anything for the little imp.

"Okay, sweet pea. Let me get changed."

She unwrapped herself from the heavenly cocoon she'd been nestled in and asked, "Where's your dad?"

"I'm right here," said a smokey voice from her doorway. Jarod leaned casually on the doorframe, as if he belonged there. Something was different about him this morning. Her heart skipped a beat at the proprietary way he looked at her. Once upon a time, she'd seen him wear that expression, but it had never been directed toward her.

His eyes glowed with azure fire, and his impressive chest was defined through his simple white t-shirt. A coat of arms, one of many hidden tattoos which marred his perfect skin, peeked out of the sleeve on his left bicep. He still wore his sleep pants of blue plaid flannel, which hung low on his hips, and his feet were bare.

Her mouth watered.

"Like what you see?"

Her startled eyes shot back to his face to meet a devilish smile.

Damn it. She mentally chastised herself for being caught ogling the perfect male specimen, but she was more than ready with a rebuttal.

"I always like what I see when you're around, Jarod. You know that."

The surprise in his eyes was worth the heat which pinkened her cheeks. She brazenly winked at him as she hugged Jessica and marched into the bathroom for her quick morning routine.

Muffled voices came through the bathroom door, and then her bedroom door shut softly. Leaving the bathroom, she hurried to change into a pair of well-worn blue jeans, another camisole layered with a pink and white flannel button-up shirt. Wool socks and tan waffle-bottom boots completed her ensemble before she headed down to the kitchen.

She was the last to enter the Saturday morning chaos which reigned supreme with the Kings.

Jessica had stationed herself on a barstool at the marble island, where Julie flipped her famous pancakes on a giant electric griddle. Camille was moving from the refrigerator to the table with armloads of condiments for breakfast.

All the men sat at the table except for Charlie, who carried a heavy platter for Camille laden with scrambled eggs, sausage, and bacon. Charlie had a special relationship with Camille, Lauren supposed. He'd lost his own mother at the tender age of twelve. Camille treated him like one of her own sons and a grandson all wrapped up into one special kid.

"Lorn! Sit here," commanded a mouth full of pancakes, and a tiny hand gestured to the barstool next to her.

"I see you've got your breakfast. How is it, sweet pea?" Lauren settled herself on the designated barstool while Jessica continued to stuff her tiny mouth with pancakes. She smiled, revealing a rather large amount of syrupy mush.

"Close your mouth when it's full, Darlin'."

Jarod's big hand gently wiped a napkin across Jessica's chin. Then he walked around and snagged the barstool on the other side of Lauren, putting her in the middle. He sat sideways with his left arm on the marble and his knees spread wide to surround Lauren's stool. He brushed a curl off of her shoulder with his right hand, and his toothy grin conveyed to her he'd gotten over her remark and was making his next move.

What is his game?

"I take it you had a good night's sleep," she said, a bit breathily.

"Actually, no, I didn't." He pointed his chin toward Jessica. "She likes to sleep sideways. I think I might have a bruised rib or two. That is, when she's not lying on top of me," he chuckled, but then, more seriously, he admitted, "She has nightmares."

Lauren nodded in understanding. She still had nightmares sometimes.

"Anything you want to share?" he asked, his expression more of concern than pleasure over the game he was trying to play.

"Not right now. Besides, you know most of the story already. Everyone in town does." Then, her confusion got the better of her. "What are you up to, Jarod? This isn't like you."

"Later," he said cryptically, leaning in to kiss her cheek. Then he stood up to collect his daughter. "Let's go clean you up, Darlin'. You missed your bath last night."

Lauren's eyes followed him as he sauntered out of the room with Jessica in his arms. That's when Lauren noticed all conversation in the room had stopped.

"What?" she asked, irritated at having the attention on her once more.

Julie grinned. "Nothing. Grab a plate and join us at the table."

Conversation ebbed and flowed around her as she contemplated the tingle on her cheek left by Jarod's soft kiss. He hadn't shaved, so a little beard stubble had grazed her skin.

As she pushed her empty plate away a micro-person climbed onto her lap. Jarod, never far behind his daughter, sat down next to her.

"That was fast."

"She took a shower," he said in disbelief. "She couldn't wait to get back down here to you."

Lauren was about to give him a sassy retort when he handed her a brush and two hair ties. "I have absolutely no idea what to do with these."

"Of course you don't," she smirked, taking the hair ties and brush from him.

"Two braids, Lorn," Jessica commanded.

"Please," Jarod reminded her.

Jessica put her little hands on Lauren's cheeks and looked her in the eyes, "Please, Lorn?"

Lauren laughed. "Turn around, silly. Two braids it is."

She brushed out and divided her hair, ignoring the stares and whispers from the rest of the clan.

LAUREN'S NIMBLE FINGERS HYPNOTIZED JAROD. SHE wove his daughter's hair into an intricate plait beginning at Jessica's crown and flowing seamlessly down the right side of her head all the way to her shoulders. When Lauren's fingers reached the end of the three raven ropes, she used one of the blue elastic bands Jessica had picked out and swiftly wrapped it around the ends, careful to keep the hair smooth. When the braid was complete, she began the whole process again on the left side. Jessica sat perfectly still through the entire process, to Jarod's amazement.

The importance of beauty rituals must be written in female DNA.

His view of her work was obscured now, so he concentrated on Lauren's face instead. She wore a smile and hummed softly, as though she and Jessica were alone in the room. When she was finished with the twin French braids, she wrapped her arms around Jessica and placed a swift kiss on her temple.

Jessica giggled.

"All finished, sweat pea."

"Thank you, Lorn."

Instead of jumping down to seek out some new entertainment, Jessica leaned her head back on Lauren's chest and placed her tiny arms over Lauren's hands, which were wrapped around her middle.

Jarod said a silent prayer of thanks that Jessica was here with them now, receiving the love and attention she so desperately needed, and he vowed he'd move heaven and earth to keep it that way. Apparently, the most immediate need Jessica had was for a mother, and it looked like she'd already picked out the lucky candidate.

Her choice was perfectly fine with him.

"What do you want to be for Halloween, Jessica?" Jason asked.

All eyes landed on her. She looked up at Lauren before she shrugged her shoulders.

"Do you know what Halloween is, Darlin'?"

She shook her head at him. Jarod shared a look with Jason and saw his own anger reflected in his brother's green eyes. However, Jason was better at schooling his features.

Jason put his arm around Julie and said, "How about we show you, princess?"

CAMILLE TASKED THE MEN TO THE BARN, WHERE A section had been cordoned off for the larger outdoor seasonal decorations. Not unlike the Room of Doom, this space was huge, but full of sealed bins of lights and outdoor garlands instead of open cubicles of dainty crafting material.

Jarod didn't have an aversion to being here because it was mainly for storage. Plus, Camille had never used the barn for her special brand of punishment on her rowdy boys.

He collected some containers marked "Halloween" and marched back to the front yard of the main house. James, Jason, and Josh were busy with the folding ladder and some tools.

Because most of their neighbor's homes were so far apart in this area, every Halloween, the Kings invited their rural community to their home for some safe trick-or-treating and neighborly fellowship. If the weather was bad, the barn would be opened up for their guests to congregate. The forecast was for clear skies and warm temperatures this year, and they hoped it would hold out until after the festivities.

The men started work on the mini corn maze and put out the welcome signs, while the women worked on the smaller décor and treats. Julie was in charge of preparing the yummy sweets to be put around on tables for their guests. Jessica, never one to pass up a sugary snack, had stationed herself in the kitchen with Charlie, who was teaching her the fine art of finagling a freshly battered spoon out of the chef's hands.

As much as Jarod enjoyed witnessing his daughter's antics, his attention was constantly drawn to Lauren. He was nervous over what he was about to propose, waiting for the right moment to clue her in on what he was thinking. He had to present his plan perfectly, or she would never agree.

"If you hurt her, you and I are going to have serious problems, big brother."

Startled, Jarod spun around to find Josh standing next to him, his gaze directed toward Lauren.

"I don't plan on hurting anyone," he answered disgustedly.

Jarod shoulder-checked his little brother on his way back to the barn for more supplies, but Josh was hot on his heels.

"Then what is your plan? To hire her as a nanny, one with *benefits*?" he sneered. "She needs more from you than that, Jarod."

He spun around, putting his nose in Josh's face. "It's none of your damn business! Now back off, *little* brother."

But Josh stood his ground. "Lauren has been one of my best friends since we were kids. She puts on a tough bravado, Jarod, but she's fragile. And we all know how gentle you are with women."

"What the hell is that supposed to mean? I've never hurt a woman in my life, and you know it!" A red haze was beginning to blur his vision.

Josh took a steadying breath. "Ever since Miranda left, you've treated women like Kleenex. You use them up and then dispose of them when you're done."

"You think you're any better?" Jarod asked, incredulously.

"Lauren is not one of your throwaways, Jarod."

"Who said I think of her that way, huh?"

"You're on the make," Josh accused.

"I'm not on the make, Josh. Far from it. I want to marry her."

They both stared at each other in surprise—Jarod because he'd said it out loud before he'd had a chance to talk to Lauren, and Josh out of pure astonishment.

In the next moment, Jarod found himself on the ground with a bloody nose.

"I won't let you use her like that!"

He'd never seen his brother so worked up, not to mention he'd never let Josh get the jump on him before.

Astonishment kept him slow, so Josh got another punch in before Jarod regained his senses and turned the tables on him. He pinned Josh to the ground, not wanting to hurt his brother.

"What the hell is wrong with you?" he yelled.

"I won't let you crush her, Jarod!"

"For God's sake, how would proposing marriage crush her?" He couldn't believe this.

"She's been in love with you since the first time she met you. Don't try to tell me you don't know that. So, since you now have a daughter... What? You're going to use Lauren's emotions against her so you can provide a mother for your daughter?"

He looked around. Jason and his father were making their way over to them in a hurry. The women were still inside, thank God. Jarod shook his head. He got up and stormed off to the barn to clean up his face—*I am not using Lauren.*

I'm not.

Jarod turned the water on in the three-piece bathroom located next to the small living space, which was used in case one of the animals got sick and needed around-the-clock care. He washed the blood from his nose and looked in the mirror. His left eye was beginning to swell.

That little shit really got me good.

Disgusted, Jarod threw his bloody washcloth in the hamper and slammed his fists on the bathroom counter.

Lauren was too good of a person to be used, by him or anyone else. He was fully aware of what her childhood had been like, and not because she'd been forthcoming. This was Timbisha Township, and secrets were impossible to keep. That's why she was perfect for Jessica. They understood each other, and he trusted Lauren would know how to handle whatever emotional problems that might come later in Jessica's life.

He'd planned on giving Lauren what she needed. If she loved him, he couldn't help it. He wasn't capable of love anymore, but he was definitely attracted to her physically. And he was more than willing and able to make her feel the way a woman should... wanted.

But because he respected her so much, he would have to be honest with her. His need for her was getting to the point of urgency, and she had to know it. She flirted with him every chance she got.

He assessed his injuries in the mirror. His nose was red and his eye was swollen. He looked like he'd been in a fight.

Just great.

He needed to blow off some steam before he faced the rest of his family, so he threw a couple bales of hay in the bucket of the compact tractor, climbed onto the driver's seat, and hauled the bales to the front yard. He stopped near the maze and hopped off. He angrily tossed the bales to the ground, got back into the seat, and headed back to the barn for more hay. He'd made five more trips before he'd gained his control.

He put the tractor away and headed into the house for lunch. Jason had fired up the barbecue; the smell of grilled meat was heavy in the air, making Jarod's mouth water. He passed through the mud room, into the kitchen, and was met with a mini body slam below the knees.

"Jar'd! Where've ya been?" Jessica held tightly to his legs, her chin pressed against his knees as she looked up at him.

He bent down and scooped her up. "I've been out front, Darlin'. What have you been up to?"

She grabbed his cheeks and looked carefully at his face.

"Didja fall down?" she asked, concern etched into her heart-shaped face.

Her expression nearly shattered his control.

"Mommy liked a wet washcloth when she fell down."

She wriggled her feet to be let down. She ran into the kitchen and yanked the nearest hand towel off the rack, then ran to the bathroom. The water turned on, and then she was back with the wet cloth. She grabbed his hand and brought him to the table, where she climbed onto his lap and placed the sopping wet towel on his face.

"All better?" she asked sweetly.

"So much better, Darlin'." He squeezed her tightly and she kissed his cheek.

LAUREN LOVED SPENDING THE HOLIDAYS WITH THE Kings, and Halloween was their kick-off to the season. It gave her a taste of what a normal family life would have been like, if she'd grown up in one.

Every year, Camille and James opened their home to anyone willing to venture out to the countryside on All Hallows Eve. It was all very Norman Rockwell.

So it was quite a shock to find Jarod in the kitchen with a black eye and swollen nose.

Surely, he and Jason didn't decide to spar, did they?

"Are you all right?"

"He's fine," Josh said with disgust.

Jarod shot sapphire daggers at Josh but couldn't do much else because Jessica was sitting in his lap, holding a dripping towel to his face.

Lauren looked from one brother to the other.

Josh gave her a look of warning before he stomped out of the room.

Jason wrapped his arm around her shoulders. "They were fighting over you, Sassy Pants."

"What?"

"Shut the hell up, Jason."

"Don't swear in front the princess, Jarod," Jason warned.

"Someone please tell me what's going on."

"Sorry, Sassy, I think you and my big brother have some talking to do."

He winked at her, then scooped Jessica from Jarod's lap. "Come on, princess. Let's go see what Jujyfruit and Nana are up to in the Room of Doom."

Lauren put her hands on her hips. "Well?"

Jarod got up and stomped into the kitchen. He threw the wet towel in the sink and glared at her, before stomping back into the dining room. He grabbed her upper arm and dragged her out of the kitchen.

He wasn't hurting her, but she felt a little intimidated. She couldn't remember whether she had ticked him off, unless he was upset about this morning, but that was their normal back and forth banter, so she didn't know how to react to this latest display of dominance.

He pushed her into a small sitting room off the front of the house. Camille normally used it when meeting new clients, preferring a more homey and comfortable atmosphere in order to put potential customers at ease.

He let go of Lauren's arm and turned to close the door. When the lock clicked, a tiny chill went down her spine.

Fearing he was going to tell her to leave and never come back, she cleared her throat and said, "I'll get my things and go, Jarod. I'm not sure what I did, but—"

"What? No, Lauren, the last thing I want you to do is leave."

"Then what's all this about?" she asked, fully exasperated.

His behavior was so out of character, she didn't know what to think. He was normally cold and calculating when he was on duty, always in complete control, but he wasn't on duty now.

When he reached up and pushed a stray hair out of her face, she realized she'd misinterpreted where this display of dominance was coming from.

"Jarod, I can't have an affair with you. It would kill me," she implored, embarrassed by the tears welling up in her eyes.

"I don't want an affair either," he softly answered.

Leaning down, he gently brushed his lips across hers and then nibbled. "I want you," he whispered, stinging her with the blue fire in his eyes.

When she didn't answer, he swooped in with a toe-curling kiss. She wrapped her arms around his shoulders and held on tight, relishing the taste of him, the heat of him, until she thought she might pass out. It went on and on until she was dizzy.

He gently pulled free. His breath billowed from his massive chest and fanned out across her cheeks.

"But right now we really do need to talk," he chuckled.

It took all of her willpower to kick-start her brain again. She closed her eyes to concentrate on getting her heart rate down.

Finally, she lifted her chin. "After *that* kiss, I certainly agree."

Still shaking, she sat down on the comfy Georgian sofa. It was burgundy and gold chenille with throw pillows to match. Contrary to what she'd said, she hoped he would sit down with her so they could continue where they'd left off but, to her disappointment, he began to pace across the Persian rug that matched the furniture.

"I never thought I'd want, or need, another woman in my life again, but I want and need you."

Jarod wanted her. Jarod needed her. She couldn't believe he'd just blurted it out like that.

But do you love me? Does it matter?

"Aren't you going to say something?"

How was she supposed to respond? Shaking her head, she asked, "Why now?" But before he could answer, she realized she already knew the reason. "Jessica."

He sat down next to her and reached for her hand. "Listen to me, Lauren. Please."

She shook her hand from his grasp and took his place pacing the rug. She wasn't angry, just disappointed and, okay, maybe even a little hurt. Of course he didn't love her—it was crazy to think so, and she knew it.

Jarod King was incapable of loving a woman because *Miranda* had ruined him for anyone else.

If Lauren could bring Miranda back to life, she'd kill her for what she'd done to Jarod and Jessica.

She loved them both so much that sometimes she thought she'd go mad. The voice in her head that told her she wasn't worthy of love was quiet now, waiting for her to make a decision. She was so tired of being alone. She wanted a family, and Jarod was tempting her with the possibility of having one.

And then it hit her: Jarod wanted it too.

She turned wide eyes to him and commanded, "Ask me."

Her spirit calmed when she realized Jarod was offering her a way to make her dream come true. It didn't matter if he loved her or not. She would be a fool not to take it and run with it until the day she died. She'd love them enough for all three of them, and then, when things got tough, she'd love him a little bit more. If he gave her more children, she'd fill them up with so much love it wouldn't matter if their father loved their mother or not. No one would know, except for the two of them. It would be their secret. It wasn't Jarod's fault he was broken.

He stood up and took both of her hands in his. "Will you be a mother to my daughter and a wife to me? Will you marry us?"

A tear slipped down her cheek and she angrily brushed it away. He didn't need to see her love right now. He was in a desperate situation and needed her help. His proposal wasn't personal, it was business. She understood the situation.

She took his hand in a firm handshake, looked her blue-eyed devil in the eye. "You have a deal."

CHAPTER 10

Hell Hath No Fury Like A Mother Scorned

Jarod pumped her hand a couple of times before it dawned on him what she'd said.

A deal?

"This isn't a deal, Lauren. I want you to be my wife in *every way*." He stressed the last part, squeezing her hand just a bit, letting her know his intentions. "I won't share you with anyone else, and I won't stray to other women. I want the three of us to be a family."

Her lip quivered and a tear escaped her eye. She tried to cover it by nodding her head and discreetly wiping it away.

"I know what you need, Jarod. I've agreed to your terms." Her voice was steady, but sadness etched her face and ate at his heart. He'd expected her to be happy because he sure as hell was.

He began to second guess his proposal when she stepped into his personal space, grabbed the front of his t-shirt with both fists, and pulled his mouth down to hers.

He didn't fight her. She was a spicy sort of heaven he didn't deserve, but he was a selfish man, and she'd agreed to marry him. He'd be damned if he was going to let her out of their "deal" simply because she misunderstood him. He would have to prove himself to her.

He had her wrapped up in his arms when she drew back and gasped for air. Still holding her, he lifted his head to smile down at her before he kissed the tip of her nose.

"Everything will be fine because we're completely compatible. You'll see, Lauren. I promise I will make you happy." As the words left his mouth he realized he was determined to make it true.

"I know you will." She shrugged a negligent shoulder at him and gave him a lopsided smile.

He'd seen this tell of hers before. It was the one she used to mask her true feelings. She wasn't convinced he could keep his promise, but on the outside all was well with the world.

She stepped out of his arms, leaving him with a damned feeling of emptiness. She took a deep breath and broke into her professional, business-like persona.

"How do you want to handle this? I mean, I don't want to steal Julie's thunder. That would just be plain rude, not to mention I don't want to hurt my best friend."

Shit, she had a point. He hadn't thought that far ahead.

"Reno?" he suggested.

"What do you mean?"

"We could drive to Reno tonight and hit a wedding chapel."

She visibly swallowed, never taking her eyes from his. Damn, she gave good blank face, and would make a good cop if the idea ever crossed her mind. It was frustrating he couldn't read her feelings as well as Josh could. He needed to know what she was thinking.

"Say something," he commanded.

She nodded her head, her expression never changing. "What time do you want to leave? Are we telling your family before we go or after the deed is done?"

"I'll make some calls, find out how many twenty-four-hour chapels they have, and I'll let you know in an hour or two. As for letting everyone know, I think Josh will probably take care of that for us. He's got a bug up his ass about you which I don't understand. He's not in love with you, is he?"

Her expression went from stoic to surprise to hilarity in a nanosecond as she burst out into loud guffaws. She even bent over and stomped her foot. It was the first time she'd smiled since he'd dragged her into this room to propose.

"Of course he's not in love with me, Jarod!" She held on to her stomach, trying to catch her breath. "We are best friends." She shook her head at him. "He's like a very protective big brother. If he's mad at you over this, then you need to address it with him. I won't marry you if the two of you are going to fight about it for the rest of our lives."

She made her way over to the door. "I'm heading back to the craft room to help your mother with her hanging spiders. I won't say anything until you give me the all clear." She stepped out of the door and was gone.

What the hell just happened?

I'VE LOST MY MIND.

Lauren tried to stay nonchalant on the outside while she had a raging panic attack on the inside. She'd agreed to marry Jarod King, the man she'd loved since she was a girl. But he didn't love her. He only needed her as a surrogate mother for Jessica. Could she live with a man who didn't love her back?

She didn't care. Jarod would be hers and hers alone. He had promised. She would make it work if it killed her.

Breezing into the craft room like she hadn't just made a deal with the devil, she sat next to Julie as if nothing of significance had just happened.

"What did Jarod want?" Camille asked distractedly as she strung spindly black legs made of pipe cleaner through a large black ball of Styrofoam.

"He wanted to know what kind of costume to buy for Jessica," she lied.

Camille put her things down and gave her a puzzled look over her reading glasses. "Why? I told him I had the perfect costume for her already." She rolled her eyes and picked up her materials again. "That boy has been a wreck since you moved back to your condo, Lauren. I hope you stay the weekend with us. I need help getting his head screwed back on straight."

Lauren noticed Julie hadn't said a word. In fact, she hadn't even made eye contact with her. Something was up with these two. She'd known both women too long not to know when they were hiding something from her.

"All right you two. Spill."

Both women were innocence personified, sputtering denials at the same time.

"I don't know what you mean."

"Finishing up with these spider legs."

Lauren laughed. "You could never pull off a crime, you know that, don't you?"

Julie looked at Camille and smiled. "Josh told us what happened to Jarod's face."

"Really? Because Jarod didn't elaborate. What happened between them?" she asked. She hoped if they talked about Josh, she wouldn't have to talk about what had happened between her and Jarod.

Julie looked to Camille for permission before she explained. "Josh is concerned Jarod may take advantage of your feelings for him, that's all."

Oh goody. Julie was in mother-hen mode. Lauren had gone from no mother at all to two in one morning.

Then Camille cut to the chase. "I hope you said yes to Jarod. He doesn't realize how much he loves you, dear."

Lauren didn't believe her, but it was a nice thought. She'd never disrespect Camille by contradicting her belief in any of her sons, especially not Jarod, but Lauren knew the score. He needed a mother for Jessica, he was physically attracted to her, and she was weak enough to go along with it.

Julie put her arm around her shoulders. "So, are we invited or what?"

Lauren burst out laughing before the tears fell from her eyes. "I don't know. Jarod's plan is to go to Reno tonight and hit a chapel. I told him I wouldn't say anything until our plans were finalized." She wiped her eyes and hugged her friend. "Oh Julie, I'm so sorry! I don't want to take away from your day. Please don't be mad at me."

"Mad? I'm only concerned that you're going to be all right." Julie hugged her back.

"So, we're waiting on Jarod to make some plans, eh?" Camille stood up. "If you girls don't mind, can you finish up these spiders? I need to have a word with my oldest spawn."

She left the craft room before Lauren could argue otherwise.

Julie started laughing outright.

Lauren just stared. "There is nothing funny about this. I've lost my mind, haven't I?"

Julie shook her head and got herself under control. "Oh Lauren, he doesn't have a clue how much trouble he's gotten himself into with his mother," she said seriously. "Jarod leaving his mother out of his wedding is tantamount to treason in this family. He must be crazy!"

Lauren sat stock still as the reality hit her. Now they were both laughing so hard they couldn't hold the spider legs together.

As Jarod stepped out of his bedroom his mother charged into his sitting room and stared daggers at him.

"What do you think you're doing?" she asked in a tone he hadn't heard since he was a boy.

"Changing?" he asked, hoping that was the right answer.

She narrowed her green laser beams at him, making him cringe.

Shit, I'm in trouble.

"I ought to take you to the craft room and make you tie ribbons around sachet packets!"

Oh God, please not that! His fingers began to cramp at the thought of all those tiny, monogrammed ribbons he could never twist into the perfect tie. The names and dates never ended up in the correct order. He barely held back a shiver of revulsion.

"Mom, I can explain—"

"Shut up, Jarod. You don't have to explain anything to me. I know you better than you know yourself, damn it."

He took an involuntary step back when she narrowed her eyes even further. Before he began to squirm too much, she softened in tiny increments on a sigh of breath.

"What am I going to do with you, son?"

At a loss, he only shrugged and gave her a sheepish smile. He was still a little intimidated by her. He didn't want to make any sudden movements just yet.

He wasn't stupid.

"Sit down, please." She gestured to his sofa.

He sat down, never taking his eyes off of his mother as she positioned herself right next to him. Damn, she was within smacking distance, and he knew how fast she could throw a backhand. He and his brothers learned to fight from their father, but they'd gotten their *speed* from their mother. She'd had to be quick raising three boys, and Jarod knew one wrong move, one wrong word out of his mouth, would earn him a swift penalty she wasn't afraid to dole out.

She removed her spectacles and stared at him for a moment.

Then, "I can't imagine how hard this past month has been for you, darling. I won't pretend everything is sunshine and roses right now because I'm as confused as you are about Miranda's death and the miracle of Jessica."

He closed his eyes in relief. This wasn't going to be a smackdown.

"But if you think for one second you can marry Lauren and exclude your family—exclude *me*—then you've got another *think* coming, mister."

Wait, what?

"If Lauren has agreed, and you're dead set on marrying her in such a rush, I'm not going to stop you. I had hoped for a church wedding for the two of you..."

"You knew I asked Lauren to marry me?" he interrupted, but she ignored his question.

"...but if you have a pressing need to marry her right this

second, you could at least let me plan a decent reception for the two of you."

"Mom..."

She held up her hand in the age-old stop gesture.

"Miranda was never the love of your life, Jarod. You only thought she was. You were far too young to know what love is, and I had no doubt in my mind Miranda was only with you because you were the heir apparent to our family's money. The proof was in the pudding when you announced you were going into law enforcement instead of working beside your father at King Construction. She left without a backward glance. That should've told you something."

He was stunned. He hadn't thought of his relationship with Miranda in those terms. He'd loved her so much, or at least had thought he had, that he couldn't see... Of course, she was a gold digger.

Wow, the realization was almost a relief.

"You couldn't see it because you were too close to it," she explained as if reading his mind. "Kind of like when Julie thought she couldn't love Jason. Her judgement was blinded by lies spun by Billy, who was competing for her affection. Miranda had you so tightly wrapped around her finger you couldn't see that she was no better for you than Billy was for Julie."

It was like a veil had been lifted. For the first time in five years, he saw things with clarity. He hadn't pushed Miranda away. He hadn't let her down as a husband. She'd never loved him in the first place.

"I love you, Mom."

"I know you do, Jarod," she replied a bit haughtily, making him chuckle.

Turning all business, she said, "Now, if you want to plan a

small wedding with Lauren, that's fine, but you WILL have a decent reception to introduce yourselves to the community as a family, and I will plan it. Understand?"

"Yes, ma'am."

"Good. Now that's settled, the girls and I will need to make some adjustments in our schedule to fit this in. When were you planning on stealing her away?"

"Tonight."

They stared at each other before she began to shake her head.

"That's too soon."

"I'm not budging. I want to marry her tonight. I've already made the calls."

"She doesn't have a proper dress! And we need to send out invitations—"

"We're getting married tonight. I've already reserved a chapel in Reno for seven o'clock this evening. I can't take time off from work right now. I was just on my way down to tell her."

He heard her blasphemous curse under her breath and quickly silenced his chuckle.

"Fine. But there will be a reception as soon as I can manage it. Understood?"

"Of course. And since she'll be my wife, she won't be able to work for me anymore, so she'll be readily available for you to torture in that Room of Doom of yours."

She cracked a grin, then stood to leave. "I left Lauren and Julie in the craft room. Will you be taking Jessica with you?"

Jarod hadn't thought about it, so he merely shrugged.

"Oh, I hate all this rushing around business," she said before she stormed out of the room, obviously irritated all over again.

CHAPTER 11
Resignation Accepted

Lauren lay on her side, rubbing the gold band around the ring finger of her left hand, mesmerized by the glint of the morning sunshine off the bevel that went all the way around it. She enjoyed the warmth on her face but relished the heat engulfing her from her head to her toes. Jarod's warm body was spooned up tightly behind her. His left arm draped haphazardly around her waist, his torso touching every inch of her naked skin along her back, and a heavy leg covered her thigh. His spicy male scent flowed over her, keeping this peaceful, dreamlike aura alive in the new sunlight streaming through the window.

As daylight began to fill the room, she knew this moment would end soon and he'd be anxious to get home to Jessica. Camille had suggested the little girl stay home with the family because Lauren and Jarod would need some time for themselves.

Camille had been correct. *God bless that woman!*

Jarod had gotten them to the chapel right on schedule. He'd worn black dress slacks, a white dress shirt, and a black tie, but had forgone a jacket. Noting his casualness, she'd worn a long, black, western-cut skirt, her only pair of cowboy boots, and her white silk blouse. There'd been no time to order flowers, but the chapel provided a simple bouquet of daisies and baby's breath.

The ceremony itself had been short and sweet, the license and other paperwork taking more time to complete than the I do's.

By seven-thirty, the minister pronounced them Mr. and Mrs. Jarod King.

Done deal.

By seven forty-five, Jarod had them checked into the hotel suite, which was an upgrade from a basic room. The front desk clerk noticed her small bouquet and asked if they'd used the hotel's chapel. Jarod had immediately said yes.

With a wink and a grin, their room had been upgraded to a spacious suite with a jacuzzi tub right in the middle of the floor and an oversized king bed.

Jarod took advantage of both, and neither of them had gotten much sleep.

Lauren didn't feel tired as she contemplated their new relationship. Morning afters stunk, and she supposed this would count as one. After all, he had proposed and married her all in the same day. The only difference was neither of them had been drunk when they'd met with the justice of the peace. She hated feeling awkward and wondered what would happen next.

She got her answer before the thought had been completed in her head when Jarod began to stir behind her. A smile slowly formed on her lips as the hand on her torso began to slide up her body to do more exploring, and she felt his body coming to full attention behind her. Whisker-roughened lips kissed her neck, gliding up to nibble on her earlobe, making her toes curl.

"Good morning, beautiful. How was your night?" he whispered in a sleepy, masculine voice.

Feeling ornery, she answered, "Horrible. I barely caught a wink of sleep."

"Horrible, huh? Maybe I should make it up to you," he said, pushing her to her back and leaning over her for a leisurely kiss.

"Yes, maybe you should," she agreed breathily.

God, Jarod in the morning was a wonderful sight to see with his short hair a little flat, and his face covered in stubble. But his eyes, peeking through dark lashes like blue fire, and they were currently focused on her lips.

"Good thing I'm up for the task, ma'am," he growled.

She only giggled for a second after he put his plan into action.

THEY HAD A QUICK BREAKFAST IN THE DOWNSTAIRS restaurant before checking out of the hotel by eleven o'clock. Lauren was still a bit dazed by this morning's activities and stunned at Jarod's nonchalant attitude. He seemed unfazed by their new circumstance.

Unfortunately, the usual panic was making an appearance, but she fought hard to keep up a happy front. For now, she would follow his lead and try not to give her uneasiness away.

"I'm sorry to rush you this morning, but I really wanted to get back home. I have to find a storage shed to rent and order a U-haul. I need to check in with Brad and Eli to let them know of the new changes in the office, and I need to post your position right away."

Like brakes screeching on asphalt, the repercussions of her

hasty marriage hit her smack in the face. His to-do list only reinforced her agitated state as her earlier peaceful calm flew right out the window. Trying to process his announcement, she addressed each item in the order he'd given her.

"First off, never apologize for making love to me, Jarod. We won't last long as a couple if you do."

He looked at her in surprise. "Sassy, I'm not apologizing for that. If I was sorry for making love to you, it would mean I never intended to do it again. Believe me, I am *not* sorry."

Okay, so he liked sex. Every man did.

"Well, then, what are you apologizing for?"

"For rushing us out of there."

"That was your idea of a quickie?" Lauren was surprised and a bit giddy at the prospect of more quickies.

He focused his bedroom eyes on her, making her tingle all over again. "That was way too quick for my taste."

Oh, goody.

Moving on to the next item on his list, she asked, "Okay, then why do you need a storage shed and a U-haul?"

"Are you kidding?"

"No." Had she missed something?

"Honey, we need to move your stuff out of your townhouse."

She swallowed. He wanted her to give up her home? But what if this didn't work out? Sure, she spent the majority of her time with his family, but still, the townhouse was hers. What if she needed some space, some time to think? What if they fought? What if he realized marrying her was a mistake and he wanted a divorce? Where would she go then?

As if he could read her thoughts, Jarod said gently, "Lauren, you are my wife. You live where I live. You sleep where I sleep."

He reached over and grabbed her hand, bringing it to his lips for a gentle kiss on the knuckles, then turned it palm up to kiss the inside of her wrist. "You are a King now, a part of my family. You are Jessica's mother. Please don't run from me— *from us.*"

The sincerity of his words made her eyes well with tears, and her heart sing with joy at his acceptance of her into his family, even under the circumstances.

"Please don't shut me out, either. I've been there and done that already." He sounded angry.

That hit a nerve. "Don't ever compare me to your ex-wife, Jarod King. I'm not a coward." She let out a breath. "I think I'm a little overwhelmed at the moment. And since when have you ever known me to run from a challenge?"

He laughed. "Never."

"Okay then." Geez, she'd just gotten Jarod, and he thought she'd give him up? Not for anything. However, her fears of abandonment lingered under the surface, so she tried to explain herself.

"When dad left me with my mother, I was all alone. My mother was never sober, and so I had to fend for myself. Don't misunderstand. I'm not complaining because it made me who I am."

He stared out the windshield, holding her hand to his thigh. He gave her an encouraging squeeze. "Go on."

"After the third stint in foster care, I made a vow to myself that when I was old enough, I would never need to rely on another person to live ever again. Buying the townhouse fulfilled my need for independence. I finally had a permanent roof over my head which no one could take from me. I have a great job and I'm financially secure."

"I get it. However, you don't need it anymore." He gave her his fiery blue gaze. "You have me."

They drove in silence for a few minutes.

"Jessica needs the security of a mother, Lauren, just like you did. If you feel like you need an escape, keep your rooms at The Estate and use them when you're sick of me or if you feel like you need space."

"It's not the same."

"I know, but it's important to me that we share the same roof. I can't explain it any other way."

He didn't need to. Miranda had spent a lot of her time away from home, especially after Jarod became a deputy. It had been no secret she'd slept elsewhere.

Lauren understood his need to keep tabs on her. For now, she would allow it because trust was important in any relationship. She hoped as time went by he'd grow to trust her and know she wasn't going anywhere.

Coming to a decision, she agreed. "I'll list the townhouse as soon as we get back." His hand relaxed over hers, making her more confident they'd successfully negotiated their first compromise as a married couple. "But I'm keeping my position as administrative assistant." She couldn't live and work in the same place. She'd talk to Camille about it when they returned.

He grinned evilly, letting her know she'd been mistaken in the negotiations.

"No, you're not. I accepted your resignation when I proposed marriage. It became effective when you said 'I do.' There's a nepotism clause in the employee handbook, honey. Sorry, but you're fired."

Damn it.

JAROD PARKED HIS RAPTOR IN ITS REGULAR SPOT AND shut off the engine. His wife—*God, how I love the sound of that* —wore her usual confident expression, the one she sported when she was confronted with something new and challenging. He'd always loved that look on her, but now he loved being the cause of it.

Not touching her wasn't an option. He was more than pleased when she came to him willingly and kissed him as voraciously as he kissed her the moment he reached for her.

Perfect.

Coming up for air with a smile, he rubbed his thumb across her plump bottom lip.

"You ready, Mrs. King?"

Her expelled breath fanned across his face, her eyes showing surprise at her new moniker. Recovering in the next heartbeat, she said, "Of course," in her famous sassy tone.

She got out of the truck before he could open the door for her and tried to retrieve her overnight bag, but he beat her to the handle before she had a chance, and lifted it out of the truck bed.

Smiling in thanks, she led the way to the mud room and passed through it to the kitchen.

No one was around.

Shrugging off the absence of his family, Jarod indicated she should head upstairs. When she got to the second-floor landing, she hesitated and looked at her bag, which was still clutched in his hand.

"Second thoughts?" he asked.

"No, I just realized I have to move twice."

"What do you mean?"

"Well, it's not only my townhouse I have to move out of. I also need to move my stuff from my rooms here into yours."

"Now you're talking." He laughed, trying to put her at ease.

She shook her head and continued in almost a panicked state, "Not to mention I have to change my name on all my legal documents."

"Good thing I fired you then. You'll have lots of time to get it all done."

She rolled her eyes at him. "I'll go to my room to get my things and meet you in yours... ours."

"I like the sound of that." He kissed the end of her nose and headed to his room to start making space for her.

Our room. God, that sounded good to him.

Not knowing what to do with the contents of her bag, he set it inside the door before taking his own overnight case into the bathroom to put his shaving gear away. He found his sink had acquired a few beauty items which weren't there before.

Sure enough, when he peeked into the shower, bottles of girlie body wash and shampoo and conditioner sat on the ledge next to Jessica's blue Cookie Monster bubble bath. He also found a purple loofah hanging from the shower head.

He picked up the amber-colored shower gel and held it to his nose. Sandalwood, heady and spicy just like Lauren, filled his nostrils. It made him want to look for her and occupy her time for about an hour or so.

"My things are missing," she announced, startling him.

His eyes clashed with hers briefly before he backed her up against the wall and began kissing down the long line of her neck, starting at her earlobe and trailing to the base of her throat. He pinned her arms above her head, entwining his fingers with hers, keeping her captive.

"Oh," she whispered and immediately came to life for him.

He pressed the length of his body along hers while he ravaged her mouth like a gluttonous man.

He slowly released her hands, smoothing his palms down her arms, her shoulders, and then the sides of her body. When he felt her arms settle around his neck, he picked her up and sat her on the counter.

She'd worn a pretty navy-blue skirt that was straight, trapping her legs. He growled his frustration and began to draw the material up so he could part her knees to accommodate him, needing to be as close as possible.

She had her hands on his waistband, digging his shirt out of his pants, when someone cleared their throat.

Lauren squealed, jerking her skirt back into place, while Jarod jumped back, feeling like a caveman, ready to fight off his challenger.

The throat clearing became a masculine chuckle and then an outright laugh. Jason raised his arms in surrender.

"I wanted to congratulate the two of you, but I think I may be interrupting the honeymoon. Shame on you for not keeping her locked away for the whole weekend, Jarod."

"Oh, I'm keeping her, all right," Jarod said.

He lifted her off the counter and hauled her up beside him, not letting her go. The possessiveness he felt was satisfied by the surprise in her eyes.

"Hey, Jason," Lauren said, sounding out of breath.

Damn, he loved fracturing her cool façade.

"Hey, sis. Let me be the first to welcome you to the family," he stated, and then he literally grabbed Lauren out of Jarod's arms and hauled her in for one of his bear hugs, lifting her off her feet.

When Lauren began to laugh, Jarod unclenched his fists and rolled his eyes.

"Let her go before you break her, you big oaf."

Jason glared at Jarod. "Everyone's downstairs in the reception hall, waiting for you guys. So if you're finished playing kissy-face, I'd like to eat. Jujyfruit fixed quite a spread and I'm starving." He pecked Lauren on the cheek and sauntered out of the bathroom.

Pompous ass.

"Oh." She began checking and straightening her clothes again and rearranging her hair. "How do I look?" she asked a bit anxiously.

"Good enough to eat."

"Jarod," she scolded.

He wrapped his arms around her middle from behind and gazed at her reflection in the mirror, resting his chin on her shoulder. "You're beautiful." He kissed her neck again and then reluctantly released her.

"You're not so bad yourself."

He held his hand out to her, and she took it without hesitation, making him feel better.

He led her out of his room and down the stairs to the massive reception room, located on the ground floor in the back of the house. This space was dedicated to holding business and social events for King Construction. The commercial kitchen was adjacent to this room for easy catering.

His mother had lined the center of the room with long tables for a buffet-style luncheon. A three-tiered cake sat directly in the center of the buffet. When they entered the room, applause erupted from more than their family.

"Jar'd! Lorn!" came a small voice followed by the tapping of small feet running across the travertine tiles. Then Jessica launched herself at him.

Jarod caught her up in a big hug and squeezed her tightly. "I missed you, Darlin'!" He kissed her cheek.

"Where'd ya go?" she asked seriously.

"We went to Reno."

She reached for Lauren, who took her into her arms now. "Why'd ya leave me?"

Lauren hugged her and kissed her cheek. "We didn't leave you, sweet pea. Your daddy asked me to marry him, and I said yes."

"Lauren is your mommy, now. What do you think about that?" Jarod announced to his daughter.

Jessica leaned back in Lauren's arms to put her little hands on her face. "Okay."

"Okay? That's it?" Jarod asked.

"Yeah, it's okay with me." Then she kicked her feet to get down. "Come on, Lorn. Joojee made a cake."

Lauren looked at Jarod and shrugged. "Julie made a cake," she stated, like it made all the sense in the world.

They followed his daughter, who had a death grip on Lauren's hand, dragging her toward the dessert tables.

<hr>

"I DIDN'T INVITE HER," JULIE SAID WHEN SHE SIDLED up next to Lauren after the wedding cake had been served.

"I would never accuse you of such a dastardly deed," Lauren laughed as they watched Marguerite work the room.

Lauren was overwhelmed by the hugs and well wishes from the people surrounding her, some she knew well and some not at all, including a small group of people from King Construction and James's security detail.

Father O'Keefe and a few people from the sheriff's department, including Marguerite, were also among the well-wishers.

"She arrived early, taking in every detail. She's been overly polite to Camille. Of course, Camille doesn't buy it for a second. It's obvious the only reason Marguerite is here is to get a look inside The Estate."

Lauren merely smiled at her friend.

"What is it?"

"Nothing," she said, keeping the tears at bay. Lauren felt wonderful and confused at the same time. However, she also sensed an air of foreboding, a strange gut feeling that something terrible was about to happen.

She smiled, though, not wanting Julie to pick up on anything. Julie had been through enough, and Lauren was sure her erratic emotions were due to the stress of a rushed marriage, losing her job, and becoming a mother within a twenty-four-hour period.

Julie put her arm around her shoulders in a friendly hug. "I'm here if you need me, you know that?"

"Yes, of course," Lauren confirmed, hugging her friend tightly. Changing the subject, she asked, "How did Jessica do last night?"

"I think she's the reason why Camille and James have bags under their eyes."

"Seriously? It couldn't be this rushed reception or anything?" Lauren said only a little bit sarcastically.

"Well, there's that, but you know Camille. She lives for this stuff."

Lauren merely nodded.

"Jessica missed Jarod something awful. I'm not sure any of them got much sleep," Julie continued.

Lauren sought out Jessica. Sure enough, she was clinging to

her daddy, head drooped on his shoulder, barely awake. One little hand intermittently patted Jarod's back, as if to reassure herself he was real.

Lauren wished she had a camera. The picture of father and daughter was too precious to forget. Jarod was perfectly comfortable toting Jessica's limp body around. It didn't keep him from speaking with people or eating. His paternal instincts had kicked in, as if he'd been caring for her since her birth, rather than barely a month.

The afternoon luncheon ran into the late evening. Julie had made a lot of food, and some of the guests seemed reluctant to leave, including Marguerite, but she wasn't lingering around the buffet tables like the rest of the remaining guests. It appeared she was waiting for something else.

Or maybe *someone*, Lauren thought.

Lauren sat next to Jarod at their designated table, Jessica still in his lap with her head on his shoulder. He was engaged in conversation with James when Josh sat down on the other side of Lauren.

"Okay, it was weird when Jason *told* Julie to marry him and she complied. I was adjusting to one of my best friends becoming a sibling and doing fine with it, but now you've blown me out of the water this weekend, Lauren." He winked at her, yet she could still sense a bit of animosity directed at Jarod.

"Are we okay?" she asked seriously.

"We have never been better," he said as he hauled her in for a hug. Before he let her go, he whispered in her ear, "Are you sure *you're* okay, though? Jarod can be a domineering asshole. I don't want you hurt, Sassy."

She kissed his cheek and answered confidentially, "You

know how much I love him, Josh. How can I not be the happiest woman in the room right now?"

He didn't look convinced. "All you have to do is say the word, and I'll knock some sense into him. AGAIN," he said loud enough for Jarod to hear. "I'm here for you, Lauren."

Tears pricked at her eyes knowing Josh cared for her enough that he would protect her from his own brother.

She hugged him back and said, "I'd never let that happen, but thanks for the thought."

"You'll never get the jump on me again, anyway, Josh," Jarod said. "Thanks for your concern. And take your hands off my wife."

He'd finished his conversation with James and was now turned toward Lauren with his arm around the back of her chair and the other holding Jessica, who had given up trying to stay awake.

Lauren almost offered to take her, but Jarod looked content just holding his little girl.

Before Jarod and Josh got too antagonistic with each other, Eli strode into the room in full uniform. She looked around for Brad, and found him leaning into Marguerite, whispering intently. They were probably figuring out when they were going to hook up later.

Lauren barely contained her revulsion. She couldn't figure out what Brad saw in that woman.

Eli approached Jarod with a purpose, but when he arrived at the table, he noticed Jessica sleeping on Jarod's shoulder. His expression softened. He altered his course and went to Lauren instead.

"Congratulations, Mrs. King," he said with pure delight as he bent to give her a peck on the cheek. Then he turned and shook Jarod's free hand.

"Jarod, I need to speak to you for a second, if it's all right. It's about Avery Decatur."

Jarod said, "Sure thing. Josh was just leaving."

"And that's my cue. I'll talk to you later, Sassy." Josh pulled the chair out for Eli to sit before he made his way back to the dessert table, where Charlie was munching his way through a plate of cookies.

"Spill it," Jarod said.

"Avery's bail was posted anonymously, and he has since left town," he said, without preamble.

Jarod met Lauren's eyes for a moment before returning his attention to Eli.

"No idea who coughed up the cash to bail him out?"

"Nope, not a clue."

Jarod said nothing, but a small grin began to form.

"You don't seem as upset as I thought you'd be," Eli said warily.

Jarod winked at Lauren.

"Why are you so happy about this?" she asked.

"I think this may be the slip-up we've been waiting for." He glanced around the room in thought. "Why in the world would anyone bail an idiot like Avery out of jail if he'd already screwed up once?"

Lauren hadn't a clue.

"Could be Avery has what they need," Eli guessed.

"My thoughts exactly. Put out a BOLO on Avery, and let's see where he leads us," said Sheriff King, which immediately turned her on.

"Sure thing, boss." Eli gave a small salute before he left the room, making a detour to the dessert table.

"Should we tuck Jessica in?" Lauren asked.

Jarod glanced at Jessica in surprise, almost as if he'd forgotten he still held her.

"Is she asleep?"

"Since dessert, which she didn't finish. Look how droopy her arms and legs are," Lauren laughed.

Jarod held up a tiny hand to kiss the knuckles, then rubbed his big hand around her back. Again, Lauren could see the reluctance to let her go.

"What if she wakes up and we aren't there? I don't want to upset her again. Mom said she was a mess last night."

Lauren wanted to laugh, but Jarod was serious. She schooled her features and said, "Whatever you think is best, dear." She winked at him to let him know she was teasing.

"Sassy pants," Jarod mumbled under his breath.

CHAPTER 12
Fruitless Search

He followed the sound of shuffling feet coming from one of the back rooms of the old, low-rent house. He could almost smell the fear. Getting closer, he heard the mumblings of the desperate man who fruitlessly searched for what rightfully belonged *to him.*

He found the man in the last bedroom going through what looked like the former lady of the house's underwear drawer.

"I never figured you for a cross dresser, Avery."

At the sound of his voice, Avery screamed.

"How'd ya git here so quick?"

"You know I'm a man of means." He gave Avery his hard stare. "Find it yet?"

Put out, Avery forgot who he was talking to and exclaimed, "No, I ain't found it yet! What do I look like, a damned bloodhound?"

He had Avery in a chokehold before Avery could finish his search through the lady's lingerie.

"You watch your mouth," the man said through gritted teeth. "There are so many holes in this desert no one will blink if they find a part of you in one and the rest of you scattered by coyotes."

"Sorry! Sorry!"

The terror in Avery's voice fed his rage.

"Just find the damned money, Avery. Look for it like your life depends on it... because it does."

He gave Avery a shove before walking out of the room.

Where the hell had Miranda hidden it all? Half a million in cash would be difficult to hide in this small house. He didn't know what he was going to do if they'd managed to move it all.

He was a big player in the scheme of things, but he wasn't the biggest fish, and his partners demanded their payout. If he couldn't deliver, well, he really didn't want to think about the consequences.

He'd been responsible for recruiting Big Mike and Avery in this little capital venture, against his partners' wishes. But he'd seen Big Mike's ability to create a quality product, and Avery's simple-minded ways were perfect for muling.

It was unfortunate Miranda had gotten herself involved, for more reasons than he could count. One was because he respected her ex-husband. Too bad Jarod had been so hung up on the bitch. She really wasn't worth any man's time of day, including Big Mike's. The bastard had served him well until Miranda's ambitions turned Big Mike against him when she'd demanded a bigger cut.

Gold-digging whore.

The man looked around at the squalor and almost laughed. Miranda had been so hell bent on marrying into money, only to ditch Jarod and the richest family in all of Timbisha Township in order to come live in this Las Vegas shit hole. All because Jarod hadn't wanted to work for his old man.

And because she'd gotten herself addicted to Big Mike's quality product.

He laughed out loud at the irony until he remembered the bitch had stolen five hundred thousand dollars from him. He drew back his fist and shoved it through the paper-thin wall of the tiny living room.

The release of violence only appeased his anger for a moment before the worries began to bubble up once more. He slowly looked around the room, eyes landing on everything and seeing nothing, until he zeroed in on a dirty sippy cup lying on the floor.

He slowly began to form a plan to recover his money. For the first time, he realized Avery wasn't the only human being alive who might know the whereabouts of his missing profits.

If Avery couldn't find the money, the man might know someone who could. He would be taking a big risk using her but, if push came to shove, he wasn't above hurting a spoiled brat to get what he wanted.

CHAPTER 13
Molly's Diner

It was the week before Halloween, and the sun was warm and bright, glinting off the plate-glass windows of the town square. Jarod wore a smile on his face and felt the pieces of his heart healing, knitting together, making him feel whole again.

He felt alive.

He felt like a man.

Jessica's room still wasn't complete. Hating to do it, he and Lauren had tucked her into sheets and blankets on the sofa in his sitting room but left the bedroom door open in case she woke up in the night.

She did.

Jarod had fallen asleep with Lauren in his arms and woken up with a warm woman wrapped around him and a steel bar jammed into his back. Jessica somehow managed to fit her tiny body sideways, ramming her little feet into his lower lumbar as he lay on his side facing Lauren. It was a strange phenomenon that happened when Jessica was in his bed. Somehow, her tiny body could fill a space large enough for an adult.

He laughed at the memory of crawling over her delicate frame so he could get out of bed. He hadn't wanted to wake either of his sleeping beauties, so he'd kissed them both softly before heading to the shower.

When he'd finally left his suite, both of his girls were still in his warm bed, nestled together as if they belonged there, pleasantly snoring away.

He drove through town now, thinking about his new life and how his outlook on the future had changed from one of dismal monochrome to something unknown and bright. Normally, the commute to work gave him the opportunity to dwell on the regrets of his past, but today was different, as if he'd reached a turning point. All he could think about was making plans with Lauren.

Inevitably, though, the case crept back into his thoughts, along with the possibility there could be some progress in catching his drug dealers. Eli's news had been intriguing.

Avery was a small-time criminal who dabbled in misdemeanor crimes, like occasionally smacking around Luanne, who gave as good as she got, and he had a couple of possession charges for marijuana. The explosion at Avery's little farmhouse had been uncharacteristic, but it could be an indicator Avery was trying to advance his criminal career to drug manufacturing. Jarod had no earthly idea where the idiot could have found a recipe for cooking meth, or the means to afford the essential ingredients. If Jarod's theory was correct, Avery had a backer.

He hadn't heard from anyone on Avery's whereabouts yet. Usually, the first thing Avery did when he was released from jail was head home for some sleep and some food. Since Decatur's house was still part of an ongoing investigation, Jarod assumed Avery spent the night in a cheap motel. Timbisha Township had a few of those. Avery didn't need to leave town to check into one.

So if Avery wasn't at home and wasn't in town, where had he gone?

Jarod released a frustrated breath. Whoever bailed out Avery had not done it for philanthropic purposes; they'd needed something from the small-time criminal. The pieces were right in front of Jarod but he couldn't make them fit together.

As he cruised up Main Street, Jarod spotted a King Construction vehicle parked in front of Molly's Diner. Jarod had skipped breakfast this morning, and Molly's had perfect coffee and even better omelets—something he'd never admit to Julie. He signaled and turned his vehicle into the parking lot, taking the last open spot.

Molly's had opened as a coffee shop back in the 1930s. It was a typical U-shaped restaurant, with the kitchen and counter in the center of the room and booths lining the outer wall of the building along the windows. Though it had been updated a few times, it still bore a resemblance to its original interior, with chrome and Formica countertops and blue vinyl bar stools and booth benches.

As Timbisha Township grew into a large mining community, Molly's had also grown, adding a small casino in the back with four floors of hotel rooms above the gaming hall. It had passed through the hands of a few owners in its day. Derek Lawlor, the newest owner, had commissioned King Construction to do some renovation work on the hotel portion.

Jarod wasn't surprised to see his dad sitting in a booth with Derek. What did surprise him, though, was seeing a third wheel at the table... his deputy, Brad Anderson.

"Good morning, gentlemen," Jarod addressed the group.

"Hey boss."

"Son."

"Good morning, Sheriff. Care to join us?" offered Derek, who scooted over in the booth, leaving space for Jarod to sit down next to him. Derek and Brad now faced each other against the plate-glass window overlooking the sidewalk, and Jarod's father was to Brad's left.

"Don't mind if I do." Jarod noted everyone's coffee mugs and asked, "Have you ordered yet?"

"Carrie was just going back for some menus. Oh, here she is now," James said.

"Morning Sheriff! Can I get you something to drink? Coffee, juice?" Carrie, always friendly, handed menus to each of them while Jarod gave her his request for black coffee.

"Be right back," she said with a smile and hurried off behind the counter for the hot carafe.

"How's married life this morning, Jarod?" Derek asked.

Jarod smiled at his menu, not making eye contact with any of the men.

There were a few masculine chuckles before James said, "Married with children, or *child*, as the case may be. Camille and I can't tell you how happy we are to have a granddaughter as sweet as our Jessica. And Lauren has always been a part of our family. Jarod did us all a favor by formalizing the relationship and making it legal."

"Who'll be taking Lauren's place in the office, Jarod?" Brad asked quietly, almost too quietly for Jarod's liking.

He eyed his deputy.

"I'll be posting the position today and plan on going through the normal procedures. Why? Do you have someone in mind?"

Brad hesitated before he said, "No, just curious is all." He smiled genially and returned to his menu.

Carrie came back to take their orders, each of them ordering the omelet special, which came with two pancakes, bacon *and* sausage, home fries, and a choice of toast or muffin. Apparently, everyone at the table was as hungry as he was.

"Marrying Lauren left you empty-handed at work, huh?" Derek asked.

"Yeah, I probably won't find the same quality of help I had with Lauren, but when a woman like her comes along, you have to keep her as close as possible, right gentlemen?"

Jarod eyed each man, knowing his father would agree. James and Camille King's romance was almost legend in Timbisha Township.

Jarod assumed Derek loved his wife, but he was curious about Brad's reaction.

Brad stared at him briefly and then raised his coffee mug in a toast. "To women you can't live without."

"Here, here," chimed James as they all clinked their mugs together.

Carrie brought their breakfasts, and the conversation turned casual, covering everything from police-blotter incidents to the renovations on the hotel.

"Are you keeping the name the same?" Jarod asked. "Molly's has been a mainstay in Timbisha for years."

"We don't want to change the name of the restaurant. Too many locals would have a fit, plus regular commuters know of this place and stop in often in their travels across the state. We're considering renaming the hotel portion, but it's all up in the air. For now, 'Molly's' will remain." Derek winked with this pronouncement.

"Well," James said as he pushed his plate away, "I gotta get going. Jason has a problem at the shopping center which needs another pair of eyes." He pulled a twenty out of his wallet and placed it on the table before he stood up to grab his jacket from the coat hook attached to their booth. "Derek, Brad, it's been a pleasure as always. Son, I'll see you at dinner?"

"Of course, Dad."

"Good," James said as he patted Jarod on the shoulder and waved goodbye to the other men.

As James left the restaurant, Jarod noticed a man in a corner booth who'd been concealed behind James for the duration of the meal. When the man in question put down his newspaper, Jarod recognized him immediately. Dane, James's head of security, watched closely as his employer left the establishment, but he didn't bother getting up to follow James out.

Jarod narrowed his eyes in thought for a moment. Ignoring Dane's presence, Jarod stood and said, "I'll be right back," and headed to the men's room, which was situated around the counter to the right. Jarod casually nodded at Dane as he passed by, not wanting to bring attention to the man, who was sometimes both a help and a hindrance to Jarod's investigations. The retired FBI-turned-bodyguard worked under the radar and used methods which were sometimes inadmissible in court. Jarod's dad liked to encourage Dane's assistance if Jarod was working a difficult case. It was annoying. Jarod liked to do things his way. If he needed help, he'd ask for it.

After taking care of his personal business, Jarod exited the restroom to see Dane still sitting in the corner booth, keeping tabs on Derek and Brad, who had no trouble making conversation with each other. *Strange*, Jarod thought, since Brad had said he didn't know the Lawlors.

Maybe Brad was trying to convince Derek to let them question Aiden? If that was the case, Jarod would leave his mentor to it. Any information Aiden could give would get them closer to finding the bastards responsible.

As Jarod rounded the counter to the left to collect his jacket from the coat hook, he noticed Eli seated on the other end of the restaurant drinking coffee, his empty plate in front of him.

The coffee shop was crowded, so Jarod decided it was possible Eli hadn't noticed them sitting at the booth—until Eli made eye contact with Jarod and continued his surveillance of Brad and Derek.

Interesting. Jarod nodded his acknowledgment to Eli but didn't make a fuss about seeing him, either.

"Well, gentlemen, duty calls. Nice seeing you again, Derek. Brad, I'll catch up with you at the station," he said, putting his own twenty on the table to help cover the bill.

They returned his goodbyes, but neither was in a rush to vacate the booth.

As Jarod walked through the glass door and onto the sidewalk, the sun didn't seem as bright and the day was suddenly less shiny than it had been an hour ago.

What the hell was so interesting about Brad and Derek to have two men watching them so intently?

THE WARM AND COZY BED FELT LIKE A SAFE SHELTER shielding Lauren from the repercussions of her hasty marriage. Lauren was exhausted thinking of all the things she needed to get done today, including writing up a job description for Jarod to post in the paper because, honestly, he didn't know everything her job entailed.

She also needed to change her name, which she was still not used to the idea.

She needed to put her townhouse up for sale. Camille would know whom to list with, which reminded Lauren she needed to pack her personal things and figure out what to do with her furniture and bigger items. Were they going to live at The Estate, or did Jarod have something else in mind?

Plus, there was all the other minutiae she was forgetting, which happened when a woman got married on the fly.

Tap, tap, tap went a finger against her cheek.

"Lorn," whispered a familiar, sweet voice.

"What?" she whispered back.

"What're ya doin' in me and Jar'd's bed?"

Lauren opened her eyes and smiled. "Sleeping, silly."

Jessica smiled broadly. "I missed you guys."

Lauren's heart swelled. "We missed you too, sweet pea."

She kissed the little girl's cheek and gave her a hug before asking, "Should we see what's for breakfast? I'm starving."

Jessica gave her a smacking wet kiss back and climbed off the bed in a rush. "I hafta go potty first," she replied as she ran into the bathroom.

Lauren laughed as she stood from the big bed and stretched before slipping on her robe. She found Jessica in the bathroom standing on a blue stool washing her hands.

"Let's brush our teeth, too, sweet pea. Where's your toothbrush?"

Jessica pointed out the blue one shaped like a puppy, and together they brushed their teeth and washed their faces. Lauren brushed out Jessica's long black hair before they left the bathroom and headed downstairs, not bothering to change out of their pajamas.

It was Monday morning, so the only person they found in

the kitchen was Camille. Jessica ran to her grandmother, who put down the newspaper she'd been reading. Jessica ended up on her lap for kisses and hugs.

"Did you have a good night's sleep, sweetheart?"

Jessica nodded her head. "Lorn was in Jar'd's bed," she informed her grandmother.

"Yes, I suppose she was." Camille glanced at Lauren, who now blushed.

Damn it.

"What would you ladies like for breakfast?"

"Pancakes, Nana," Jessica suggested with her most serious face. Then she added sweetly, "Please?" with her little hands folded tightly in prayer under her chin.

"How about if I do the cooking this morning, Camille? I feel a bit out of sorts."

Camille gave her an assessing look and then nodded her agreement. She turned to Jessica, asking, "What do you say? Should Mommy make your pancakes?"

Jessica turned wide eyes to Lauren. Even though Jessica had said it was "okay" that Lauren was her mommy now, the child had yet to use the term. Lauren held her breath and swallowed, refusing to let the tears suddenly flooding her eyes fall down her cheeks.

Jessica nodded her agreement and laid her head down on Camille's shoulder.

Camille winked at Lauren as if to say, *Give her some time. It's all going to be all right.*

"Okay then," Lauren said under her breath and went to the cupboards as if she knew what she was doing.

Who was she kidding? The only food she knew how to prepare was spaghetti. This was definitely going to be an interesting morning.

LAUREN DROVE THE CAR DOWN MAIN STREET toward the sheriff's office, trying to shake off the last remnants of frustration the department of motor vehicles had bestowed upon her.

She'd been dealing with bureaucratic red tape for the past two days. Who knew you had to jump through so many hoops when you got married?

Getting her legal name changed was only part of what caused her uncertainty. Since Monday, both James and Camille had been calling Lauren "Mommy" whenever Jessica was around, trying to make the little girl comfortable with their changed circumstances. Lauren knew they meant well, but she hoped it wasn't pushing Jessica too much. Jessica had refused to call Jarod "Daddy" for the past month, and now she was being pressed into calling Lauren "Mommy" overnight, even though Jessica's initial reaction to them getting married had been positive.

Lauren took deep breaths, a breathing technique she'd practiced in yoga, to calm down the racing thoughts and panic straining to be let free. She had to keep it cool if she wanted to be a good wife and mother.

Her erratic thoughts were still racing when flashing lights filled her rearview mirror. A fire truck four cars back had everyone pulling over to the right to make room for it.

As she maneuvered her car to the shoulder to let it pass, more emergency vehicles followed behind the pumper truck—an ambulance and Jarod in his cruiser.

What on earth?

Curiosity piqued, she followed Jarod to the scene a few blocks down and three over from Main Street. A crowd had already gathered in the parking lot of the one-story Restful Night Motel.

Smoke billowed from one of the rooms through the broken picture window of the unit. Firemen hosed the blaze. It didn't look like it had been burning for long.

She parked next to Jarod, who spoke into his radio. Eli canvassed the crowd, taking statements. Josie, the motel manager, wrung her hands and shook her head back and forth in disbelief.

As Lauren approached him, Jarod looked up at her in surprise while he finished his radio call.

"Just get here when you've finished up, Brad. I don't know what exactly we're dealing with yet, but I need your eyes here at the scene." He put the mic down and stood up, drawing her in for a quick hug and a peck on the cheek.

"Hey," he said smiling. His blue eyes were covered with his mirrored sunglasses, but she knew they smoldered with memories of their wedding night. She could hear the heat in his voice and feel it in the way he rubbed his thumb over her bottom lip.

"Hey back," she answered, a bit breathlessly. "I followed you from Main. Got my new driver's license. I'm all legal now."

"Yeah? Did you think you weren't legal before?" He teased her ear with his whispered question, which made her giggle.

"You're in a good mood, considering a burning motel room is only a few yards away. Anyone inside?"

His dimple showed before he switched to cop mode. "The fire department was first on the scene. No one saw the renter leave this morning, so we think—"

"One dead, Sheriff. Looks like someone left a burner on in a makeshift kitchen." The fire chief had approached them without Lauren seeing him.

Jarod turned all of his attention to the fire chief now. "Show me."

"Not safe yet. Give us some time to secure the structure, and then you can have at it." With that, the chief walked back to the smoldering room.

As Jarod turned back toward Lauren, Eli made his way to them from the crowd surrounding the scene. His expression was grim, and Jarod tensed up before schooling his features.

"What do you have for me, Eli?"

"Inconsistencies, shadowy figures, and a possible round of gunfire." Eli shook his head and slapped his notebook on his thigh. Lauren had never seen him so frustrated.

Jarod nodded once in understanding before turning his attention on her.

"You can't be here, Lauren."

That stung.

"I know," she assured him with a nod of her head. "Is there anything you need before I head back out to The Estate?"

He seemed to struggle with something before he crowded into her space. "You mean before you go *home*?" he clarified.

She took a deep breath. Licking her lips, she confirmed, "Yes, before I go home."

"Just this."

Before she knew what he was about, he jerked her to him and gave her a kiss that would have her dreaming about him all day long.

JAROD FOLLOWED LAUREN WITH HIS EYES UNTIL SHE was safely in her vehicle. She smiled and gave him a small wave before she backed out of the parking lot and pulled out onto the road to head home.

Home.

As he began to imagine her waiting for him Eli cleared his throat.

Jarod shook off the spell his woman cast upon him every time she was around and gave his attention back to his deputy. Scrutinizing Eli's demeanor, especially over the past few days, Jarod realized he was looking at a man with something on his mind. Eli was a rookie, but he had proven his investigative skills over the past few months, collaring criminals who hadn't been on Jarod's radar.

"What's your gut feeling? And don't hold back."

Eli hesitated, unsure about something. Was it mistrust Jarod saw in the man's eyes? He was about to give him another nudge when Eli finally spoke.

"All right. My gut tells me the body inside is Avery Decatur and that his death isn't accidental."

"I agree. What else?"

Jarod watched the surprise in Eli's eyes before he regained his composure. "I also think this incident is related to crimes involving our current meth problem," Eli said, clearing his throat again. "But I have nothing to back it up."

Jarod looked him in the eye and said, "My gut tells me the same thing, Eli."

Eli's phone rang before either of them could get down to the nitty gritty. He checked the screen and answered with a smile.

"Hey, baby. Everything okay?" Caroline Wallace's voice could be heard on the other end. A smile formed on Jarod's face as Eli began to break out in a sweat.

"What? Are you sure? Okay, I'm on my way right now."

He stuffed his phone in his pocket and took off toward his cruiser.

"Eli?" Jarod yelled.

He stopped in his tracks and ran back to Jarod. "She's in labor... I ... I need to go." Eli was already out of breath.

Jarod patted his shoulder. "Go on, now. Drive safe, and I want an update every hour. Got it?"

"Copy that, boss." Eli turned back to his vehicle and screeched out of the parking lot with lights flashing, scattering the growing crowd of onlookers who were still curious about the fire.

Jarod allowed himself a chuckle before he made his way to the motel room to have a peek inside.

It didn't take a DEA agent to figure out that the "makeshift kitchen" had been hastily put together to represent a meth lab. Jarod was no fire expert, but the equipment didn't look like it had ever been used. It looked too clean, even after being in a fire. There was debris and smoke damage all over, along with water from the sprinkler system and fire truck. Most of the damage centered around the bed where the charred body lay.

The stench turned his stomach.

"Is that gasoline?" Jarod wondered aloud to no one in particular.

"Yes, some sort of accelerant was used, Sheriff. My nose says gas, but we'll have to wait for testing to confirm," the fire chief said. "Thanks to the recently overhauled sprinkler system, the fire didn't spread and it was put out within a half hour."

"Josie had work done recently?"

"Yeah, she didn't make code on her last inspection, so she had it updated about a month ago." He looked around the room before continuing. "I'm no forensic doctor, but the body hasn't been dead for too long."

"No, he hasn't, has he?" Jarod murmured, taking a closer look at the body on the bed. What he found was disturbing.

"Got here as quick as I could, Jarod." Brad said as he sauntered into the room. "Good lord, that stinks."

Jarod looked up at him and asked, "What do you make of this?"

Brad walked over to the body. "Fool lit a cigarette around combustible drug paraphernalia."

"You find the butt?"

Brad raised his eyebrow at Jarod, then looked around the bed and nightstand. Both had considerable damage. "No, but there's a melted ashtray here." He reached for a box of latex gloves and slipped some over his hands. He picked up the ashtray gingerly and studied it.

Jarod scrutinized his friend for a moment before continuing his perusal of the room.

It was clear to him an accelerant had been poured over the body and bed. There was a blackened pathway burned into the cheap motel carpet leading from the bed to the fake lab equipment. It was obvious someone staged the scene—due to the obvious bullet hole in the victim's skull.

He'd seen crime scene photos of two other burned bodies with bullet holes in their skulls recently. They'd belonged to his ex-wife and Michael Trapp.

Jarod now had two problems: a killer who was executing his victims before burning their bodies, and an unsolved drug ring running amuck in Timbisha Township. The victimology suggested they were connected, but Jarod was damned if he knew how. Had Trapp been Avery's backer, and had the deal gone sour? But that didn't make sense because they'd both been killed in the same way. The two criminals had been murdered by the same unidentified suspect, Jarod was certain.

Jarod and Brad worked the room in silence while the fire-fighters and the medical examiner did their thing. The sun was setting when the coroner finally removed the body from the room and hauled it away to the morgue for autopsy. Hopefully, a bullet would be recovered, since none had been found in the room.

They still hadn't found anything to ID the victim, but Eli was right. The fire hadn't burned the corpse entirely because of the new and improved sprinkler system. When the body had been lifted from the bed and moved to the gurney, the under-side of the corpse was briefly revealed, showing minimal fire damage.

Avery had a large dragon tattoo on his upper back and neck. When the techs moved the body from the bed to the bag laid out on the gurney, Jarod could just make out one of the talons on the back of the victim's neck, behind one ear.

He noticed Brad messing around behind one of the nightstands.

"Find anything interesting?"

"No. I thought I saw something, but it's just this old Book of Mormon." Brad lifted the warped and soggy tome and placed it on the nightstand.

Jarod nodded. There wasn't much left for them to do. The forensic team still collected evidence and took pictures. Jarod and Brad were in their way at this point.

"Fine. I'm heading back to the station to finish up my reports, and then I'm calling it a night. You coming?" Jarod asked.

"Yeah, I'll follow you back."

The hairs on Jarod's neck stood up. For years, he'd trusted

Brad Anderson with his life. Throughout his training, Jarod relied on Brad. He respected his mentor. But, for whatever reason, the thought of having Brad at his back now triggered all kinds of warning bells.

Jarod's damn gut feeling was back with nothing to base it on. He decided to start listening to his gut and looking outside the box. Suddenly, Monday morning's breakfast with Derek flashed through his mind.

Was Derek Lawlor somehow involved? Could it be that Brad had a lead but like Eli, he didn't want to share it until he had all of the information first? And why the hell hadn't Brad mentioned the bullet hole—that had been so obvious to Jarod —in the victim's skull? Was it possible he just hadn't seen it?

Jarod had no answers but he sensed he was getting closer to solving Miranda's murder. He could feel it in his bones.

CHAPTER 14
Waking Up In A Trunk

"How many pumpkins are we carving?" Charlie asked, covered from head to foot in stringy pumpkin slime and seeds, which dotted his hair and shoes as well.

"How many do we have so far?" Josh replied with a question of his own. Lauren could almost see the horns growing on his handsome head, and the ornery look on his face guaranteed Charlie was about to get punked.

Charlie looked disgustedly around the yard at all the pumpkins surrounding them.

Lauren had lost count of how many they'd carved so far. Her hand was beginning to cramp, but she was enjoying the warm sunshine and the idyllic setting of the fall day. The sky was a brilliant blue, and not a cloud marred its azure perfection. The trees surrounding the main house were in vibrant shades of red, gold, and orange—colors signifying Timbisha Township had officially reached the other side of summer. The sage and rabbit brush were yellow, their nasty pollen a problem for some people, but not Lauren. The crispness in the air warned that winter wasn't far away. For now, the Old Man still slept.

Charlie, on the other hand, looked like he was getting ready to quit.

"A lot. Where are we putting them all?"

"Mom wants them lining the drive," Josh said matter-of-factly.

Lauren groaned. "That driveway is almost a mile long! How far apart are we spacing them?"

Camille would never want so many jack-o'-lanterns.

"Are you kidding me, Josh?" Charlie whined.

"Nope."

Josh never looked up from the pumpkin he was working on, but Lauren caught the shake of one shoulder, the telltale sign Josh was fibbing.

Charlie's shoulders sagged. "I'll grab the next few from the bin."

When he had gone, Lauren narrowed her eyes. "She doesn't want them lining the driveway, does she?"

"Hell, no." Josh laughed outright now. "She wants them placed sporadically around the yard this year. I want to see how long he'll do this before he figures it out."

"You're a sick man, Josh King," Lauren said, as she finished up the face she was carving.

"I am not sick," he said stubbornly. "I just like pumpkin seeds, and I know Julie is going to roast them."

"Josh, we have like... twenty pumpkins already done. How many seeds do you need, for crying out loud?"

"As many as I can get. Hush now, he's coming back."

Lauren shook her head. Charlie would do anything for Camille, and Josh knew it.

Boys.

Charlie placed five more pumpkins on top of the makeshift plywood-and-sawhorse tables and began cutting into another pumpkin. He had a renewed look of determination on his face, the one he wore when he didn't want to disappoint someone important to him—someone like Camille.

"Holy cow, Josh! I'm going to be roasting seeds 'til Thanksgiving!" Julie announced as she brought a tray of iced tea to the tables. Jessica followed behind her with a plate of cookies that her little blue eyes never left.

Worried the child might trip, Lauren reached with sticky hands to help, but before she could intervene, Julie turned to extricate the plate from Jessica's tiny hands.

"Thank you, sweetheart," Julie said.

"You're welcome, Joojee," Jessica said, eyes following the cookies to the table as if they might get away.

Josh scooped her off her tiny feet and began tickling her. Jessica squealed, "Hunkle Josh! Sto-o-o-op!"

"You were eyeing those cookies like a hawk eyes a mouse, princess! Don't these people feed you around here?"

Julie handed her a cookie before she scolded, "I take insult to that question, Josh. Just look at her. She's grown a foot in the time she's been here."

Josh rotated Jessica in his arms so she was horizontal to the ground, one of his big hands on her chest and other on her thighs. He began to lift her up over his head and down again, like a barbell.

"I don't think she's grown a foot, but she's definitely put on a pound or two."

Jessica laughed without fear as Josh lifted her up and down a few times before placing her on his shoulders. She grabbed his hair with one hand, keeping a tight hold on the cookie with the other.

"Do it 'gain, Hunkle Josh!"

Lauren's eyes misted over. It wasn't that long ago Jessica had been afraid of everyone and kept her giggles and smiles to herself. Now, she was blossoming and learning her place as the princess of the Kings.

"Char-lee, you got icky stuff in your hair."

Charlie put the carving knife down and began to run his pumpkin-smeared fingers around his head. "I do, huh?"

Jessica squealed, "Oh no, you're makin' it worse!"

Charlie gave a quizzical look to Josh and then held up his slimy hands. "I am? Maybe you should help get it out." Then he put his hands up as if he were going to touch Jessica.

Josh laughed before dodging Charlie's hands, all while holding on to his overhead cargo.

"Don't let 'im touch me, Hunkle Josh!"

And away they went, Charlie chasing Josh and Jessica around the yard.

"Charlie must've figured out Josh was messing with him. He would never abandon a job for Camille," Julie said with a fond smile for her little brother.

"You were in on it? What a mean sister you are, Julie Armstrong, my soon-to-be-sister-in-law." Lauren had her hands on her hips in mock reprimand, with a big grin on her face.

Julie sighed with pleasure. "I cannot wait to be Mrs. Jason King."

Before Lauren could reply, a gruff male voice said, "Me either."

Jason, who had suddenly appeared, wrapped his big, tattooed arms around his fiancée and kissed her soundly.

"What are you doing here so early?"

"It's Nevada Day, Jujifruit. Everyone's off today." He kissed the tip of her nose and then turned to Lauren. "What's the plan of attack, Sassy?"

"I think Camille has some ideas about the castle this year."

"Of course she does," Jason said with a wry smile, while he looked around the yard. "Where's my idiot brother?"

Julie laughed. "He's not an idiot! He's playing with Jessica and Charlie."

Jason grunted when the trio ran past them, Jessica squealing and keeping a death grip on Josh's hair. But when she caught sight of Jason, she screamed louder, "Hunkle Jason!"

"Hey, Princess." Jason snatched her from Josh's shoulders so swiftly that she didn't have time to let go of Josh's hair, and he let out a yelp.

Josh gave Jason a dirty look. "Watch it, you big oaf," Josh grumbled, rubbing his battered scalp.

Jason ignored him and gave all his attention to Jessica. "How's Princess Jessica doing today?" He kissed her on the cheek. Jessica proceeded to explain her day to her hunkle Jason, while Julie and Lauren stared avidly.

"My God, that's hot," Julie whispered.

Lauren gave her a knowing look. "Uh huh."

"There's just something endearingly sexy about a hunky, tattooed man who knows how to talk to little girls," Julie sighed.

Lauren could only nod. It was amazing to her how such a strong, gruff man could be so gentle with a tiny person.

"Yeah, there really is. Wait 'til he's holding his own child. Then you'll understand how I feel about Jarod."

She noted Julie's startled expression right before Jarod's cruiser pulled into the driveway and parked in its normal spot on the other side of the house.

Suddenly, all Lauren wanted was to be in his arms. She rushed toward him. The moment he caught sight of her, his footsteps picked up their pace as well.

When she reached him, she didn't hesitate to throw her arms around his neck and hugged him tight. His strong arms enveloped her, making her feel safe and secure. She pulled back to smile at him, but when she did, he pressed his lips against hers, demanding a more passionate welcome.

She gladly accepted. She felt a little dizzy when he ended the kiss with a satisfied smile.

"Hello, my wife."

"Hello back," she said, clearing her throat. "Are you done for the rest of the day?"

"With kissing you? Hardly," he teased and kissed her again.

She laughed and said, "No, are you done playing sheriff for the day? We need help setting up."

"That's what I'm here for." He kissed the tip of her nose, then took her hand to lead her to the house. "I need to get changed first. Maybe you could help me out of this uniform?"

From the blue blaze in his beautiful eyes, she'd be helping him with a lot more than a change of clothes. "I'm happy to oblige, Sheriff."

THE LAWMAN IN JAROD HAD NEVER BEEN A FAN OF his family's traditional Halloween festivities. He saw the potential for danger everywhere. There were always too many people coming and going, and too many hiding places to count. Normally, he'd set his apprehensions aside because they lived in a small community which was normally non-threatening. With the recent murders and the case he was working on, however, he had a bad feeling about the coming night he couldn't shake off.

He eyed Dane, who was situated near James at the other end of the yard. Jarod should have met with the ex-FBI man before the trick-or-treaters began to show up, but he hadn't had time.

He'd been too caught up in Lauren to think clearly.

After absconding with her that afternoon, his mind had been on other things. It was the first time since his daughter arrived that he'd put off greeting Jessica in favor of getting reacquainted with his new wife.

Now he regretted his decision as his home was overtaken by ghosts and goblins. Even some of the adults wore costumes.

Shaking off his regret at not insisting on tighter security measures, he surveilled the growing crowd as dusk began to lengthen the shadows across the yard.

The jack-o'-lanterns were lit up, giving the area an eerie glow. White lights had been strung up in the trees, offering enough backlighting for everyone to see where they were going and whom they were talking to, and some security lights had been set up along the makeshift parking lot in the empty field between the house and corn maze, but it still wasn't enough for Jarod's peace of mind.

His mother always took into consideration the variety of guests who would show up on Halloween night. She made sure that, from stroller to walker, her guests would be entertained and enjoy themselves. Therefore, she had incorporated the arts-and-crafts hay bales for the littler guests, similar to the arrangement Lauren made at the parish dinner. It was situated near some folding tables and chairs so parents could keep their eyes on their children. Near it was the refreshment table, where Julie and Jason were stationed.

They also set up a corn maze for the majority of the trick-or-treaters who entered at one end, got lost a little bit inside, and finally arrived at the other end, where they held their bags out and yelled "Trick or treat!" upon completion. Charlie and a couple of his friends were in charge of the maze.

Jarod and Josh got stuck with haunted castle duty—not Jarod's favorite. The haunted castle was geared toward the older kids and younger teens who liked to get the tar scared out of them. Thankfully, his mother forbade any kind of gore, allowing only jumping out at kids in the dark, tapping them on the shoulder when they least expected it, and chasing them down the dark passageways, which were right up Josh's alley.

Jarod thought it made everything more chaotic, playing on his last nerve.

After getting Jessica dressed in her Cinderella costume, complete with tiara and blonde wig, Lauren sought him out for his inspection.

"Bibby bobby boo, Jar'd!"

"And what is your name, princess?"

"I'm me!" Jessica laughed.

"Is that you, Darlin'? I didn't recognize you with all that blonde hair."

"That's cuz Cinna-rella has yellow hair. And I'm Cinna-rella t'night," she informed him.

"Oh yeah? Well, did you know you're my princess every day?" Jarod bent down on one knee to give her a hug without knocking off her yellow hair.

Jessica hugged him with her little arms tight around his neck.

Lauren's look of admiration fueled the ardor Jarod felt toward her but, in light of the crowded surroundings, he pulled himself together.

"You know you're good with her, right?" Lauren said.

"I..." He didn't know how to respond to her praise. He merely shrugged and kissed her nose. "Thanks for saying so."

"I wanna see Char-lee in the corn. Will ya come with us, Jar'd?" Jessica had one hand on her hip, the other bent with a plastic pumpkin in the crook of her elbow.

"Daddy has to stay at the castle, sweet pea, but I'll take you," Lauren assured her.

"Okay," she pouted, a tiny lip sticking out and her shoulders drooping.

"Charlie has candy," Lauren sing-songed.

"Oh!" Jessica said, doing her happy dance.

"Are you all right? You look like you just sucked on a lemon," Lauren chuckled to Jarod.

"I hate Halloween."

"I didn't know that." She seemed so surprised he had to kiss her again.

"Take care of my princess while I get back to scaring the kids."

"Ten-four, Sheriff." She gave him a sarcastic salute before taking Jessica's hand and leading her to the corn maze.

"Sassy," he muttered.

As his eyes followed their progress across the yard to the maze, Derek and Brad landed in his field of vision. They were having an argument not far from the parking lot. He scanned the rest of the area and found Debbie Lawlor lingering near Camille and some other women from church, but there was no sign of their son, Aiden.

Maybe he was in the castle or maze?

Thinking of the castle, he remembered he needed to return to help Josh. The screams were getting louder, and God only knew what his brother was up to.

Rolling his eyes heavenward in a plea for sanity, Jarod went back inside and got busy scaring the kids.

———

"You know, your face is scaring the kids more than anything I can do in this castle."

"Kiss off, Josh."

It had been two hours, and Jarod's last nerve had been picked at, tossed to the ground, and stomped on. He didn't need Josh's smart-ass remarks goading him into another fight.

"I'm only saying you need to loosen up. What the hell is with you?"

Jarod sighed. Taking in Josh's concerned expression, Jarod admitted, "I'm fine, really. I need to switch with someone. Think Charlie would want in on the castle this year?"

Josh smiled with pride. "Yeah, probably. He's getting ornery enough for it."

Jarod relaxed. Finally, he could leave to find his wife and daughter. "I'll go tell him."

"And leave me here unsupervised? Are you sure you want to do that?" Josh laughed and clapped him on the shoulder as Jarod walked away.

Taking a deep breath of the cool air, he sought out his wife and daughter first. Not spotting the two of them right away, he hurried to the corn maze, stopping every four or five steps to greet members of the community who wanted to wish him a happy Halloween or discuss problems in their neighborhoods. He couldn't blow them off, so by the time he made it to Charlie, he was more than irritated.

"We're switching. Where's Lauren?" he asked gruffly.

Charlie just laughed his bad mood off. "Okay, and I have no clue. What happened to your costume, Grumpy?"

Jarod's first reaction was to snap, but this was Charlie, who unfortunately was taking more and more after Josh. Jarod relaxed his facial muscles into a smile and shook his head at himself for his bad mood. "Sorry, kid. I need a break. Do you mind switching with me?"

"Not at all. Actually, Josh is over in the castle, right?"

"Yeah."

"Cool." Charlie grinned evilly and whistled to two of his buddies from school. When he had their attention, he said, "He's alone. Let's go." The trio started laughing.

"Should I worry about my little brother?"

"Not any more than you normally do, Jarod," Charlie said with a laugh, and they took off toward the castle and the unsuspecting Josh.

Picking up the candy bowl where Charlie set it on the ground, Jarod began handing out candy to the kids filing out of the maze. From this spot, he could see most of the yard and the people still enjoying themselves.

Lauren and Jessica were nowhere in sight.

Getting a prickly feeling, he dug his phone out of his pocket and dialed Lauren's cell. No answer. Then he dialed Jason's.

"Yo," Jason answered.

Without preamble, Jarod asked, "Have you seen my girls?" From his vantage point, he could see Jason looking around the grounds, then he leaned in to Julie, who shook her head and served another piece of pie.

"No, Jarod, I haven't, and neither has Julie. Do you think they went back inside the house? Maybe Jessica had another episode?"

That was Jarod's thought, too. He needed to find them but couldn't leave his candy post.

"Can you send Dad over here? Charlie left me at the maze alone."

"Sure thing." Jason hung up, and Jarod watched as his brother approached James with their request. James got up and headed for the corn maze. Relieved, Jarod put the candy bowl down, not wanting to wait another second to look for his wife and daughter.

He entered the house and called out to them, but no one answered. He checked the Room of Doom, thinking Lauren may have needed more supplies, but upon inspection from the doorway, the room was empty.

He launched himself up the stairs, thinking Jessica may have gotten tired and needed to rest.

"Lauren? Jessica?"

The bedroom was empty. He dialed Lauren's number again. Her cell phone rang from the bathroom. He found it happily dancing on the counter. Putting his hands on his hips, he wondered where they'd gotten to and decided to seek out his mother.

She knows everything.

He found Camille by the crafting tables with the little kids. Jessica had to be there.

"Mom, have you seen Jessica and Lauren?" He cringed at the quaver in his voice.

Turning in surprise, she assessed his harried expression and immediately went on alert. "No," she shook her head. "I thought they were with you?"

Truly beginning to panic, Jarod said, "No, I haven't seen them since they went to the corn maze a couple of hours ago. When's the last time you saw either of them?"

Neighbors listened in on their conversation, and a few even told them when they'd seen his girls last.

Word quickly spread that Lauren and Jessica were missing, and soon their neighbors were all involved in the search. Josh closed down the castle while Charlie and his friends searched the fields. Josh was easy to spot, as his hair was now a glittery shade of pink. Jarod did a double take before getting back to the search.

The minutes ticked slowly by, making Jarod think all kinds of crazy things. Twenty minutes passed before Dane approached him in a rush, followed by the rest of the King family.

"I've got a couple of kids saying they saw Jessica following a boy to the parking lot."

"What?" Jarod almost yelled. "Who? What boy?"

Dane put his arms up in a "calm down" gesture and continued, "By all accounts, the description fits Aiden Lawlor."

Charlie said, "I knew he was up to something. He was acting weird when he got here."

"What do you mean?" Jarod asked.

Charlie shrugged. "He's been quiet since he got busted last month. But tonight he wouldn't even say hello or anything. He didn't go in the maze or the haunted house. He kept looking around like he'd lost something."

Charlie's best friend, Marco, spoke up. "I saw him go in the house, though. I thought he was using the bathroom."

"He was in the main house? Not the portable outhouses we brought in?" James asked.

"Yes sir," Marco said.

"Why do you think he was using the bathroom in the house?" Jarod asked.

Marco shrugged. "Well, I had just heard Lauren explaining

to Jessica that there wouldn't be a line in the house. I figured Aiden must've overheard them and snuck into the house to use one of yours."

Dane spoke to the crowd. "Has anyone seen Aiden?"

Everyone shook their heads.

Jarod's heartbeat sped up.

"How about Derek and Debbie?"

Again, no answer.

Dane leaned into Jarod's ear. "Your deputy was pretty worked up with Derek earlier. Have you seen him lately?"

Jarod's blood turned to ice. "No, but I witnessed the argument as well."

Dane's phone buzzed. He glanced at the screen and excused himself from the group to return a call. Before Jarod lost all semblance of calm, Dane was back and addressing Jarod's father, which really chapped Jarod's hide.

"GPS is up. They're heading south on 95. They've got a good hour's lead on us," Dane announced.

"Who is? Dad, what's going on?" Jarod was livid.

But James ignored him. To Dane he asked, "Why did it take so long to locate her?" He was as furious as Jarod.

"The bug in the tiara just went live, along with the one in her tennis shoe. They're both moving in the same direction, so we know she's wearing both. No telling what the signal problem was, sir." Dane looked distraught.

"What the hell is going on?" Jarod repeated, having had enough of their subterfuge.

James sighed. "I made sure if something happened to Jessica, we'd be able to find her. I asked Dane to place GPS implants in her shoes, her toys, her tiara... in case something like this happened."

Jarod stared his father down before he turned and ran for

his Raptor. An hour was a long time to make up, but he'd break all traffic laws to find his wife and daughter.

As he shoved his keys in the ignition, Jason and Josh slid into the cab. He glared at both of them.

"We're still deputized, remember?" was Jason's only explanation, reminding Jarod he'd deputized them during the Billy debacle. He wasn't sure if their deputized status would stand when he crossed county lines. He didn't care, though. Deep down, he was happy to have their support.

With a nod of his head, Jarod tore out of the parking lot. His father and Dane wouldn't be too far behind, Dane doing whatever it was Dane did. Jarod needed to calm down a little before he let Jason fill him in on what other "security" measures their father put in place behind his back. And Jason would know, too, because James told him everything.

Right now, the only thing that mattered to Jarod was getting his wife and child back. They were his only focus, and by God, if one hair on either of their heads was damaged, there would be hell to pay.

***

Nauseating pain.

Darkness.

Where am I?

The whine of tires on pavement and more pain as the car bumped over ruts in the road.

Lauren mentally took an inventory of her body and found the only pain she suffered was in her head. She could move her fingers and toes, which she thought was a good sign. However, her wrists were bound behind her back, and her face itched around her mouth.

Duct tape!

She was on her side in the trunk of a car, facing the tail lights. She could see the emergency release handle near her feet. It had been cut. She could also make out Jessica's wide blue eyes and tear-streaked face.

She was nestled against Lauren's chest, silently crying. Lauren tried to soothe her, but with the tape on her mouth her words came out as muffled gibberish.

"Mommy!" Jessica cried and hugged Lauren as tightly as her small arms could reach.

"Mff mffkah," Lauren mumbled through the duct tape, as she tried to swallow her panic at their situation. How the hell had they gotten here?

Jessica looked up at her again and said, "What?" through her tears before proceeding to rip the duct tape from Lauren's mouth.

Lauren gasped. She wouldn't need to see her aesthetician for a while.

Before she could ask why Jessica wasn't taped up too, the little girl put her index finger to her lips and whispered, "Sshh. We hafta stay quiet or we getta nuther smack."

Horrified someone had hit Jessica, Lauren's nausea turned to rage.

"Can you untie my hands?" Lauren whispered back.

Without a sound, Jessica reached over Lauren's body to tug on her wrists. She grunted and pulled, but the binding wouldn't come loose. Jessica began to cry silently again as she slid back in front of Lauren.

"Can't get it," she whimpered.

"Baby, it's okay. Don't cry anymore. We'll think of something."

Jessica cuddled up next to her again and silently cried herself to sleep.

WHAT MUST HAVE BEEN HOURS LATER, LAUREN tensed when she felt the car turn onto a dirt road. Her body hurt from being in the same position for too long, and her head still throbbed. The temperature in the trunk had risen to a stifling heat, and Lauren knew the sun was fully up by now. She could see light coming through the seams of the trunk lid, and the tail lights were no longer lit up.

Then the car came to a complete stop and the motor turned off.

Jessica stirred but didn't make a peep. Lauren heard her breaths coming in pants now, and she tried to calm her little girl down. "It'll be okay. Daddy will come as soon as he can," she whispered.

And then a familiar voice said, "We're here, ladies."

When the trunk opened, Brad's handsome face peered in at her.

Her eyes opened wide in surprise. Before she could let him have it he reached in and placed one large hand over her mouth and the other roughly around her neck.

"Jessica. Did you take the tape off of Lauren's mouth?" he scolded. "Tsk, tsk, tsk. You know what happens when you don't do as I say."

Jessica put her small hands to her own mouth and began to silently cry.

"I'll tell you what. If Lauren doesn't make a sound," and here he squeezed her neck to emphasize each word, "then I won't punish you. But if she does," he yanked Lauren out of the trunk by her neck and hair and brought her up to his face, almost nose to nose, "then I'll have to smack you both."

Lauren just glared at him.

"Okay, then," he said as he let her go with a small shove. "Get out of the car, Jessica. You know the drill."

Lauren winced when he roughly grabbed her bound elbow and pulled her toward an old house. It had chipped yellow paint and a squatty, flat roof that reminded her of 1950s military housing.

Lauren took stock of her surroundings. They were in an old neighborhood with houses of similar condition, shape, and size. There were no sidewalks, and most of the driveways were dirt. The yard had probably once been covered with lawn at some point because broken cement mow strips still circled the old trees.

As they kept walking, the trees parted between the houses and she could just make out the Las Vegas skyline on the other side of the valley.

"Hurry up, Jessica. You're trying my patience, girl."

Jessica hurried to lift up an old pot in the dirt next to the cement porch leading to the front door. Lauren looked around, but found no other vehicles on the street and no movement from any of the homes. Jessica retrieved a key and reached up to the doorknob.

Brad pushed her out of the way to work the key and opened the door. He shoved Lauren inside, never taking his hand off of her arm.

Her shoulders ached from her arms being tied behind her back for too long. She wriggled her hands and fingers until they tingled a little. She subtly pulled her wrists apart to loosen the awful tape. They were still held together tightly. The adhesive was strong, and she could feel all the hairs on her arm being yanked out of her skin. She ignored the pain and kept flexing.

"Get your little ass in here, Jessica, and shut the door!"

Jessica scrambled in and slammed the door.

Lauren, not really a patient person when she was being kidnapped, snapped. "What the hell are we doing here, Brad? And unbind my hands right now!"

With lightning speed, Brad backhanded her, causing her to see stars for a moment. Jessica ran to Lauren where she landed on her rear. Tears fell freely down the child's precious cheeks.

"Jessica, explain to Lauren what happens when she speaks without being spoken to."

Jessica looked her in the eyes and whimpered, "You'll getta smack."

Tasting blood, Lauren glared at Brad, who raised an eyebrow at her. He sauntered over and squatted in front of her, his hands casually resting on his knees.

"Now, Mrs. King, I understand this is new to you, so I'll explain the rules. It's very, very simple, so listen up. You do what I say, when I say. You do not speak unless I give you permission to do so. And any attempt to leave my company will be met with harsh punishment."

She looked at Jessica and saw the beginnings of a bruise on the little girl's temple. Lauren glared back at Brad and saw only his smug expression.

She summoned all of her will to remain calm and think this through without trying to kill Brad herself. She didn't know how long it would take Jarod to get here, so she had to bide her time and remain alive until he did. She had no doubt her husband was on his way.

She breathed through her nose and out her mouth very

slowly. Then she gave Brad a curt nod, indicating she understood his "rules."

His smile would have been beautiful if it weren't for the cruelty in his eyes. How had she never notice it before?

He reached down and toyed with her hair. "You're a very pretty woman, Lauren. Jarod is one lucky son of a bitch." Then he grabbed a handful of hair, his fingernails scraping her scalp in the process, and brought her up to his face once more.

"It would be a shame to have to rearrange a few of your lovely features, wouldn't it? And make no mistake, Lauren. I will hurt you."

He shoved her back to the floor and stood up.

"Well," he clapped his hands once and rubbed them together. "Shall we get started then?"

CHAPTER 15
Secret House

"Slow down before you kill us, Jarod."

He gave Jason a hard look before he acquiesced and let up on the accelerator. He watched the speedometer needle fall to eighty-three miles per hour and grunted.

His brothers had been quiet for a while, and Jarod was thankful for the time to think. The problem had been under his nose the whole time, but he just couldn't make the pieces fit together. Or maybe he didn't want to. The uncomfortable theory that somehow Brad Anderson, his mentor and friend, was involved in a drug ring seemed too far-fetched to consider. The man had passed up being sheriff and basically handed the job to Jarod. Why had he done that?

"I know that face," Jason said. "Out with it, Jarod, before you pop a blood vessel."

When Jarod continued to stare out the windshield, he felt Josh's hand on his shoulder.

"I want to find her as badly as you do. If you have any ideas, let's hear it. Maybe we can help figure this out."

Glancing at his little brother in the rearview mirror, Jarod tried to sort out the situation as best he could. Before he could say anything, Jason's cell phone rang.

"You find out anything, Dad? Yeah... That's good news."

Jarod glanced at him with a raised eyebrow. "What is it?"

"Dane's contacts say Jessica's GPS signal has stopped moving. They have an address. Hold on... what, Dad? Say that again?"

Jarod sat impatient as Jason took his sweet time talking to James. Again, Dane had come to the rescue.

"What should we do, then? Okay, I'll let him know. What's the address?" Jason used a pen he'd found in a cup holder to write something on his hand. "Got it. Yeah, we just hit Indian Springs, and Jarod's foot is getting heavier the closer we get to Vegas. Yeah, see you then, Dad."

"Well?" Josh asked.

Jason actually chuckled, pissing Jarod off.

"You think this is funny?" he asked disgustedly.

"No, it's not funny at all," Jason replied.

"I swear to God, Jason, I'm coming over this seat and kicking your ass if you don't spit it out!" This from Josh.

Jason turned in his seat and glared green sparks at their little pink-haired brother, whose glittering coiffure was a distraction, to say the least. "Yeah, like that's going to happen, Bubblicious." Jason tsked and shook his head.

"Charlie's a dead man," Josh muttered.

Jason rolled his eyes before turning back to Jarod. "Lawlor has been under federal investigation for several years."

Jarod squinted at Jason. "For what?"

At the same time, Josh asked, "What does that have to do with Lauren and Jessica?"

"Shut up and let me finish. It seems Derek has been padding his books. The few mines he still keeps operational aren't producing as much as he's been reporting. He's getting money from somewhere, but no one knows where. Dad suspected something after Derek paid us his deposit in cash but then asked for the terms of the contract to be changed after we started work on Molly's. The IRS suspects tax evasion and money laundering, but they don't have enough evidence, whatever that means. They keep auditing him, but he's been a clever bastard. Isn't that lovely?" he asked sarcastically. "But because the feds have been focused on Derek and his business ventures, Timbisha Township became fascinating to the DEA."

"Meth," Jarod muttered.

"Exactly. And somewhere along the line, Derek's name came up in an undercover sting in Vegas," Jason paused. "When Miranda was killed, it started the whole thing in motion."

"Are you saying Derek kidnapped my daughter?" Jarod was getting frustrated.

Jason shrugged and said, "Dane said two other names are also associated with the DEA task force investigating the Lawlors—Avery Decatur and your deputy mentor, Brad Anderson."

They were on the outskirts of Las Vegas now, and Jarod lost all of his patience before Jason had even talked to James.

Snapping at his brother, he demanded, "Where's my family, Jason?" Jarod didn't care about the murders or the case anymore. He just wanted his girls back.

"The GPS in Jessica's sneaker is blinking happily at the address I've got right here," he held up his palm. "But Jarod, Dane's sources say it's at the same location as one of your department's county vehicles."

Jarod saw red. "Brad's?"

"Yes."

"If he's hurt them, I will kill that son of a bitch."

"You won't get near him. The feds are already on site. Here's where we need to meet up with Dad and Dane."

"How are they there already?"

Jason shook his head and chuckled. "Plane, you idiot."

"We could've flown? Are you serious?" Josh was completely put out.

Jarod said nothing. His county had been under federal investigation for years, and no one from the government had contacted him. He wondered who the undercover agent or agents were. He'd like to give them a piece of his mind.

Once inside the city limits, Jason put the address in the Raptor's GPS mapping system. Josh seemed more relaxed in the back seat now that they knew help had already arrived. They would be late to the party, so to speak. But if the plane had gotten there so early, why hadn't they apprehended Brad already? What were they waiting for?

LAUREN SAT ON THE DIRTY FLOOR AND WATCHED Brad through new eyes. He wasn't the handsome and charming deputy Jarod relied on. No, he was something altogether different, and Lauren was having trouble coming to grips with this new persona. Her natural defense had always been a smart mouth and feigned confidence. She couldn't use either of those now to get out of this mess, especially not with Jessica to protect.

Brad had just insisted they should start whatever the hell he planned on doing, but given no further direction. She badly wanted to tell him to screw off but she wouldn't risk Jessica being hurt if she spoke without his permission.

Scumbag.

So she glared with all her might... which was nothing in the grand scheme of things. It made her feel better to let him see her wrath, though. Because as soon as she got the opportunity, she was going to kill the bastard.

Or die trying.

Jessica clung to her with her head hidden away from Brad against Lauren's shoulder. It was difficult with her hands still bound behind her, but Lauren managed to give Brad the evil eye while quietly rocking her little girl back and forth.

At last, he grinned. "All that anger is turning me on, Mrs. King. Hmm, that name really doesn't fit you. I prefer your old name, Lauren Lockwood. That's a porn star's name if I ever heard one."

He was baiting her and she knew it. She took a deep breath and schooled her features. Reacting to him wouldn't be smart, and since his comment didn't require an answer, she held her tongue.

Assessing them as they sat on the floor, he said, "Where did they hide my money, Jessica?"

Jessica tightened her hold on Lauren. She slowly turned around to look at Brad.

"I dunno," she whispered, shaking her head back and forth.

Brad squinted at them for a minute before he looked around the filthy house. Lauren couldn't believe this was where Jessica had come from.

Finally, Brad perked up and asked, "Where did the police find you hiding when Miranda died?"

Jessica's eyes opened wide and her lip quivered, but she shook her head again.

Lauren didn't see the backhand coming before it collided

with the side of her head, the pain momentarily leaving her blinded. Again.

Jessica screamed.

"Quiet down." Brad's voice was deathly calm, but there was no mercy in his eyes. "You want me to kill this mommy, too?"

Lauren's eyes flared. Had he admitted to killing Miranda? If so, they'd both be dead as soon as he found what he was looking for.

"Not this mommy! Don't hurt my Lorn mommy!"

"THEN TELL ME WHERE YOU WERE HIDING!"

Brad balled his fingers into a fist and cocked his elbow back, ready to strike. Lauren braced herself for the punch that would knock her out.

"It's a secret!" Jessica yelled, tears streaming down her baby bird face. "Mommy made me promise." She cried in earnest now.

Brad dropped his fist and talked to Jessica like she was his new best friend.

"You made a promise to your dead mommy? Well, I understand promises. But it doesn't count anymore because she's dead, Jessica. You can tell me where you hid and show me what else is hidden there." His voice became a hard edge when he talked about his money.

Jessica looked at Lauren. She gave her an encouraging smile, and whispered, "It's okay, sweet pea. Show him what he wants to know." Lauren swallowed as the big fat tears fell down Jessica's face.

Anger swept over her, and before she could stop herself, she said, "Don't worry, Jessica. Daddy will be here soon." She looked Brad in the eye and saw his fear momentarily before his cruelty took over again.

"Yeah, Jessica. You can leave when *Daddy* gets here," he sneered.

Jessica was unsteady, but when Brad grabbed her behind the neck, she picked up her feet and started into the other room.

Lauren began to fight the bindings in earnest now. No way was she going to let that monster be alone with her little girl.

Feeling wetness around her hands, she knew she was bleeding as the tape ripped from her skin. She slid one hand free and nearly screamed as pain shot through her shoulders. Her arms had been bound for hours, and she didn't know if they would be of any use for a while.

Searching for something to use as a weapon, she rummaged through the filthy kitchen until she found a paring knife. It was small, but it was better than nothing. It might give her time to get away from the maniac.

She wrapped her fingers around the sticky handle to make sure they still worked. Her grip was loose. She shook out her arms, wincing at the pain, and tried again. The more she worked her hands, the stronger her grip became.

She'd been slowly making progress down the dim hallway as she mastered her grip on the handle of the tiny knife.

Some heroine I am.

Shoving her insecurities back, she listened for voices. She heard Brad's harsh demands and Jessica's whimpers before something ground against the floor in one of the bedrooms.

She peeked in one of the doorways in the middle of the hallway and spied Brad dragging a large wooden box out of the closet.

"This is where you hid?" He pointed at the box with disbelief in his voice. Lifting the lid, he said angrily, "There's nothing in here but dirty blankets and this old bear."

Jessica stood with wide eyes. "That's my secret house," she whispered. "Teddy lives there."

He threw the bear at her, hitting her in the face. It knocked her down, but Jessica scrambled to pick up the bear and hugged it to her with all her might. "There there, Teddy," she cried into the bear's ear.

Lauren had seen enough. Before Brad could do anything else to hurt Jessica, Lauren let out a roar, surprising him. When he whipped around, he reached behind his back for something, but she shoved the dirty knife into his right shoulder with all of her might. She didn't stop to see whether she'd killed him or not. She used her momentum to scoop up Jessica, and she ran out of the room and down the hallway as fast as her weakened legs could take them.

"YOU BITCH!" he screamed, but she'd already made it through the front room. She was out the front door before his heavy footsteps ran down the short hallway behind her. She jumped off the front porch and heard a gunshot come from the house at the same time a tree branch snagged her arm. The pain was like a hot poker stabbing through the meat of her bicep, but she didn't falter.

Before she cleared the yard, flashing lights and men with assault weapons surrounded the property.

Two things happened at once. She dropped to the ground as a tactical team pointed their guns at the house and yelled into a bullhorn, "PUT DOWN YOUR WEAPON." And, from behind her, Brad yelled, "You're dead, Mrs. King!"

Both parties opened fire as she and Jessica huddled on the ground, Lauren's body covering her little girl's. What felt like hours were only seconds before strong hands lifted her from the ground and a male voice asked, "Are you hurt, Mrs. King?"

She looked at the man in black tactical gear. "I'm fine, we're fine. Where's my husband?"

Not waiting for an answer, she tried to step away from the stranger to look for Jarod.

"Ma'am, you're bleeding. Let's get you looked at," he said as he lifted her arm and escorted her to an ambulance.

"What? No, I'm fine. I just need my husband." She jerked her arm away from the man, nearly dropping her daughter. She would never let her go again. She didn't want these strangers touching her or Jessica. She wanted to find Jarod. He would take them home.

Where the hell was he?

Starting to feel a bit dizzy, she had to fight to keep her hold on Jessica, but she needn't have worried—her little girl was wrapped around her like a spider monkey, the teddy bear sandwiched between them. People were talking to her, but she tried to fight them and get away. She didn't want these strangers.

She wanted Jarod.

She thought she heard someone call her name, but she spun around and couldn't find any familiar faces. They were leading her back to the ambulance when she heard it again.

"Let me through, that's my wife!"

She turned a full circle and there, quickly striding toward her, was the man she'd loved all her life but who did not love her in return. That was okay, though, because he was here to take her home.

"Jarod, there you are," she murmured, right before the lights went out.

JAROD BROKE OUT IN A SPRINT WHEN LAUREN'S LEGS buckled beneath her. The men surrounding her didn't allow her head to hit the ground, but he didn't want them touching her.

She's mine.

One of the S.W.A.T. men caught Jessica before she fell from Lauren's arms and set her safely on the ground. When she spied Jarod, her little feet ran straight into his arms.

"Daddy!"

Jarod had longed to hear her call him that but wished it were under different circumstances. "I'm here, Darlin'. Daddy's here," he cooed as he followed the stretcher carrying his wounded wife to the ambulance. Bruises covered Lauren's face and there was blood all over her. Jessica was covered in blood, too. "Are you hurt, Jessica? Is this blood yours?"

He began to examine her when he noticed the teddy bear. It was a cheap stuffed bear, much like a carnival prize. It looked clean and new except for his wife's blood mixed into the blue fur.

"Where'd this come from, Darlin'?"

"It's Teddy. He couldn't come with me before, but now I got 'im and I'm keepin' 'im safe from now on," she informed him.

He kissed her forehead and hugged her tightly as he approached the ambulance, and asked one of the technicians, "What's wrong with my wife?"

"She's suffered some head trauma and she has a gunshot wound to the upper arm. We're taking her to UMC Trauma Center, sir," said the EMT who was currently setting up an I.V. bag.

"I'm coming with you," Jarod said, as he attempted to climb into the ambulance.

"Sir, I'm sorry, there's no room. We need to work on your wife. I promise we're going to take good care of her. We need to leave now."

"Wait a—" Jarod began to argue, but the doors shut in his face and the vehicle pulled out onto the street, its siren whirring.

"Come on, son. We need to get to UMC. Give your keys to Jason." His father held out his hand. "He'll follow us in your truck."

Stunned, he reached into his pocket and grabbed his keys while he kept a death grip on his daughter.

"Don't worry, Jarod. I know Sassy. She's going to be fine," Josh said, his voice breaking every other word as he followed Jason back to the Raptor.

While Josh and Jason climbed into his truck, James got them buckled into the back of a government-issue black Escalade. Dane sat behind the wheel as James got into the back-seat with Jarod and Jessica. Without a carseat, they managed to buckle her into the center space while she clung to Jarod's side.

He didn't mind. If he'd had it his way, he would've held her all the way to the hospital, carseat laws be damned. What would they do, ticket him?

He shook his head at his rambling thoughts.

"What happened to Brad?" Jarod asked dully. He felt Jessica tense up at the asshole's name, and Jarod barely kept his control leashed.

"Suicide by cop," Dane said. "Well, maybe not suicide. It didn't look to me like he was paying any attention to the authorities surrounding him. His main focus was on Lauren."

At the mention of his wife's name, Jarod's worry came back tenfold. She'd risked her life to protect his daughter. But more than that, he didn't know what he'd do without her. All he could see was her smiling face and hear her self-assured wit, even when she wasn't so confident—and all he wanted to do was hold her close and never let her go. If she died, he'd never live through it.

I can't lose you now, Sassy.

"What do you have in your hands, Jessica?" his father gently asked.

Jessica rubbed her nose on Jarod's shirt before turning toward her grandfather.

"Teddy," she whispered.

"Yeah?" He smiled. "I had a teddy bear growing up. He was my best friend for a while. Is he your friend?"

"Uh huh," she said, and then in barely above a whisper, "He guards the treasure."

Jarod looked down at his daughter before raising an eyebrow at his dad. "What treasure, Darlin'?"

"Mommy and Big Mike's treasure. Teddy is very brave. He hadda have a op-ray-shun an' everything."

"An *operation*?" James clarified.

"Uh huh. Mommy had to put stitches in his tummy. See?" She held up her toy to her grandpa.

James reached out to take the bear, but Jessica pulled it back protectively. "Ya hafta be careful with 'im, 'kay Papa?"

"Of course, honey. I promise I'll be very careful," he said.

Jarod watched as his father squeezed the bear between his forefingers and thumbs. Both men heard paper crinkling inside.

James confirmed, "I feel something small and hard in there as well." Then he handed the bear back to Jessica. "Thank you for letting me examine your teddy."

"Welcome," she said, hugging the bear and turning to put her head back against Jarod's side. "I wanna see Mommy."

"We're going to see her now, Darlin'," he confirmed. He just hoped she was awake when they arrived.

AN ADMIN ASSISTANT USHERED THEM TO A BLESSEDLY quiet waiting room. Jessica kept asking for her mommy and cried when told she couldn't see her yet.

Jarod understood how she felt. If they didn't let him see Lauren soon, he was going to punch something.

"We got us rooms at the Belagio," Josh said, once he was seated in a plastic chair.

"Good," James answered. "I'll call your mother when we have more information on Lauren."

"Where'd you two run off to?" Jarod asked Jason, who sat down across from them and handed Jarod a bag.

"We went to Walmart to pick up some clothes for the princess."

"Thank you." Jarod hadn't thought beyond getting his wife and daughter back. Taking a closer look at his little girl, he grimaced at the dried blood and filth covering her Cinderella costume.

"I picked up some of those wipey things, too," Josh said. "At least we can wash her face and put her in some clean clothes."

Jarod found the wipes and tried to get the dirt off of Jessica's face, who didn't complain, even when Jarod discovered a few bruises. Rage unlike anything he'd ever felt rolled off him in waves. When he met his father's and brothers' eyes their expressions matched what he felt. None of them said a word in deference to Jessica, who'd been traumatized enough.

For her, Jarod kept his cool. Brad was dead. There was nothing left to do about it.

As a satisfying thought of smashing Brad's skull floated through his mind, a nurse entered the waiting room. "Mr. King?" she inquired.

"Yes," all four of them answered.

Jarod rolled her eyes. "I'm pretty sure she means me."

"Are you Lauren's husband?"

"Yes, how is she?" He stood up while Josh finished dressing Jessica.

"She's stable. The bullet in her arm went straight through and no bones were broken, and there was no substantial bleeding found. She has some abrasions on her wrists from the duct tape she says was used to bind her hands behind her back. She's in some pain, so we've given her meds to control it."

"Is she awake?" Jarod asked.

"Yes, and she's been asking for you and your daughter. We're moving her to a room as soon as she's finished with her CT scan. The doctor wants to rule out any skull fractures or brain hemorrhage due to her concussion, which is substantial. We're keeping her overnight as a precaution."

"How long before she's in her room?" Josh asked. He'd finished dressing Jessica, who was now safely ensconced in Jason's arms.

"Give us thirty minutes or so, but you all can head up to room two-twelve right now to wait for her." She smiled as she left for parts unknown.

Josh and James began gathering up the bags as Jason reassured Jessica she would see her mommy soon.

CHAPTER 16

Lost And Found

She felt the weight of her body press into the gurney's thin mattress when the narcotics from the IV entered her vein. She hated the feeling, but it was better than the burning in her arm and the massive jackhammer pounding through her skull. She could have sworn her nurses were twins before she realized there was only one of them.

That can't be good.

Where's Jessica? Where's Jarod? Why isn't he here with me now?

She hated hospitals. She hated being sick. She needed him, but then she remembered he didn't love her, so it would make sense for him not to be here.

Still, she wished she could gaze into his blue eyes and let them lull her to sleep so this headache would go away.

"Mrs. King, we're taking you to your room now. The doctor will see you again after he's had a chance to look at your scan," one of the twin nurses said.

"Is my husband here?" She hated to sound so whiny, but she really needed him. Her panic sat patiently waiting to consume her behind the thin curtain of chemical pain relief now flowing freely through her circulatory system. She breathed deeply, but the oxygen made her dizzy.

Good thing she was already lying down.

"I don't know, but I'll have someone check the waiting rooms for him."

Lauren watched the fluorescent lights pass by one after the other until they made a white blur along the ceiling. She really needed to concentrate on her surroundings if she was going to find Jarod.

How did I get here?

Frightening images flashed in her mind, like someone surfing channels on the television. She wanted control of the remote so she could focus on only one picture and remember. She'd forgotten something important, but for the life of her she couldn't recall what it was. She closed her eyes for a moment and a beautiful blue hummingbird hovered in front of her mind's eye.

No, that's not right.

It wasn't a bird.

A tiny face with blue eyes appeared. It smiled and called her "mommy."

"Jessica!" Lauren nearly toppled off the gurney looking for her daughter.

"Whoa, Mrs. King. Please lie back down. We're almost to your room."

"No, you don't understand! I've lost my daughter," she pleaded. "She's just a baby, please, I have to find her!"

Lauren began to get off the gurney, but the nurse was having none of it. "Lie back down, Mrs. King. We'll find your daughter," she coaxed.

"Mommy!"

Lauren looked around and saw Jarod and Jessica rushing down the hallway. Relief made her collapse back to the gurney, but Jarod was there with Jessica in his arms before she had time to hit the pillow. He gathered her to them for the best group hug ever.

"Mommy, mommy, mommy," Jessica said over and over as Jarod allowed the little girl to slide onto the gurney with Lauren.

"My God, woman, I thought I'd lost you," he choked out. He showered her with kisses, making her feel as though she'd gone to heaven.

"Please, Mr. King. Let me get your wife settled in her bed," Nurse Ratched said, pushing him back.

Lauren really didn't like her anymore.

"Of course," he said before clearing his throat.

Is he crying?

Nah. She was still dreaming from the wonderful poison dripping through her IV line.

The nurse maneuvered Lauren's gurney into a private room where all the King men waited, along with the elusive Dane. After making the transfer from the gurney to the bed, which was no easy task with five large men, one small girl, and an IV stand to dance with, the nurse heaved a sigh of relief and left with the empty gurney.

Jessica had transferred along with Lauren onto the hospital bed and made herself at home cuddled up to her side. Relieved she'd found her little girl, Lauren let the tears slide down her cheeks.

Jarod, now at her side, didn't waste time wiping them away.

"Do you want me to move her? Is she hurting you?"

"No, she's perfect. I just missed her." Lauren looked into Jarod's eyes and admitted, "I missed you, too... so much."

He smiled at her and continued to trail the backs of his fingers over her face, careful not to touch the sore spot on her cheek or her swollen bottom lip.

Someone at the foot of the bed rubbed her foot through the thin hospital blanket. Her gaze shifted to Josh, who smiled weakly.

"Good to have you back, Sassy."

"It's good to be back."

"What happened?" Jason asked. "How did Brad snatch you?"

Lauren closed her eyes, not wanting to rehash the nightmare that had led her to a hospital bed in Las Vegas. But if she didn't get it out, it would haunt her.

Jarod still gently stroked her head, making her feel safe, while Jessica was tucked up tightly to her side. Lauren glanced at Jessica's perfect little face and noted she'd fallen asleep. A tear squeezed out of her eye, stinging a trail down her cheek, where Jarod wiped it away.

"You don't have to talk if you don't want to," he whispered.

"No, it's all right. I need to get this over with," she sniffed, mentally preparing herself for the story.

She smiled, indicating to Jessica before her explanation. "She had to go potty and was getting pretty adamant about using one of the rented blue outhouses." She paused, remembering the little argument they'd had and chuckled. "This girl is obsessed with the color blue."

"We know," they all said together.

She let out a small laugh before she continued, "Well, she was doing the pee-pee dance, and I figured she'd never be able to hold it long enough to make it to one across the yard. The line was pretty long, too. I knew she didn't want to have an accident in her costume, so it was easy to get her to go in the house, which was much closer."

"Pee-pee dance?" James asked

"It means she had to go really bad, Dad," Josh laughed.

"Oh."

"Anyway, after using the bathroom upstairs, Aiden met up with us in the utility room on our way out. He said Charlie asked him if he could fetch Jessica and bring her back to the corn maze to see him."

"Aiden Lawlor?" James clarified.

Swallowing the lump in her throat caused by her embarrassment over such stupidity, she nodded her head. It took a moment to calm her emotions.

Josh rubbed her foot again and encouraged, "You're doing great, Lauren."

Trying to push the horror of seeing Jessica heading to the parking lot instead of the corn maze with that horrible boy, she continued to explain what she'd witnessed.

"He spoke to her like he knew her, and she went willingly, with no signs of panic like she'd displayed at the harvest dinner. I thought she was fine. I'm such an idiot. Jarod, I'm so sorry." She started crying and clutched Jessica tighter, who snuggled more deeply into the side of her body.

Jarod bent down and kissed her forehead, whispering, "You couldn't have known, love."

The endearment had her heart speeding up for all to hear, thanks to the monitors attached to her blood pressure cuff, which had chosen that moment to take a reading.

"What happened next, Mrs. King?" said Dane, who'd been

quiet until now. Lauren had forgotten about the man until he'd spoken up.

"I tracked their progress halfway to the corn maze when my attention was distracted by some kids screaming in the haunted house. I only took my eyes off of her for a moment, but when I looked back, they were no longer heading for the maze. He'd switched direction and was heading toward the parking lot, so I ran to catch up. By the time I got there, I yelled at him. He stopped and turned, but before I could ask him where the hell he thought he was taking her, something smashed into my head. When I woke up, we were in the trunk of a car."

Jarod entwined his fingers in the hand she had resting on Jessica's back and kissed her knuckles. Her wrist was bandaged where the duct tape had worn away her skin. He gently placed soft kisses on the gauze. "I'd kill that son-of-a-bitch all over again if I could," he said through clenched teeth.

"I know," she whispered.

"No one else was there? Just Brad?" Jason asked this time.

"Yes. He was alone." She thought for a moment, remembering Jessica's terror and her knowledge of the *rules*, which Lauren explained to everyone.

"Jessica already knew him, Jarod. She was terrified of him."

Jarod glanced at his little girl and frowned.

"That explains her behavior at the dinner, too," James said. "Brad had come in with Eli before you'd arrived. He must've spoken with her, maybe threatened her."

"He's dead now. We'll never know what happened," Jason confirmed.

She watched as light dawned in her husband's eyes and he shook his head. "Why didn't I see it before?" he asked himself quietly.

"Because you were too close to it," Dane said. "He'd

manipulated the situation from the start. He put you in a position he could control because you trusted him. He banked on your friendship to blind you to what was really happening in Timbisha Township. If it weren't for the FBI's informant, we wouldn't have known exactly where to look."

"What do you mean by 'we'? I thought you were retired?" Jarod asked.

Dane sighed. "I am, but when my niece came to me with suspicions about the sheriff's department being connected to Timbisha's drug problem, I made some calls. I've been consulting on the task force for a while now." He grinned. "But I'm glad it's over now."

"Your niece?" Josh asked.

Dane looked around the room. Lauren wasn't sure whether he wanted to speak or not, until he admitted, "When my sister's husband died, I came to Timbisha Township to be near them. However, in order to do that, I had to take an early retirement from the bureau. Thankfully, James hired me on so I was able to stay near the only family I have left."

Lauren asked, "Marguerite Theroux is your niece, isn't she?"

Dane chuckled. "Are you sure you don't want to go into private investigation, Mrs. King?"

"She's sure," Jarod answered for her. He kissed her forehead and sighed. "Keep going, Dane. The pieces are fitting together now, but I want you to confirm Brad's relationship with Derek."

With a nod, he continued. "It's a simple one, really. Derek had the means to distribute the meth through his mining company, and Brad took advantage of Derek's need for cash." Dane ended on a shrug.

"And Trapp? How did he and Miranda play into all of this?" James asked.

"I can answer that one, Dad," Jarod said. "Michael Trapp was the producer." At his father's blank stare, he added, "The cook, like the Walter White character in *Breaking Bad*. He was the scientist behind the production of the drug. I knew Trapp in school. He was pretty smart in science and chemistry, but he hung out with the wrong crowd, made a lot of poor choices growing up. Miranda knew him from school, too. I'm sure once she realized how much money was involved, she began to take a piece for herself."

James thought for a moment and said, "We need to find out what's in that teddy bear."

"What teddy bear?" Lauren asked. When James pointed to Jessica, Lauren noticed the blue stuffed animal stuck between the two of them. "She had this when we ran out of the house." She fished it out from between their bodies. Jessica didn't seem to realize it was gone, she was so deeply asleep.

Lauren kissed her forehead. They'd been through so much in the past twenty-four hours it was no wonder Jessica had crashed.

"Let me take that, Mrs. King," Dane said.

She handed it to the ex-FBI agent and watched as he squished the bear between his fingers. Right before Dane was about to pry open the stuffed toy's belly, James cleared his throat.

"You can't rip it open like that. My granddaughter will be devastated, and she's been through enough. We need to find someone with some scissors and thread to repair it."

Dane raised his eyebrows in disbelief before nodding his agreement.

"I'll go see what the nurses can do for us," Josh said before he left the room.

Lauren smiled to herself. If anyone could persuade a nurse to do surgery on a teddy bear, it would be Josh. He'd probably get a phone number or two in the process.

JAROD WATCHED AS JOSH HURRIED OUT OF THE ROOM to charm a nurse into doing his bidding. His eyes swung back to Lauren and his rage came back in full force.

A bruise ran along the side of her left cheek and her swollen bottom lip was cut. The bruises on her neck were unmistakable —fingerprints where Brad tried to choke her.

Jessica hadn't fared any better. The bruises he'd uncovered in the waiting room had grown more pronounced, but her emotional state suffered the most damage. She now clung to her mother like a lifeline. Her little fingers tightened and loosened in Lauren's hospital gown. Even in sleep, she burrowed into the shelter of her mother's protective body. Every now and then, a small whimper would issue from her lips.

How he wasn't breaking things and howling like a madman was beyond him. Somewhere between Timbisha and Tonopah, he'd realized he couldn't live without either of them. Speeding down Highway 95 into Las Vegas, he'd vowed to never let Lauren go. He'd lost one wife and, by God, he wouldn't lose another one. Lauren had become his everything.

Even bruised, beaten, and shot, she was the most beautiful thing he'd ever seen. Watching Jessica claim her as her mother made him realize how much he loved them both.

Love?

He thought he would never love another woman, but

damn it, he *loved* Lauren more than he'd ever loved another woman in his life.

His mother was right. What he'd felt for Miranda had been nothing more than a teenager's infatuation, as immature as the boy he'd been. He'd let the divorce sour his outlook on the female persuasion, another sign of his immaturity.

Now, looking at the two battered and bruised women lying together in the hospital bed, his soul ached. They were his, and he'd failed to protect them. He vowed never to risk them again.

Giggles from the hallway drew him out of his rumination. Josh's low voice was charming as he and a very blonde nurse came through the doorway. She was attractive, even in her nurse's scrubs, and she carried a small kit in her hand.

"Valerie has agreed to perform surgery on Teddy," he said.

"Surgery," she giggled while shaking her head. "Let's see the patient." She then turned startled eyes to all the men in the room and whispered an "Oh my" under her breath.

James handed her the bear while issuing directions to preserve the toy as best she could, for his granddaughter's sake.

"Let's see what we've got in here," she murmured as she delicately cut the seams.

All eyes in the room watched as she broke through the threads and opened up the teddy bear's stomach. She pulled out a white envelope. With a question in her eyes, she handed it to Jarod.

Josh said, "Thank you, Valerie. You have a delicate hand, but do you think Teddy will have a scar?"

Jarod kept his chuckle to himself. Josh knew how to get women to do what he wanted without even trying.

Once the nurse was finished sewing up Teddy, James took the bear from her and carefully placed it back in Jessica's sleeping arms, while Josh walked the flirtatious Valerie back to the nurses' station.

As if just noticing, Lauren murmured, "Why the hell is his hair pink?"

James and Jason said matter-of-factly, "Charlie."

"Ah," she said, tried to nod, and winced.

Jarod turned the object over in his hands. It was an average, legal-sized white envelope that had been folded into thirds. He slid his finger through the top, tearing open the seal. He retrieved a key, a blue card, and a sheet of paper containing the name of a bank, a safe deposit box number, and what looked like passwords along with a short list of names on the page; Brad Anderson and Derek Lawlor were among them.

There was nothing else.

"What is it?" Lauren whispered as Josh returned from his errand.

Jarod held up the key and explained, "According to this, they put a safe deposit box in Jessica's name. Her social security card is here, too," he said in amazement.

"We better give it to my people at the bureau," Dane said, holding out his hand. When Jarod stared him down, Dane sighed. "Jarod, it's evidence in a federal investigation and you know it. You weren't planning on keeping the money, were you?"

Actually, the thought *had* crossed his mind. There was a certain poetic justice in keeping the cash. Brad had killed Miranda, Trapp, and Avery, and then kidnapped his wife and daughter before dying over it. The irony that Jessica would beat him at his own game wasn't lost on Jarod.

Plus, he didn't like taking orders from Dane. He eyed his father's bodyguard for a moment, trying to take an unbiased look at the man. Dane was usually one or two steps ahead of

Jarod on cases, which had always irritated him. But if it hadn't been for Dane's past, his contacts with the FBI, and his niece, Jarod wouldn't have gotten his family back.

"Thank you," he said, handing over the envelope. "My wife and I owe you one, Dane."

Dane looked down for a moment before clearing his throat. "Just doing what I can, Jarod."

There was an uncomfortable silence before Jarod smiled and said, "Next time, fill me in on what you know so we can work together. I can use the help now that I'm down a deputy."

CHAPTER 17
The Wedding

Sound sleep was impossible, thanks to the nurses who kept prodding her awake every hour or so. Lauren would just feel the Sandman's tug into peaceful sleep when she was nudged back into painful consciousness.

At least they'd let Jessica stay, thanks to Jarod's insistence. It surprised her that he'd opted to sleep in the uncomfortable chair next to her bed, instead of heading to the hotel room with the rest of his family. She'd only spoken to Camille and Julie once via Jason's cell phone to reassure them she was fine.

Jessica squeezed her every now and then, as if to reassure them both they were together, though she didn't wake up. Her brave little girl had endured enough in her short life. Lauren would be damned before she'd make her uncomfortable ever again. Bending over to kiss Jessica made the room shift in her concussed head, but she needed the contact. As soon as her lips swept across her forehead, Jessica relaxed a tiny bit.

"She loves you, ya know," a husky male whisper proclaimed in the dark.

Without skipping a beat, Lauren admitted, "I love her,

too." A tear slipped from her eye, but she ignored it, letting it fall into Jessica's dark hair.

Jarod left his chair to stand near the bed. He leaned a hip on the mattress and braced himself with one arm on the other side of Lauren's hip, making Jessica the filling in their family sandwich.

He gently bent down and kissed his daughter's head before moving his lips to Lauren's. His kiss was gentle and sweet, an offer of comfort. Another tear slipped from her eye, and he kissed that one away. It was sexy the way he ran his tongue over his lower lip to taste the tear, but there was no sensual heat in his eyes. No, something different glittered in their blue depths, something she'd always wished to see but had been too afraid to ask for.

The corner of his mouth turned up into a little smirk before he kissed her a little more passionately, but just as gently as he had before. When he was through making her pulse jump around on the monitors, he smiled his killer smile—the one he so rarely showed to anyone anymore.

"Jarod...," she began.

"Jessica isn't the only one who loves you, Lauren."

Her eyes widened and his handsome face began to blur through the tears pooling in her eyes.

"She's not the only one who needs you, either." He gently played with a matted curl lying on the pillow.

God, she must look atrocious!

As if reading her mind, he chuckled. "Good God, woman," he whispered. "How can I ever live without you? You make me crazy, you know that?" He leaned in closer to her ear, "You are the most beautiful creature I've ever had the misfortune to meet. You're confident, but insecure at the same time. You love without reservation, but you don't put up with anyone's crap, either. You fight for what you want, and you don't stop until you get it and, Lauren, believe me… you've got me."

When he lifted his head to meet her gaze, she saw in his sapphire eyes the truth of his words and all the love she'd hoped for. He put his lips to hers again. This was no gentle kiss.

It consumed her.

It claimed her.

When he finally came up for air, he said, "I love you so much it's hard for me to breathe." Then a tear slipped down his own cheek as he implored, "Please don't ever leave me."

She hiccupped before she answered, "Never, Jarod. You're the love of my life. You're the only man I've ever wanted, and I promise I will *never* leave you."

The tears came in a torrent now, flowing down her cheeks while she wrapped her free arm around Jarod, hugging him to her as closely as their position would allow without crushing the precious gift sleeping soundly between them.

Or so they thought.

"I love you too, Daddy," Jessica whispered.

"It's okay, Mommy. I like the yellow part flat."

Lauren laughed. "Well, it's a good thing, because I can't flip an egg to save my life, sweet pea."

Jessica kicked her little feet back and forth on the bar stool as she stuffed as much of the flat egg into her mouth as possible.

Josh had purchased Lauren's townhouse but rented it back to them while he renovated the upper east wing of the King Estate. He was turning the whole floor into a penthouse.

They'd been living in the townhouse since she was released from the hospital two months ago.

Lauren smelled Jarod's cologne before she saw him. He was fresh from his morning shower and looking like sex on a stick in his plain white t-shirt and low-slung Levi's that had seen better days. When he kissed Jessica's head, Lauren almost swooned.

There was just something about a man kissing his child that turned her on.

"'Mornin', Darlin'. Are you ready for the big day?"

"Yup," she said around a bite of toast. "Mommy said we're gettin' our hair and faces done with Joojee 'fore the wedding."

Lauren smiled at the twinkle in Jarod's eye.

"Are you boys getting your faces and hair done, too?"

"Uh no, Sassy, we're not. Thank God," he smirked. "Can I get a flat egg, too?" He'd come around the counter into the kitchen and wrapped his arms around Lauren's waist from behind.

"How many do you want?"

"A couple. I'm starving." Then he whispered in her ear, "Someone kept me up all night, so I've got quite an appetite this morning."

She smiled before gently shoving her elbow into his ribs. "Sit down at the bar and I'll fix you a plate."

When she turned from the stove to deliver his breakfast, Jarod and Jessica sat next to each other on bar stools with their heads together, having a private father-daughter conversation. The Norman Rockwell-esque picture they painted reminded Lauren of dreams she'd once had as a child. And she vowed to keep this family together no matter what.

"D-D-DO I L-LOOK ALL RIGHT?" JULIE'S VOICE quavered as they all watched her reflection in the stand-alone mirror in an anteroom of the church.

"All right?" Lauren queried. "Honey, you look beautiful."

Camille carefully wrapped her arms around Julie. "You are a vision, dear. Beautiful inside and out, and my son is lucky to have you."

They continued to study her from head to toe. Her wedding dress shimmered like frost, almost as if tiny bits of glittery ice were embedded in the material. She wore her auburn hair up, with a few strategically placed curls flowing down around her shoulders and face. There'd been some discussion about whether or not the dress needed a veil but, in the end, she'd decided to wear a crystal tiara with green emeralds interspersed in a delicate winter-themed pattern.

Jessica had been delighted when they placed her own mini tiara on her head, but instead of emeralds, Julie had added tiny blue sapphires. Their bridal party's dresses were in a frosty blue-green, so the two different gems worked well together.

"You look lovely, Julie. I'm honored to be a part of your big day," said Melissa Theroux, who was Marguerite's younger sister.

Jason's groomsmen had outnumbered the bridesmaids, so Julie had been desperate to even out the numbers. Melissa had been a couple of grades younger than Lauren and Julie in school, and while her older sister had never been one of their favorites, Melissa had always been sweet... that is, when she spoke. Melissa was painfully shy. Lauren had been surprised she'd agreed to be a part of the wedding at all.

Josh poked his head into their dressing room. "Almost time, ladies. Oh my God," he said, as he stepped in the room. "Julie, you look ravishing."

"Ravishing, Josh? Really?" Lauren said, one eyebrow raised.

"Yes, Sassy. *Ravishing*. Anyone can say 'beautiful,' but I know Jason. Believe me, once he sees her in this dress, all he's gonna to want to do is—"

Camille cut him off. "Behave, Josh. Jessica is in the room," she admonished, pointing her finger into his chest.

Jessica looked at Julie with a crinkle in her forehead before she put her little hands on her hips and said, "Hunkle Josh, she don't look like a radish. She looks like Hunkle *Jason's Princess*."

Before Josh could retort, he was shoved from behind by Charlie. "Dude, Jason is going to pummel you if you don't get back out there. Father O'Keefe is about to start the procession to the altar."

"I needed another look at the beautiful woman who is about be my sister, and was sidetracked by a whole roomful of beautiful ladies." Josh picked up Jessica and smacked a kiss on her cheek, making her giggle before he leaned over and whispered in Julie's ear. He hugged her gently and made her cry.

Damn it. Lauren hurried over to fix Julie's mascara.

Then, to Lauren's dismay, he hugged Camille, making her cry as well. On his way out, he complimented Melissa, who proceeded to turn three shades of red before turning away from Josh.

They'd never get out of this room in perfect condition.

WHEN LAUREN HEARD "SECRET SMILE" BEING PLAYED on the piano, it was time for the bridal party to proceed to the altar.

"You know I love you, right?" Julie said to Charlie, who was giving her away.

Charlie sniffled but manned up right away. Then he whispered, "I love you, too, Sis."

On cue, Melissa went down the aisle first, with not a red blotch in sight, thank God.

Lauren gave last-minute instructions to Jessica before she turned to follow Melissa into the sanctuary.

As Lauren approached the altar, she admired all of the King brothers, who proudly stood waiting: Jason as the delighted groom, then Jarod and Josh. They were all so handsome, with Jason looking proud and imposing as usual, but in all of his wedding finery, he looked a lot more menacing... until he winked at Lauren.

As she took her spot at the altar to await Jessica, who was now proudly tossing silk petals hither and thither, Lauren caught Jarod's eye. His blue eyes shown bright as he mouthed the words *I love you*.

Ignoring the quiver in her lip, she mouthed the words back to him, right before Jessica made it to her side with a bright smile on her tiny face. Out of nowhere, she yelled, "Hi Daddy!" to the congregation's delight.

The music broke before a sweet, modern version of the Bridal Chorus began to play. Everyone stood as Julie and Charlie made their way down the aisle.

Father O'Keefe began the introductory words and spoke of enduring love. Then he asked, "Who gives this woman to this man in marriage?"

Charlie stood tall and proud, answering clearly, "I do." Then he kissed Julie on the cheek and sat down next to James and Camille. Because Charlie and Julie had lost their parents, the Kings were their only family. But that didn't keep the church from being a packed house. Both sides of the aisle were filled to capacity, and by the time Jason kissed his princess in a most inappropriate fashion, there wasn't a dry eye in the building.

THE RECEPTION WAS HELD AT THE COMMUNITY center, which had been transformed into a grand winter wonderland, complete with ice sculptures, crystal chandeliers, and sparkling fake snow. Light-blue back lighting illuminated behind the white silk which curtained the walls to hide the generic look of the room. The tables were adorned with frosted pinecones, white linens, and tall white limbs decorated with twinkle lights. Strategically placed small candles added to the soft winter ambience.

In Lauren's opinion, Camille had outdone herself with the décor and the speed with which she'd put this wedding together. Thanks to the style of Julie's dress, no one but family noticed the small bump in Julie's abdomen, the reason they'd pushed up the date of the wedding.

The wedding feast was served in four courses, beginning with a five-onion soup served in a cored onion; Greek salad with fresh greens, Kalamata olives, red onion, and feta cheese; petite filet mignon with baked potato and Italian vegetables; and lastly, apple cobbler, a dish the bride couldn't get enough of lately.

To absolutely no one's surprise, Jessica ate most of everything. She'd insisted on sitting between Jason and Julie at the head of the wedding table, reasoning that she wore a tiara like Joojee, therefore she was a princess, too.

Jason had agreed.

When dinner was over and the wedding traditions of cutting the cake and throwing the bouquet and garters were performed, the wedding party was asked to join the bride and groom on the dance floor.

Jarod held out his hand to Lauren. When she took it, he twirled her to the dance floor and began leading her in a smooth transition into the crowd, slow dancing their way around the floor. Julie and Jason stayed in the middle, while Camille and James two-stepped the perimeter, awaiting their turns to dance with the bride and groom. Charlie danced with Jessica, and her giggling voice floated around with the music. Josh and Melissa looked uncomfortable together, which struck Lauren as strange. Josh, usually a smooth operator with the ladies, appeared he couldn't charm Melissa out of her shyness.

"You look beautiful," Jarod whispered in Lauren's ear.

"So do you."

He chuckled.

Since their return from Las Vegas and his declaration of love, he'd opened up his heart to her every day. He frowned less and laughed more, and she fell more and more in love with him, knowing that he'd made her wish come true. She was married to Jarod King, and he loved her with all of his heart. For the first time in her life, she felt complete.

They danced with their foreheads together, only glancing around every now and then to check on Jessica. When Lauren noticed Jason secretly rubbing Julie's bump, she wondered whether now was the right time to share her own secret with Jarod.

Nah, she'd wait until they were alone later that night.

DEAR READER,

Thank you so much for reading *Jarod's Heart*. I had so much fun reliving the toilet paper pumpkin scene with sweet Jessica. This was a real activity I'd worked on when my son was in grade school. The looks on the his classmate's faces had been worth the tedious time taken to cut mini pumpkin leaves out of green felt, and stuff rolls of TP into brown paper sacks! I loved sharing this memory with you.

I hold this family close to my heart. You can find more *Trouble In Timbisha Township* antics in *Jason's Princess*, *Josh's Challenge*, and *Marguerite's Redemption*.

To stay up to date on new releases please follow my newsletter *Happy Distractions*

Sincerely,
Elise

www.elisemanion.com

Excerpt from Josh's Challenge

Chapter One

"How long have you had a stalker, Miss Theroux?" Timbisha County Sheriff Jarod King asked as he examined, with gloved hands, a white box filled with chocolates and a syringe filled with liquid.

"Cut the formal crap, Jarod. She's upset enough," said her landlord, Josh King. He was also the sheriff's youngest brother.

Missy stared, speechless as usual, while two sets of perfect blue eyes glared at each other. She took a cautious step back in case the brothers' reputation for fighting were to explode on her front porch.

"Excuse me, gentlemen, but I don't have a stalker," she denied in a shaky voice. Unfortunately, Harold's face flashed before her eyes.

"Who's Harold, Missy?" Jarod asked less formally, interrupting her thoughts.

Crap on toast, did I say his name out loud?

"Melissa?" Josh asked with so much concern in his voice it stole her breath. When he reached up to touch her shoulder, she moved out of his reach, and flushed with embarrassment.

"Harold Klein was my philosophy professor."

"You had an intimate relationship with one of your teachers?" Jarod's tone wasn't judgmental, but the question annoyed her anyway.

"Of course not. He asked me out and I said no. When he kept harassing me, we obtained a restraining order. He backed right off after that." She crossed her arms protectively over her chest, the reminder of the awkward situation making her feel small.

"Who's 'we'?" Jarod asked, not skipping a beat.

"Me and my roommate."

"So you do have a stalker," Jarod confirmed.

She let her shoulders fall. Did she? Harold didn't live anywhere near Timbisha Township. He didn't even live in Nevada. He'd never left "gifts" like the one found on her porch this morning. Shaking her head, she asked, "How do we know the chocolates are intended for me? I just moved in."

"She's got a point, Jarod. There isn't a name on the box," Josh said.

"Exactly," she agreed. "You see, Sheriff, I was just about to take a jog when I found it on the porch—"

"Don't call him 'sheriff' when he's acting like an ass," Josh interrupted.

"The only ass on this porch is you," Jarod answered.

Before Josh could counter his brother, Missy pressed on. "Maybe it was intended for the people who used to live here?" Then she turned to Josh. "Do you know how to find your previous tenants?"

Josh and Jarod shared a look with each other before the sheriff cleared his throat. "Well, that's an interesting theory, since I used to live here. Actually, it was my wife's townhouse before she was my wife... Oh, hell." Jarod rolled his eyes heavenward.

Josh turned to face Missy. "I bought the townhouse from Lauren but rented it back to them after they got married so I could remodel their suite at The Estate."

"Oh, I see." She really didn't, and his vague explanation still didn't answer the question as to why someone would leave a potentially lethal box of chocolates on her porch.

As if reading her mind, Josh said, "The syringe we found in the box does suggest it could be tied to the drug dealers you cleared out of Timbisha Township, Jarod. Maybe this is residual fallout from some of Brad's associates?"

Missy shuddered at the reminder of the awful story her sister had recounted to her; the kidnapping of Jarod's wife and daughter, the meth, the murders... all things Missy never thought would happen in her small hometown.

"When you called, you said there's a syringe inside the box, Missy. I don't see it," Jarod asked as he lifted the lid.

"Yes, but we didn't touch it. When we saw the syringe, Josh quickly closed it and called you. It's small."

Jarod tipped the box a little to the side. "Found it." He took the syringe out of the box, gave it a cursory glance before placing it in an evidence bag. He set it aside and then checked under the bubble wrap covering the chocolates.

"What the hell is that?" Josh asked. Missy didn't miss the anger in his voice.

"It looks like each candy has a paper letter pinned to it, but they aren't in order," Jarod said quietly.

"Like a word jumble?" Missy asked.

Jarod raised his eyebrows. "Yeah, maybe," he said, shrugging as if considering her theory. "Won't know anything until I can get this analyzed." He took some photos of the box, of the lettered chocolates and syringe, before replacing the lid. He then stuffed the whole thing into another evidence bag and sealed it. "I would prefer you not be alone. Can you stay with your mom for a while?"

"No!" Missy declared before she could catch herself. Jarod and Josh raised their eyebrows at her outburst. "I mean, of course I'll be careful, but no, I can't stay with Mom. Marguerite's moved home to take care of our mother while she's sick, and I don't want to impose on either of them. I'm sure this," she indicated the toxic chocolates, "will turn out to be nothing, right?" She hoped it would be nothing.

"Hey." Josh put his arm around her shoulders. She realized she was shaking with an oncoming panic attack. Surprisingly, his comforting touch stifled the onset. His next words, though, brought on a different sort of embarrassment. "Look, I'm right next door. You've got my number. All you have to do is call me, Melissa."

"Of course," she whispered. Missy had never been good at conversation with humans. She related more to animals than people, which meant she'd spent most of her life with creatures who communicated by behavior. Josh, handsome devil that he was, made her fumble for words with his amazing blue eyes, his easygoing personality, and a lady-killing smile. She was always flummoxed when he was near.

The sheriff studied her for a moment before finally relenting. "Fine. I'll talk to Dane. In the meantime, Missy, I want you to keep your doors locked. Here," he handed her a card, "this is my personal cell. Don't hesitate to call me for anything, day or night. Understand?"

"Yes, sir." She took the card and tucked it into her pocket.

"Josh, that goes for you, too. I have a bad feeling about this."

"Yeah, me too."

She followed Jarod to his cruiser, the offending box of chocolates under his arm, while Josh tagged along on her heels. "Thank you."

"You're welcome, Missy. I'll be in touch." Jarod put everything in the trunk before getting in—ignoring his brother, she noted—and pulled away from the curb.

When he was out of sight, Josh turned her toward him. "I mean it, Melissa. Call me anytime, and don't be shy about it. It doesn't matter if the box was meant for you or not. Things got crazy around here last fall and, I swear, if anything happened to you..."

His sincerity took her by surprise. However, she wouldn't feel comfortable imposing on him, especially if he were entertaining one of his many female admirers. Now that Jarod had departed, the hideous awkwardness which had plagued her since childhood was creeping in. It was an unwelcome social anxiety that usually happened when she couldn't think of a thing to say to someone she'd known for most of her life. Before her affliction got the better of her, she cleared her throat and said, "Of course, Josh. Thank you."

That was a proper response, wasn't it?

His smile was beautiful as he patted her shoulder before leaving for his townhouse. She studied Josh's confident swagger until she felt the heat in her cheeks. Embarrassed, she entered her own townhouse and immediately tripped over a damn cardboard box, stubbing her toe.

"Dang it, I hate moving," she mumbled as she hurried to pick up her ringing iPhone. She snatched it off the counter and slid her finger over the screen. "Hello?"

"It's me. Are you all right? What happened?" Marguerite said in Big Sister Interrogation Mode.

"I know it's you, your picture was covering the home screen. I'm fine," Missy sighed.

"Oh, no you don't. Explain why Jarod had me call a courier to run a dubious box of chocolates, and a syringe for God's sake, to a forensics lab in Reno! Chocolates, I might add, found on your front porch?"

Missy rolled her eyes. Obviously, her sister already knew what was going on, so why was she making her rehash it? "We don't even know if they were meant for me, Marguerite. The message was jumbled..."

"What message? Jarod was tight-lipped about the whole thing."

"It might've been meant for him. Josh thinks it could be a warning for finding the drug money in Vegas last year." God, please let it be about the drug money.

"Or," Marguerite countered, "it could be Harold's doing."

"Harold isn't stalking me!"

"Oh yeah? Then why did you get a restraining order against him?"

"Because he was a little too persistent," Missy explained weakly.

Marguerite's disgusted grunt came loud and clear. "Same difference." There was silence on the other end. Missy imagined the cogs rotating in Marguerite's brain. Her sister was a smart cookie who hid behind the false persona of a dumb blonde. Behind the Estee Lauder mask and salon-colored hair was a sharp, analytic mind.

Finally, Marguerite admitted, "I guess it could be possible some moron hadn't realized Jarod and Lauren moved out of the townhouse. What did the message say?"

Missy sighed. Marguerite wouldn't quit until she had all the facts. "You guys'll know before I do." She paused before she admitted, "Josh was the one who opened the box and called Jarod."

"Is Josh in the habit of stopping by early in the morning, or did he stay the night?" Marguerite asked in a knowing tone.

"No, he did not stay the night. Sheesh!" Her sister always assumed things were naughtier than they actually were.

"Keep going," Marguerite commanded, back to being all business.

"Okay, so I guess I was just standing on the porch not moving, holding this box of candy. Josh must've seen me. He came out of his townhouse and ran over to check on me. As soon as he saw what was inside the box, he called Jarod. You know the rest. Satisfied?"

"Not until I know for sure who that box was intended for, and what was in that syringe," Marguerite answered with some heat. "I'm calling Uncle Dane just in case."

"No need, I think Jarod's going to do that."

"Really?" Marguerite sounded surprised.

"Yes, why wouldn't he? He knows Uncle Dane is ex-FBI, and didn't you both say they worked together last fall?"

"Never mind about that." Marguerite was quiet for a moment. "Do you think Harold could've sent the chocolates?"

"Marguerite! I told you, I took care of him."

"We'll see," she said. "I have to go. Jarod needs help with the lab forms."

"Fine. I'll see you later. Please don't tell Mom about this. I don't want to worry her."

"I won't. I love you, Missy."

"I love you, too, Marguerite."

Missy ended the call and looked around her cluttered living room. She hadn't unpacked a thing in two weeks except the necessities. Her bedroom furniture and clothes were in place, but she hadn't bothered with the rest of the condo, which currently resembled a storage unit. Not wanting to think about what needed to be done, she reached back to her messy ponytail and tugged at it to make sure it was secure. All she needed was her iPhone for music and her earbuds. Exercise was her drug and running was her preference. She did a few stretches before heading out the front door once again.

He was stalking her.

Josh leaned his forehead against his living room window and groaned. How could he, Josh King, Timbisha Township's ladies' man extraordinaire, have been reduced to spying on his neighbor, his tenant? Full of self-disgust, he turned away from the window. Women had always come easy to Josh. Twenty-six years of dating earned him an ease with women even his brothers were jealous of, but only one girl twisted his guts in a knot and made him feel like an adolescent who was nervous about asking his first crush to the dance: Melissa Anne Theroux.

Josh had tried to ask her out many times in high school because she was unlike the other girls vying for his attention, but Melissa would blush an adorable shade of red before running away. Three years younger than him, he supposed the age difference had been the cause of her embarrassment, but the sting of her rejection followed him through his college years anyway. When he returned to Timbisha Township after graduating, she'd been out of state pursuing her veterinary degree. He hadn't seen her again until six months ago when she'd been a bridesmaid in Jason and Julie's wedding. All grown up, she'd been elegant but still bashful. Unfortunately, the more he'd poured on the charm during the customary dance between groomsmen and bridesmaids, the further she'd withdrawn from his reach, daring him to win her over.

After the wedding, she'd immediately left home again to finish school and returned two weeks ago when she accepted an offer to work for Timbisha Township's one and only veterinary hospital. He hadn't believed his luck when she'd submitted her application to rent the townhouse from him. Accepting it on the spot, she'd moved in after going over the rental agreement, a document he'd paid little attention to because he'd been too focused on her dark, auburn hair, the light dusting of freckles dotting her nose and cheeks, and violet eyes which almost seemed purple.

Now she lived next door, where she spent a good portion of his day clogging up his mind with images of the two of them dancing together under twinkle lights and around ice sculptures. He couldn't get her out of his head. He was obsessed and it made him feel edgy... and a little creepy.

Melissa is the ultimate challenge.

Josh waited until she started her morning jog before he started his own run. He watched her lock her door and take off around the corner. He tied his shoes and stood. He usually jogged earlier, but the present left on her front porch had delayed both of their morning runs. He didn't like to socialize when he ran, so he never bothered her during hers. Jogging cleared his head, so hitting on Melissa during her workout would be hypocritical. Sometimes he followed her at a distance and sometimes he didn't. Either way, they usually made it back home at about the same time. It was in those moments while they caught their breaths, that he cherished. They'd both be coming off their post-run highs, and she seemed happy to smile and talk briefly.

She's just shy.

He'd waited a few minutes before taking off on his own and was now about three blocks behind her. Just like a stalker. God, he was pathetic, but the "gift" she'd found had him on alert, and he wanted to make sure she was safe. He usually ran about five miles, and he wondered how far she would run today after everything that had happened earlier. He never used the same pattern twice in a row, for safety's sake, and was relieved Melissa exercised the same caution, especially in light of this morning's potential threat.

He wondered a lot about Melissa.

While his eyes enjoyed the lovely bounce of her soft behind, his mind was stuck on the box of chocolates. Was it just a prank sent to goose Jarod for breaking up the meth ring last fall? Josh had no answers, but he'd make damn sure Melissa stayed safe on his watch, which didn't make him a stalker at all.

He hoped.

By his calculation, they'd run almost two miles when something caught Melissa's attention. She veered off the road down into a ditch and out of sight. He immediately picked up his pace and sprinted to the point where she'd disappeared from view. As he got closer, he heard a low growl followed by Melissa's melodic voice quietly telling a small creature everything was going to be okay.

"What is it?" he asked quietly, not wanting to spook woman nor beast.

Judging by her raised eyebrows, his appearance had

surprised her. She pointed into the culvert. "It's a kitten, about six months old. Looks like it's hurt."

He ambled down into the ditch and, sure enough, a mangy orange cat with its leg twisted at a weird angle hissed and spit at Melissa.

"Need some help?"

"Um. Actually, yes. I've got a dozen boxes in my garage. Do you mind getting one? I'll stay here with the kitten and try to make friends. I don't like the look of that leg."

"No problem. I'll be right back." He ran to their complex, getting in a good sprint to finish off his jog. Glad to be her landlord, he quickly keyed the garage code, grabbed an empty box, and then headed for his pickup. He'd been gone under fifteen minutes, but in that time she had, indeed, made friends with the kitten. It was curled up in her lap, crooked leg and all, while Melissa stroked its fur.

"Oh, thank you," she said when he handed her the box. With gentle precision, she secured the mangy creature inside the container and then gracefully stood up, looking at him expectantly.

"Where are we taking him?" he asked as he helped her out of the ditch and to his waiting pickup.

"Uh," she began, looking unsure, "I already called Doc Brown. I start work at the clinic tomorrow morning, but until then I'd like to take it home, if it's all right with you? I'll pay an extra pet deposit—"

"Don't give it another thought," he reassured her. "This little guy needs our help. Besides, I trust you."

"Thank you," she said with a relieved smile. "I have a feeling the poor thing has been out here alone for quite some time. I don't know how it's managed to survive with its hind leg twisted so badly." She murmured the last part to herself.

Josh nodded while assisting her into the passenger seat and then placed the box on her lap. She was being uncharacteristically confident. She'd always been shy, but it seemed animals were the key to her heart. He made a mental note of this new information as he closed her door and headed for the driver's side.

"Excited about working with Doc?" he asked once they were on their way back home.

"Yeah. Doc's the reason I wanted to be a veterinarian," she said a bit wistfully.

"You specifically came back to work with him, right?"

She hesitated a moment, making him wonder again about the box of chocolates, before she smiled, "Yes. Of course, that's why I'm here."

Hm. She had a secret she didn't want to tell. Josh could spot a fibber a mile away, and now his curiosity was piqued. "Are you sure? Because there for a second it sounded like you weren't," he teased.

When she glanced his way, he saw her guard come up, and the awkwardness returned in a flash. He felt it like a slap. She was shutting him out again.

"Melissa," he began as he pulled into the driveway, but she ended the conversation before he could finish.

"Thank you for the help."

She quickly opened the door and jumped out, barely waiting for him to shift into park. Without a backward glance, she darted for her townhouse, keeping a tight hold on the box. She was inside before he could say goodbye.

Damn it. He'd felt the beginnings of a connection while she helped the animal, but as soon as he turned on the charm she bolted.

He hoped to figure her out soon because now that she was

back—all grown up and living two doors down—he wanted to get to know her a whole lot better.

He knew women better than either of his brothers. Grim determination took hold as he plotted his strategy. If he couldn't get past her skittish ways, no one else could.

He'd get her to go out with him by the end of the week or his name wasn't Josh King.

Acknowledgments

I'd like to thank Mr. Tony Spencer of Yateley, England, for naming the fictional small town and county where the King family resides.

* A special note of gratitude to Lynda Bailey, my partner in crime and all things Indie. Thank you for your patience, criticism, advice, and most of all, friendship.
You're the *Naughty* to my *Nice* ;)